SECRETS
of
STONE
and
SEA

ALSO BY ALLISON K. HYMAS

The Explorer's Code
Under Locker and Key
Arts and Thefts

ALLISON K. HYMAS

SECRETS of STONE and SEA

ROARING BROOK PRESS

New York

Published by Roaring Brook Press
Roaring Brook Press is a division of
Holtzbrinck Publishing Holdings Limited Partnership
120 Broadway, New York, NY 10271 • mackids.com

Our books may be purchased in bulk for promotional, educational, or business
use. Please contact your local bookseller or the Macmillan Corporate and
Premium Sales Department at (800) 221-7945 ext. 5442 or by email at
MacmillanSpecialMarkets@macmillan.com.

Library of Congress Cataloging-in-Publication Data is available.

First edition, 2022
Book design by Veronica Mang
Printed in the United States of America by Lakeside Book Company,
Harrisonburg, Virginia

ISBN 978-1-250-79947-0 (hardcover)
1   3   5   7   9   10   8   6   4   2

For my family—past, present, and future.

"RISE, OCEAN,"

A Song Sung by Seaspire's Fishermen,
18th and 19th Centuries

A sailor came to the stony point,
Bringing his loaf of bread.
With a heave and a throw he hurled it below,
And saw the ocean's mouth fed.

CHORUS

Rise, the ocean rise,
Rise and greet the shore.
With red and bread, he feeds on the dead,
And meets you at the door.

A sailor came to the stony point,
With salted pork in his hand.
When the poor beast's meat the waves did greet,
They surged and gnawed at the land.

CHORUS

A sailor came to the stony point,
Bearing the sweat from his brow.
When the salt of he met the salt of the sea,
The devil's own wind did blow.

CHORUS

A sailor came to the stony point,
With his own stubborn self at his side.
With bond and with blood they nourished the flood,
And the land succumbed to the tide.

CHAPTER 1

WELCOME TO SEASPIRE

PETER

Twelve-year-old Peter Syracuse found himself breaking into a cemetery.

It hadn't been his idea, of course. But that didn't mean he wasn't there, shuffling his feet, as his twin brother Kai searched for handholds on the old brick wall that surrounded the graveyard.

"This is a bad idea," Peter said for the thirtieth time.

"Someone has to get the Frisbee back," Kai returned. He pulled himself a step up the wall, Grandma's wooden cane hanging from a belt loop on his shorts.

"I know, but—" Peter didn't know what he wanted to say.

It had been Peter's idea to join the Frisbee game in the park when they'd seen the other kids playing. And he understood that since it was his pass to Kai that had gone wide, landing over the wall of the old, locked cemetery that rested beside the white-painted church, it was their responsibility to get it back. But . . .

But climbing over the wall seemed risky. And surely the cemetery had been locked for a reason.

Not that Peter believed the stories the other Frisbee kids told about the ghost of a Revolutionary War soldier haunting the grave-yard. And in any case, it was day, and sunny. No ghost came out to play during the day.

Still, the coastal town of Seaspire, Massachusetts, had an eerie quality to it. Not right now, when the sun danced brightly on the slate rooftops and the blue summer sky matched the endless blue of the sea, setting off green trees and red brick in a merry way. It was the perfect day for a picnic, which was what Peter and his family were doing when Peter spotted the Ultimate pickup game.

But at nightfall, or when rain clouds shrouded the sun, every-thing took on a sinister tone. The bricks became jagged, and white paint revealed its cracks. Even the colorful fish-man painted on the Fudge Kitchen window changed from friendly to malevolent. When the light faded, the town forgot its merriment and felt like it was waiting for the worst to happen. Peter couldn't help but wonder what that might be.

He shook his head and brought his mind back to the present. No, Peter didn't believe in ghosts. He was more concerned about the person who cared for the graveyard coming after them. They were trespassing. He said as much to Kai.

"Don't worry so much," Kai said, finally reaching the top of the wall and swinging a leg over. "We'll get in and out before anyone sees us."

"But what if they do?" Peter looked around. Behind him, the park glowed green in the summer sun. Families milled around, enjoying picnics and playing at the small playground—a mix of new plastic slides and an old, wooden swing set.

And the other kids waited in the field behind them for their Frisbee to come back.

Abandoning the Frisbee ran its risks. Peter and Kai had three more weeks in Seaspire. Making the other kids angry by losing their Frisbee meant isolating themselves with their family for nearly a month.

But continuing this could mean getting into serious trouble.

Peter was tired of getting into trouble.

"I see it," Kai said from his perch on the wall. "It landed on a mausoleum."

"Oh, well. We tried."

"No, we can still get it. Together." Kai shifted his weight and leaned down, hand extended. "Come on up."

"I will not."

"This is the only way. I can reach the Frisbee if I climb on your shoulders, but first we have to be on the other side of this wall. So come up. It'll be an adventure." He grinned, flashing a tooth that had been chipped many years ago. The one casual acquaintances used as a way to differentiate between Peter and Kai, who were identical. Same light skin that held a tan easily, same dark hair, and even the same freckles. However, Peter's hair was a little bit curlier, and Kai's eyes had a little more green in their hazel.

Kai waved. "Come on! We need to hurry."

Peter looked back at the kids waiting behind them, and then up at Kai. What should he do?

He did what he always did: follow Kai. Though a bitter taste developed on his tongue.

Matching Kai's movements on the wall, Peter climbed up and sat beside his twin. Beneath them on the other side of the wall was the little cemetery. Well-kept grass was interrupted by gray head-stones reaching skyward like fingers. The church stood on the other side of the yard, a door connecting it to the graveyard. And there was the mausoleum with the red Frisbee on the roof.

A cloud passed over the sun, and Peter shivered.

Kai, on the other hand, looked enlivened. Eyes gleaming, he adjusted Grandma's cane. "Let's do this," he said, jumping off the wall before Peter could shout out.

Fortunately the wall wasn't too high, so Kai just stumbled and collapsed when he landed. Peter didn't move, wondering if he should turn around and go back to the park before it was too late. But he didn't want to go back without the Frisbee.

Which move was right, and which one would lead to disaster?

Kai was already at the mausoleum. "Peter, hurry up!"

But Peter didn't come.

So Kai threw his hands in the air, drew Grandma's cane from his belt loop, and reached up to fish around on the mausoleum roof for the Frisbee.

When that didn't work, Kai climbed onto a nearby headstone and bent his knees. With a lurch, Peter realized that he was about to jump.

"Don't!" he called.

"There's still time to come down here," Kai sang back.

Peter gripped the edge of the wall, about to jump, but then released it. As much as he wanted to bring back the Frisbee he'd tossed over the wall, he couldn't banish the vision of himself and Kai being dragged back to Dad and Grandma by the priest or whoever was in charge here, embarrassed and in trouble *again*.

Had Kai even thought about that before jumping in feetfirst? If history was any indication, no, he hadn't.

Kai's tooth had been chipped when he, at six years old, had tried to rescue a friend's sister's kite from a tree back home in Ohio. He'd failed to notice one of the branches was cracked. And in fourth grade, Kai raced into the street to heroically retrieve the neighbor's ball. Only the quick reflexes of the driver had saved Kai from being hit by a car.

Peter could have managed if it was just that. But a few weeks ago, when school let out, Kai had proven how reckless he really was. Their mom, Thera Regas Syracuse, had just left on her summerlong expedition. Probably another one to the Mediterranean; because Mom's parents were from Greece, she tended to prefer digs that related to ancient Greece.

Dad had decided it would be fun to take the family rafting while Mom was gone, so they could all have an adventure. Peter and Kai, and their older sister, Sophie, were even allowed to bring friends.

Sophie and her high school friends were on one raft. Dad and the boys and a couple of their friends, Geoff and Milo, were on the other one. The river was pretty mild, so Dad said it was okay to get out and swim if they wanted to. This wasn't a white-water-rafting excursion. At least, it wasn't supposed to be.

After hours of floating, Sophie's raft got caught on a fallen log. Dad got out to unstick the teenagers, but Kai and Peter and their friends floated away while he was working. This shouldn't have been a problem, but then they lost sight of Dad and it soon became clear they'd taken a branch of the river they weren't supposed to take.

They'd tried shouting for Dad, but got no answer. Geoff and Milo started to worry. They were lost and alone on the river. Peter wanted to pull over to the side, stay put, and use Dad's cell phone to call for help. But Kai had a different plan.

According to Kai, the branch would come back to the main

river. He'd seen it on a map. He could guide the group forward, and they'd meet up with Dad again. It sounded so easy, when Kai said it, and the truth was, it never took much to convince Peter to go along with Kai's plans. They were twins, after all. Best friends for life.

So they did it. They floated ahead, with Kai at the front of the raft like George Washington crossing the Delaware. Before long, all four boys were splashing and laughing again.

And then they saw the bridge pylons. And heard the roar of white water.

Up ahead was a bridge, and below it, a drop. Geoff and Milo started yelling, and Peter brought out Dad's phone to call *someone* for help. But who could he call? Who could come in time?

Kai began to paddle hard, trying to steer the raft away from the bridge and waterfall. But it was too little, too late. They went over.

The drop was about seven feet. The raft capsized. Peter felt like a linebacker had tackled him from behind. Dad's phone slipped out of his fingers and fell to the bottom of the river. All around him, Kai and their friends choked on water and flailed, trying to get out of the bubbling spray they found themselves in.

No one was hurt. But everyone was scared and they weren't able to right the raft. An hour later, Sophie found them hanging on to the side of the raft, minus one cell phone and more than a little traumatized.

After she'd found Dad and the other boys had gone home, Dad delivered a blistering tirade to Peter and Kai about safety and sent them to their rooms for the rest of the evening. And the next day, he announced that they were going to visit his mother in Seaspire for a whole month. He never said it was because he didn't trust his sons to stay out of trouble, but he didn't *not* say it, either.

The whole raft thing had been Kai's idea, not Peter's. Yet Peter had almost drowned, and then shared Kai's punishment all the same.

He should never have decided to follow Kai's lead. And Kai should never have tried to be the hero and save everyone when he didn't have all the facts, like the existence of that bridge and the waterfall.

It was so easy to make the wrong choice, a dangerous choice, when you didn't have all the details.

Back in the Seaspire cemetery, Peter stayed on the wall. He didn't know where the cemetery groundskeeper was, or if they'd get into trouble, or if giving up and getting down on the park side would land him in turbulent water with the other kids, so he didn't move. He didn't have all the facts.

Kai leaped from the headstone to the mausoleum and was hanging on to its roof by his fingertips. As he tried to swing himself up, the church's door opened and Peter's heart lurched in his chest.

Kai let go of the mausoleum, and Peter swung his leg to jump back down on the park side. But then they both stopped.

Two figures had emerged from the church. One was a gray-haired man carrying a stepladder, and the other was a dark-haired teenage girl in a bright pink shirt.

Sophie.

Sophie waved at Peter and came over to the wall as the old man went to Kai. "Bet you have a good view up there," Sophie said. Holding out a hand, she added, "But maybe we get down now?"

Peter nodded, and Sophie helped him jump down off the wall and into the graveyard. He sighed. "How much trouble are we in?"

"Oh, lots," Sophie said, grinning. "We're talking military school, Mom and Dad disowning you both. You're going to wish the earth and ocean would rise up to swallow you whole." She laughed and nudged Peter's shoulder, and they went over to join Kai.

Kai was busy watching the old man step down from the ladder with the Frisbee. "Happens all the time," the man said, handing it to Kai. "But you know, you boys could have just asked for help."

Peter's ears burned with embarrassment. He hadn't even wanted to climb the wall! But he hadn't thought of just asking, either.

Kai, on the other hand, wasn't fazed. "Thanks!" he said, taking the Frisbee.

The old groundskeeper folded up his stepladder and gave a meaningful look to Sophie. Then he went back inside the church.

"This way," Sophie said, waving them toward a wrought-iron gate. It unlatched from the inside, so she opened it and led the way out.

"How did you know we needed help?" Peter asked, his neck still burning.

"I saw you."

"You saw me?"

"Anyone looking could see you sitting at the top of that wall," she said. Her dark eyes glinted. "*Anyone*."

Peter's shoulders tightened. "Dad and Grandma?"

Sophie twirled a lock of hair around her finger. "I may have encouraged them to go back to the car to search for Grandma's cane after I spotted you so I could get the groundskeeper and get you out of trouble." She glanced at Kai. "What kind of monster steals a cane from an old woman?"

Kai scoffed. "She said I could look at it. It was fine. Anyway, I refuse to take criticism from someone who wears that ungodly color every day."

Sophie snorted. "It's not that bad." She tapped her shirt, her work uniform for the Fudge Kitchen. It was bright pink with a stylized swirly taffy piece on the chest.

That was Sophie. Junior class president last school year, AP student, did three sports, and over the summer had signed up for extra tutoring to prepare for college. And, of course, once she arrived in Seaspire she got a job to "make the most of their trip." Yet, somehow, she still found time to rescue the boys from the cemetery.

At least she hadn't applied to the Seaspire Whale Watching Tour company. She brought home reject taffy and day-old fudge instead of fish reek.

Feeling a lot better since Sophie got them out of the church cemetery, Peter grinned. "It's pretty bad. Is that color even from Earth?"

Sophie snorted. "It's *magenta*." She checked the time on her phone. "Speaking of which, I'd better go. My shift starts in ten minutes. And Kai, go return Grandma's cane. Not even I can save you from everything."

"Fine." Kai sighed and handed Peter the Frisbee. "Take that back to Todd and the others, will you? Thanks."

Peter flipped the Frisbee in his hands, watching his sister and brother walk off to the picnic table where Dad and Grandma were once again sitting. It had been so easy for Sophie to just ask and get help, but Kai had to be dramatic and climb the wall. And Peter had just gone along with it, even though he hadn't wanted to.

Peter sighed. When they'd arrived, Grandma had taken them down to the beach and warned them about riptides: invisible currents that could drag you along the beach, pulling you farther and farther out to sea until you were miles away from where you wanted to be.

Whether Peter liked it or not, Kai was a powerful riptide.

CHAPTER 2

A HOT DOG BY THE SEA

KAI

As Peter ran back to restart the Frisbee game, Kai went to return Grandma's cane.

He hadn't *stolen* it. She'd told him he could look at it. He just decided to look at it again when they lost the Frisbee. They would have needed a long stick like that if the Frisbee had been lodged in a tree, and if Grandma was sitting at the picnic table, she didn't need it.

Grandma used a cane to get around Seaspire. She had walked with a limp since before Kai's dad was born, although asking about it yielded a variety of answers.

"This is what happens when you don't stretch before a marathon."

"I had polio as a child."

"Shark. Big one."

On reflection, it was pretty thoughtless to take Grandma's walking stick. Kai would make sure to apologize.

He passed Sophie, who had grabbed her purse and smiled as she hurried away to work, and approached the table. Where Grandma and Dad were having an argument.

"I don't see the issue, Alexander," Grandma was saying. In her hand was a knife with a pattern of silver swirls on the blade. It looked like it belonged in a museum, not in the hand of a grandmother wearing a pastel T-shirt painted with waves and seashells. "It's my knife, and I can do with it as I please."

"That is *Damascus steel*, Mom," Dad said. He scratched at a peeling sunburn, creating a patch of pink against his white skin.

Grandma nodded, making her short, gray curls bounce. "The genuine thing." She sounded proud. "At least five hundred years old, from Persia."

Kai stopped and admired the knife. The metal rippled like flowing water, strange and beautiful. Under the crumbs and mayonnaise spots, of course.

Dad snatched the knife from Grandma and wiped it on a napkin. "You can't use a five-hundred-year-old knife to cut sandwiches," he said as he worked. He muttered something about "Beowulf" and "utterly priceless" and "show some respect."

"Honestly, Alex," Grandma said, snatching the knife from Dad. "How would you have me 'respect' these blades? Leave them to rust in a glass case? Bah. They're weapons. Tools. They were made to be used." She spotted Kai. "Ah, so there's my cane."

"Yeah, I borrowed it. I'm sorry."

Dad turned his exasperation on Kai. "We looked everywhere for that."

"And now we have it back." Grandma's eyes gleamed with

mischief. "Kai, tell me. How closely did you look at it? Did you notice this?"

And with that, she slid a thin blade out from the wooden cane.

Kai's eyes widened, and he started laughing. He should have expected it.

At first glance, Grandma Syracuse seemed like anyone's stereotype of a "sweet, cookie-baking granny" up until she took those cookies out of the oven with a fourteenth-century gauntlet, its interior lined with hand-knitted material. She owned *many* knives, swords, halberds, axes, maces, shields, pieces of armor, and other assorted weaponry from every age and location, all collected during her time as a history professor. They used to be locked in the attic, but because, this summer, the boys were old enough to "know better," Grandma had moved the weapons to cupboards in her sitting room for "easy access."

This had started their dad off on his first rant of the summer about protecting valuable artifacts, and their grandmother on a retort about how "respect" was better than "protect."

Kai didn't care one way or the other. He just knew that his grandmother was the coolest old woman in the world. He'd noticed the cane as soon as they arrived at Grandma's house, but he would never have guessed a sword lurked inside it.

Grandma turned the blade over in her hands. "It's a Victorian dueling cane," she explained.

"Why do you have that?" Dad asked her, sounding exhausted.

"Protection," Grandma said simply. "Here, Kai, want to give it a swing?"

Kai reached for it, only to have Dad pull his arm away from the sword.

"Don't even think about it," Dad said. "It's not safe."

Shoulders slumped, Kai watched Grandma slide the sword back into her cane.

Peter took after Dad. They were both so cautious. Dad had totally overreacted when Kai and Peter got separated from him on their rafting trip, and since then Peter had lost his sense of adventure.

That's why this trip to Seaspire was so wonderful. The town was magic. A cool breeze floated off the richly blue ocean, which was visible just past the gray slate roofs of the buildings in town, sun sparkling on the waves. The air smelled like salt and freshly cut grass, with a touch of caramel from the Fudge Kitchen across the street. And of course, they were staying for a month with a grandmother who owned a cupboard full of swords. Surely here Kai could remind Peter that nothing was ever gained without taking a risk or two, that adventures were all about taking a chance.

Then they could be twins again, united in more than their appearance.

Grandma had pulled over the platter she'd brought the sandwiches on. "This should be *perfectly* safe to look at if you want, Kai."

The perfectly reddish-gold dish didn't look like any platter Kai had ever seen. "Grandma," he said, picking up the dish, "where did you get this?"

"A former student sent this to me years ago," Grandma said, her cheeks flushed with pleasure. "No idea where it came from, but I suspect Greek, by the style."

Dad choked. "That's ancient Greek? And you covered it in mayonnaise?"

Grandma scoffed. "Mayonnaise keeps the metal shiny. All these years, and I've never had a spot of corrosion."

Kai turned the empty platter over and traced the etchings on its domed side, some lost language. Flipped like this, it looked like a Frisbee.

The game!

"I gotta go," Kai said. "We're not done with our game."

"Go play. We can 'discus' this later," Dad called as Kai ran off.

Dad was an English teacher with a love of wordplay. Sometimes his puns were clever. Most of the time, not.

Kai found Peter and the others chasing the Frisbee. He waited until the game play slowed and approached Peter. "How's it going?"

Peter shrugged. "We're just messing around. Todd had to refill his water bottle, and we were waiting for you. What took you?"

"Grandma's cane has a sword in it!" When Peter's eyes bulged, Kai continued, "And she cut our sandwiches with this old knife. Like, half a millennium old." Kai tilted his head. "Do you think that knife would make sandwiches taste like death?" Realizing what he said, Kai added, "I mean, they don't. Taste bad. Like death. Grandma's sandwiches taste amazing."

Peter said, "Maybe that's because the souls of the dead add just the right seasoning to the tuna." He laughed, easing Kai's tension. "What would the soul of a medieval warrior taste like?"

"Scurvy," Kai said, grinning. "And illiteracy."

"You're back!" Todd, a lanky dark-skinned kid, said as he

approached the twins. He glanced between them. "Which one is Kai?"

"I'm Kai," Kai said, smiling and revealing his chipped tooth.

Sure, it got a little annoying having to reintroduce himself to people he only recently met. Being a twin had its drawbacks, but also its perks. If this was the price he had to pay for always having Peter in his corner, he'd pay it.

And Peter would come around. Kai would show him how to take action and have fun again.

"Okay," Todd said to Kai. "We've already split the teams. We put you and your brother on the same team so we don't get confused who to throw to. You get Natalie. I get Liz and Sabina."

"Sounds perfect."

"Don't get too cocky," Todd said. "My name means 'fox,' so get ready to be outsmarted."

"Yeah?" Kai laughed. "Well, mine means 'sea.' So you'd better get ready to be swept away."

Todd just waved it off. "And you," he said to Peter, "don't throw toward the graveyard anymore." Then he went back to his own team.

Kai turned to Peter. "This will be fun."

"Do we always have to play on the same team?" Peter asked.

Kai started. Where had this come from? "We're better together." Weren't they? That had always been true. Peter had Kai's back, and Kai had Peter's. But since that raft trip, Peter had become distant, almost like he didn't want anything to do with Kai.

That was unacceptable.

Kai bumped Peter's shoulder with his own. "If you want to

switch teams, go ahead. But I think we should teach Todd a lesson for blaming you for losing the Frisbee."

Peter nodded. "Yeah, let's get him."

Perfect. They'd be back in sync soon.

The game began. Kai always started by rushing right up to the line with everyone else. It was where the action was, and offered the best view of the field. Kai was pretty good at analyzing each team, knowing where people would move and who could be in range to catch his throws.

But today, he was trying to encourage Peter to move forward more. Peter kept hanging back, finding places where no one passed to him or threw to him. Kai tried, over and over, to pass to Peter, but his twin was so out of the way that the Frisbee usually went wide or was intercepted.

After Kai made yet another accidental pass to Todd, the other boy called, "What's the matter? Off your game?"

"I'm only off from school!" That had sounded a lot better in his head.

On the other team, Sabina had the Frisbee. Kai watched the field, letting the pattern fall into place.

Sabina liked to throw long and far, deep into the end zone of the other team. Kai watched Todd dash back and forth. He wasn't worth worrying about; he couldn't ditch Natalie covering him. Sabina wouldn't throw to Todd.

But farther back? There was Peter, shadowing Liz. He was in the perfect place to make the interception. But would he? He'd have to run backward to be ready.

Natalie snapped off the pass. Kai saw the Frisbee float in the air, hovering like a seagull.

Just like he foresaw.

There was a pattern to everything if you knew what to look for.

And, in that pattern, Kai realized Peter wouldn't make the play. He'd hesitated too long, scooting around in a small circle like he didn't know what to do. Liz was moving into position. They were going to lose this round!

Move! Kai thought. Peter still didn't fall back.

So Kai dashed for the Frisbee. The new pattern unfolded in his mind: Kai passing Peter to intercept the Frisbee and snap it back to Natalie, who would score. The play would be perfect. The others might even cheer for him!

There it was, right there. Liz was almost on him, but Kai knew she wouldn't make it in time. The Frisbee was his.

Kai leaped for the disk. But, suddenly, so did Peter. Kai's nose smashed into Peter's skull, and both boys fell. The Frisbee settled peacefully in Liz's hands.

"Time!" Todd called, running over. "You okay?"

"I'm fine," Peter said, rubbing his head. "Kai?"

Kai touched his nose. His fingers came away red with blood.

Todd sighed. "Guess you're out, then."

Kai pinched his nose. "Yeah, thad's brobably smart."

"I'm out, too," Peter said. "I was done, anyway."

"Beat ub your brother and walk away. I ged it." Kai grinned at Peter, who grinned back.

"That's me. Mighty assassin, the Frisbee my weapon of choice. One day Grandma will be serving cookies off a plastic disk."

The boys laughed, which made Kai's nose bleed harder.

"Now that the game is over," Todd said, "we can go to the haunted lighthouse."

Kai's ears pricked. "The whud?"

Todd grinned. "No one told you about the haunted lighthouse?" He pointed to the north of Seaspire, to a forest that rose to a craggy promontory with a blue-and-red-striped lighthouse. "It's right there, at the Point."

"It's really haunted?" Peter asked.

"Maybe. The first lighthouse keeper, some guy named Roger MacHale, left, reporting headaches and nightmares about the ocean flooding the lighthouse. He also complained he heard voices in the wind. Maybe he did. Apparently, before the lighthouse was built, there was another building in that spot. Like, an ancient kind of lighthouse or guard tower. No one knows why."

Todd leaned forward. "And not just that," he said in a whisper. "Nothing ever grows there. Like, *ever*. Seaspire's Community Cleanup Committee keeps trying to grow flowers, or gardens, or bring trees closer, but it doesn't work." He stepped back. "Maybe the Point is cursed. Maybe that's why the lighthouse is really there. To protect *us* from *it*."

Grandma was on that community committee. Kai vowed to ask her if she thought the land was cursed. "It sounds neat."

"We're heading up there now. Are you coming?"

Peter stepped back. "I don't know. A condemned lighthouse . . ."

"Oh, it's not condemned, just empty. And we're not going *into* it. Just up to the Point. It's safe. You get a good view of the Spire the town is named after."

"Ah. Sounds fun." Peter smiled, and Kai felt a surge of hope. Maybe Peter wasn't as passive as he seemed.

Then Peter added, "We should probably deal with *this* first." He gestured to Kai's streaming nose.

Todd nodded. "If you can make it, we'll see you later." He and the others waved goodbye and left.

There was a small snack shack near the park, the kind of place that sold lemonade, nachos, and hot dogs. Peter pulled Kai over and shoved a handful of napkins into his hands.

Kai, grateful, held them against his nose. When the bleeding stopped, Kai checked it. Still sore, but it didn't seem broken. Good. "What was that about, back there?"

"What was what about?"

"You were just standing there, letting the Frisbee fly over your head."

Peter shrugged. "I wasn't sure if it was in my range. I thought I'd wait and see if it looked like I could get it."

This was typical Peter. Kai couldn't count how many times Peter missed out on getting a role in the school play, or making a team, or even just going to Cedar Point with friends because he wanted to "wait and see."

If Kai didn't push him to take some action, now and then, he'd just sit on the couch and do nothing until he was older than Grandma. But these days . . .

Now, Peter was waiting again, looking at the snack shack's menu. Kai would have to give him another push. "You hungry?"

His twin nodded, and Kai said, "Me too. Let's get something and then head over to the lighthouse."

"Oh, you want to see your namesake?"

"Or yours. The Spire is a big rock, after all."

Peter scowled. Kai's name meant "sea," but Peter's meant "rock." Which led to their dad calling him "Rocky," a nickname Peter claimed to hate but never pushed to be dropped.

Kai approached the snack shack. "A couple of roasted dachshunds." When the teenager working the stand looked horrified, Kai rephrased. "Two hot dogs, please." It was their usual order at places like this.

Peter stepped up. "Uh, I kind of wanted nachos today."

There was that distance again—they were out of sync. Peter pulling away.

So Kai pulled back. "Hot dogs will be easier to carry."

"That's true." Peter kicked at the sidewalk. "A hot dog's fine."

Kai smiled. Odd distance between them or not, he still knew his brother!

They paid for their hot dogs and headed the way the others had gone. Kai took the lead. "Let's go past the beach, not through the forest," he said. "To get a view of the ocean."

"So you *do* want to see your namesake."

They headed out of the park, walking through the tourist center of town past a row of shops that sold soaps and jams. When they reached the Fudge Kitchen, Kai waved at Sophie past the grinning fish-man on the window, but she was busy with a customer and didn't see him.

On the way down to the sea they walked through a street of redbrick buildings. On the sidewalk, a couple of local girls were skipping rope. The girls chanted a rhyme Kai hadn't heard before:

One poor sailor dressed in red,

Brought some pork and brought some bread,

Fell asleep out on the stone,

When he woke up, not alone.

Made a new friend, and then,

Had to do it over again!

Then the girls spun the rope fast and counted until the girl jumping tangled her arm in the rope.

"Creepy rhyme," Peter said as they passed.

"Yeah," Kai said. "Do you think it's about anything?"

Peter pretended to duck for cover. "Careful! You don't know when Dad might be listening. He'll tell us the true story behind 'Ring Around the Rosie.'"

"Again."

"Again." Kai checked his nose. It had clotted well. "So, where's that ocean?"

They left the girls behind, following the cool salt breeze to the shore. As Kai ate his hot dog, which *did* travel more easily than nachos would have, he thought about how different the beach in Seaspire was than the ones he'd imagined when he was back home in Ohio.

He always thought beaches were hot, sunny, flat, and covered with people sunbathing. Here, though, while you did see the occasional beachcomber, the beaches were small, and jagged, broken up by huge stones that shattered roaring waves. The whole thing filled Kai with a soaring sense of excitement.

And the biggest stone was the Spire itself, poking like a huge, wicked tooth out of the sea beside the Point.

With his half-eaten hot dog, Peter gestured up the Point at a small lighthouse nestled on the edge of the tree line. "There it is."

"Let's go!" Kai pushed past Peter and ran as fast as he could off the beach and up through the piney forest to the lighthouse. Panting, he arrived on a barren patch of gray rock overlooking the dark, wild sea. To his left was the lighthouse, paint chipped, almost swallowed by the forest but still keeping vigil over the expanse of stone and sea in front of it.

Peter appeared a moment later, wiping sweat off his forehead with his wrist. "Could you wait a moment?"

"For this? Never." Kai watched as a sudden huge wave crashed on the Spire, white against slate gray. "This is amazing."

"Yeah." The ocean wind sent Peter's sweaty hair dancing. "Looks like Todd and the others already left before we got here."

"Their loss. We're awesome company." Kai crossed the wide promontory in front of him and sat down, dangling a leg off the cliff's ledge. Small wafts of spray hit his ankle.

"You shouldn't do that," Peter said.

"What, is the ocean going to reach up and pull me down?" Kai waved. "Come on. It feels nice."

Peter frowned, but edged closer to the cliff until he could also sit and hang one leg over.

"Huh." Peter patted the ground. "It's true. Look back at the lighthouse. The trees are sprouting all around it, but look at the base. See that square?"

Kai did. It looked like the foundation of an old building to him, but that could have been because Todd had told them there used to be an even older tower in this place.

"Nothing's growing there," Peter said. "Not even weeds."

"Weird." Peter was right. Kind of spooky, but not exactly haunted. After all, if it *was* the foundation of an older building, it must be pretty rocky. Hard to grow plants in stone.

Though you'd think there would be grass or moss, at least.

Kai looked at Peter's half-eaten hot dog. "Hey, you going to eat that?"

Peter looked at the hot dog, and held it out. But before Kai could take it, Peter grinned and used it to wipe his sweaty forehead. Then, beaming, he handed it over.

"Peter, why?" Kai dropped the hot dog, repulsed. A gust of salty wind, sounding like a gasping breath, caught him in the face, and he sneezed. Red splattered the rock and the hot dog.

"I thought you'd stopped bleeding."

"The sneeze sed it off again." Kai pinched his nose. "God any napkins?"

"Yeah, one." Peter passed it to Kai, who wrapped it around his nose. "Well," Peter said, standing. "I guess no one's eating the rest of that."

"Bud id's one-of-a-kind now," Kai said, laughing. "Don'd you want to daste by soul?"

The wind flapped at the napkin in his hand. The air was colder now, as though a cloud had moved over the sun. Looking up, Kai saw that one had. In fact, the sky was full of gray clouds, blotting out the summer light. When did that happen?

The trees behind them rustled as the gusts grew. Kai understood the lighthouse stories better now; when the wind blew through the branches, they sounded like ghostly voices, calling and pleading.

He shivered. Maybe it was time to go home.

Kai pulled the napkin away from his nose. The bleeding hadn't been as bad this time. He picked up the ruined hot dog and tossed it into the water. The waves swallowed it up like a ravenous monster. Waves leaped and crashed in the sea below.

"Maybe some fish will like it," Kai said.

"I'm glad you got someone to taste your soul." Peter pushed himself back from the edge, then stood up and looked around. "It's getting stormy. We'd better go. Get up, Kai."

But before Kai could stand, a huge gust, larger than any before it, sent him skidding away from the edge of the sea.

CHAPTER 3

RISE, OCEAN

PETER

What the heck was that? Peter had just enough time to ground his toes when the wind tore at him and bowled Kai over. As Kai sat up, nose once again dripping, Peter watched the sea out past the cliffs.

Before, the ocean had been a rich navy blue, coolly reflecting the blue sky. Now, the sky swirled with clouds that bubbled with sick grayish-green light, making the sea look as dark gray as the Spire itself.

"We should go!" Peter called. Whatever was going on, it wasn't like any kind of tempest Peter had ever seen. He didn't want any part of it.

But Kai was already crawling back to the edge. "Oh, man," he said. "You have to see this."

One struggling step at a time, Peter fought against the storm. He dropped and crawled over to Kai, who was clinging to the edge of the rocks. Peter did the same, wind whipping his hair.

The sea below churned and foamed. The waves roared like a beast. That sick green energy in the sky snaked through the water like electric eels toward the Spire. Between the Spire and the promontory, the sea swirled.

"What is this?" Kai yelled over the howling wind.

"The storm getting worse?" Peter called back. "We need to get out of here!"

The whirlpool below thundered and shot a jet of water straight into the air. As much as Peter wanted to run into the woods, away from the water, he remained transfixed, desperate to see what happened next.

The pillar of seawater swirled, veined through with bolts of green energy. They crackled so loudly that Peter wished he didn't need his hands to hold on against the wind, so he could cover his ears. The sound grew, and grew, until Peter couldn't stand it anymore.

And then the world shattered.

Water slammed against the boys, hurling them back. Wind shrieked around them.

Peter lay still, ears ringing, head aching. Then he sat up, spluttering, and looked at the sea.

They were no longer alone.

A figure stood on the edge of the Point. No, *over the sea*. On air.

And "standing" wasn't really accurate. That would imply legs and feet.

Hovering in the air over the ocean was a being that could have slithered out of Peter's nightmares. It was at least ten feet tall. Instead of legs, it had a scaly greenish-gold tail, like a snake's but with jagged, dark green fins at the bottom. At the waist, that tail morphed into something that was almost human and covered in armor that looked like it was made out of seashells. Claws glittered like mother of pearl.

Instead of hair, the creature had tentacles that writhed like tongues tasting the air. A scaly face with no nose, and eyes set wide on the head, like a fish's. Those eyes were yellow with a snake's slitted pupils. At first, those eyes roved, and if Peter had to put a word on it, he'd say the creature looked lost.

But its eyes found Peter and Kai, and it smiled. Peter shuddered. The thing's teeth were needle sharp and crowded in its mouth.

The creature spoke, but Peter didn't understand a word. Gaping, he slapped blindly for Kai, finally finding him huddled on the rock just an arm's reach away.

"What the . . . ? What happened?" Kai mumbled. He sat up, shook his head, and saw the creature. "Oh."

For a moment, time froze: the wind whistling, the sky dark with storm clouds, the boys staring at the creature, the creature contemplating the boys. Then it spoke again.

"You bleed still?"

Peter would have expected the words to hiss, like a snake or like water receding from a sandy beach. But instead, this creature's voice rumbled, deep and melodious.

Kai touched his nose. "Um, yeah. I guess I do."

The creature didn't move. Those snaky eyes peered at the boys, then flicked around to the lighthouse. "This place," it said. "Much has changed since I was cast away, and yet they still build their towers to keep watch. Why have you brought me back, if such towers remain?"

"Brought you?" Peter felt like he was caught in a dream. Nothing made sense, but what could he do but let it sweep him along?

"It was you who called me," the creature said. "And you who bleeds, so you must have opened the gate to my prison." He waved at the swirling water behind him.

Although the creature mentioned Kai's bloody nose, it never took its eyes off Peter. Like it thought *Peter* was the one bleeding, or something.

"Look," Peter said. "I'm not bleeding. Kai is. And we didn't open any gate."

"Yeah," Kai said, standing. "So, Fishface, you can go back where you came from."

The thing didn't appreciate that. Thunder boomed, and the sea rippled with huge waves. "Would you so soon return me to where I was bound?" the creature growled. "You, foolish human, who lies when you say you did not open the gate, and bid me rise?"

"Actually, *I* said we didn't open any gate—" Peter started.

The creature wasn't listening to him. "I had dreamed of humans who would not take back what they once gave so freely. Who would honor me, and what I could bring them, instead of giving in to their greed."

It snarled, and a huge gust of wind bowled Kai back to the ground.

"But I was deceived," the creature said. "I feel the land's disgusting power, and I see the way you cling to it as you demand my departure. But I will not be dominated. I will make no mistake this time."

It lifted its fist, and another pillar of water shot out of the sea.

Peter yelled but couldn't hear himself over the rushing, swirling water.

The creature looked furious. "Your kind summoned and then feared me, cowering behind your filthy *land*. This time, you shall not fear without reason."

The water surged beneath them. Peter screamed as the water crashed down. Kai grabbed him and rolled, pulling them both out of the way.

"Let's go!" Kai yelled. Peter nodded. They both rose and ran.

Peter clung to Kai as they weaved through the trees. They took the trail that led back to the park. The wind screeched, and behind them, timbers moaned and creaked.

Don't look back. Don't look back! But then, a river of seawater, mud, and broken branches burst through the woods, directly in their path.

Despite his own warnings, Peter looked toward the sea. The forest had become a stormy twilight, and through the trees, he could see the creature hovering above the cliffs, an enormous wave rising behind it. It should have been a special effect in a movie, or video game. But this was a real wave.

This was so much worse than the rafting trip.

"Should you escape me," the creature said, "know that when the moon lends me her strength, I will blast the land with my power. I will send waves and floods until the mightiest mountains are brought low. This is my vow, human, and this will I keep!"

Thunder boomed, and the giant wave started to fall.

Kai wrenched Peter's arm. "Go! Go!"

Peter didn't need telling twice. He scrambled over fallen trunks, breath ragged in his throat. Just a little farther, and they'd reach the park at the edge of the forest and be safe with their family.

But how far could the creature send the wave?

As Peter and Kai, gasping, neared the park, water slammed into their backs like an enormous hand swatting two mosquitoes. Peter's breath was knocked out of him, and, disoriented, he swirled through filthy seawater. Salt stung his nose and eyes, and oddly, all he could think was, *If it hurts my nose, I bet Kai's really hurts.*

Something hard brushed Peter's grasping fingers, and he clutched on to it as sand and twigs grated his skin. Something strong grabbed his ankle, but all he cared about was holding his breath and praying nothing big, like a log, took his head off.

The water receded, and Peter found himself soaked, battered, and dirty, clinging to the picnic table his family had eaten at not long before. Salt water trickled in streams through the grassy fields.

The park was deserted. People must have seen the storm coming and taken shelter inside, their family included.

Good. No one else was hurt.

Kai slumped on the ground, coughing, his hand holding the table beside Peter. Splinters stuck out of his shirt.

"How bad is it?" Peter asked.

Kai waved a hand. "Nothing broken. I think."

Peter looked around. Seaspire's streets were as abandoned as the park. Rain pelted the twins, huge, heavy drops that felt like hammer strikes. Lightning split the sky, and thunder boomed. The town looked like the setting for a horror video game, especially with the storm raging.

They had to run. They had no idea how far the creature's power reached. Peter knelt beside Kai. "We have to get home," he said, yanking on Kai's arm.

Kai pushed him away and stood, still coughing. He nodded, his shirt stained pink with diluted blood.

Holding Kai's arm, Peter pulled his brother toward their grandmother's house. Behind him, the storm roared, howling words that Peter couldn't understand. Trembling, Peter ran, desperate to escape the next blow.

But no further attack came. Blinking rain out of their eyes, Peter and Kai stumbled into their grandmother's house, slamming the door on the tempest raging outside.

CHAPTER 4

SOMETHING WICKED

KAI

Kai, aching and stinging, tripped over the spiked mace Grandma used as a shoe scraper. As Peter frantically bolted the door, Kai huddled on the ground, trying to get something resembling clarity.

His eyes blurred with salt, and after getting hit with that wave, he felt like he was breathing sand. Something hard hit his shoulder; he realized it was the floor. He'd toppled over without noticing.

Kai sat up, blinking, and Peter sank to the ground and rested his head on his knees. "We're safe," Peter wheezed.

For now. The house creaked like the wind was trying to tear the walls off.

Kai rubbed his face with shaking hands and hissed as he brushed raw skin and splinters. He was covered with dirt and sand. His shirt had absorbed what his nose had bled out and was currently acting as a bandage for other cuts and abrasions.

"What *was* that?" Kai asked.

Peter just shook his head. His own shirt was missing a sleeve, and a huge scrape ran along his chin. He put his head in his hands. "I don't know. I don't know. Some kind of sea god? A hallucination?"

Kai snorted. *Hallucination?* Hallucinations didn't send waves to flatten forests.

A large splinter stuck out of his thumb. Carefully tugging it out, he thought of his dad, reading Shakespeare's *Macbeth* aloud to their family last winter.

By the pricking of my thumbs, something wicked this way comes.

For some reason, that made Kai laugh, which turned into a coughing fit. Water from his hair trickled past his ears, and he thought he'd never feel dry again.

What *was* that thing? Kai replayed the creature's arrival in his memory, letting it run all the way to when the wave finally caught the boys. Its power was incredible, a force of nature. What could they do against that?

There was only one thing to do. "Where's Dad? We need to tell him what happened out there."

Peter shook his head, spattering Kai with water. "And he'll do what? What can Dad do that doesn't end in him getting nearly drowned, too? Besides," Peter said quietly, "this isn't our problem."

Kai couldn't believe his ears. "Not our—not our problem? Seriously? Were you listening to that . . . that thing? It said *we* summoned it!"

"And how do you know it wasn't lying?" Peter squeezed the handle of Grandma's shoe scraper mace. "It must have been lying. We didn't do anything. How could we have called that thing?"

Kai stopped. "I don't know."

Peter was right. They didn't *do* anything. They went to the lighthouse, but they hadn't said any spells or lit any candles or whatever else Kai had seen people do on TV when they were summoning monsters or whatever.

Still, Kai couldn't believe it was a coincidence. "We must have done something. Creatures like that don't just appear. And it *said* we brought it back. Why would it lie, right before sending half the harbor down on our heads?"

"I don't know," Peter said. "But it doesn't matter. *This isn't our problem.* It's not."

"Then whose is it?"

"I don't know! A wizard, or scientist, or something. Someone who won't mess it up."

"Who says we'd mess it up?"

"Kai, we barely got away alive now. We'd fail. I know we would. Let's just . . . pretend this didn't happen, and we got caught in the storm with everyone else. Let someone who knows how to deal with it take it from here."

Kai looked over at Peter shaking, holding that mace like a lifeline. "Okay," he said. "But first, we tell Dad."

"Kai!"

"Dad might know someone who can help. If we don't say anything, then how would we get a message to them in time? That creature said it was going to drown the land. We can't just sit by."

Surely Peter understood that.

Peter opened his mouth, then shut it. "Fine," he said finally. "But Dad's not going to believe us."

"Why not?" Kai used the door to pull himself standing. "I haven't made a habit of lying to him. Have you?"

As Peter shook his head, Kai led the way toward the stairs. Maybe Dad was up there.

They'd only taken a few steps when the front door flew open and a very soaked Dad and Grandma stepped inside.

"Who bolted the door?" Grandma looked up and smiled at the boys. "See, Alexander, I told you they'd be here."

Dad rushed over. "We couldn't find you in the park when the storm started, and you weren't hunkered down with Sophie at the Fudge Kitchen. Where were you? What happened? Did you get hurt? What happened to your shirt?"

"Kai got a bloody nose at Frisbee," Peter said.

Dad sniffed. "I smell seawater. Did you go swimming? In the middle of a storm? You should have told us where you were going."

"We didn't go swimming, Dad," Kai said. "We were in the woods."

"Then why do I smell—Well. I'm glad you're safe." Dad smiled at them, which made Kai feel worse.

"We're not safe, Dad," Kai said.

Dad's smile melted. "You want to rephrase that?"

"Not this time. We're not safe."

From the living room, Grandma called, "Have you seen this?"

Dad went into the living room, followed by the boys. Grandma was watching the news. On the screen, there was the forest by the park, flattened and splintered.

"What happened?" Grandma breathed.

Dad turned to Kai. "You said you were in the forest?"

"Yeah. We got hit with a tidal wave! I have the scrapes and cuts to prove it!" He held up a cut arm.

"A tidal wave . . ." Dad shook his head. "That's impossible."

"It happened. We're fine, just a little battered. But there's more," Kai said. "There's a monster in the harbor. Peter and I went to the lighthouse, and when we were there, this . . . fishy snake guy appeared and told us we summoned him. Then he said he was going to flood the land, um, when did he say, Peter?"

Peter sighed. "Something about when the moon gave him the power to do it."

Kai nodded. "And that's when we ran. Through the forest by the park. And he threw a tidal wave at us. It blasted us out of the trees and into the park. I thought I was going to get the skin peeled off my bones, leaving my guts hanging out."

When Dad looked sick, Kai wished he hadn't described it so graphically.

Dad looked at Peter. "And you saw this happen, too, Rocky?"

Peter nodded, not even objecting to the nickname.

Now was the moment of truth. Would Dad believe them? Would he know how to help?

Dad pulled Kai, and also Peter, into a hug. Which hurt. "It must have been traumatic. Like a monster's attack."

"Dad, we're not lying, and this isn't a metaphor," Kai said. "There really is a monster out there."

Kai threw a glance at Peter. *Help me out here.* But Peter didn't say a word. How could he let this go? A monster was coming for them. They had to do more to fix this!

Their dad released them and shared a skeptical glance with their grandmother. "Neither of you are liars. But, being from Ohio, we're not used to these sudden sea storms. A tidal wave . . . no, it was probably just a big swell. While I'm sure it was terrifying, next time, stay farther away from the water whenever you see a storm coming in." Dad released them, and then said, "Now. Both of you, dinner is soon, and you smell like a reef. If you're both really feeling all right, then go wash up and get some dry clothes."

"But, Dad—"

"You'll feel better after drying off and eating spaghetti and some nice, hot garlic bread. I know I'm already gar-licking my chops." With a gentle pat on each of their shoulders, Dad returned to the kitchen to start dinner.

Kai followed him, about to argue again, but Peter just grabbed his arm and pulled him away. "I told you he wouldn't believe us," he murmured.

"He might have if you'd tried a little harder to convince him," Kai returned.

As Kai and Peter went upstairs, Kai heard Grandma mutter to Dad, "That didn't look good, Alex. The forest by the park was hit by something more than a big swell."

Their dad breathed out loudly through his nose. "Thank heavens, then, that the boys escaped with just some scrapes. Poor kids. Must have been horrible."

Kai resisted the urge to run back in and make his case again. But what good would it do? Sure, he and Peter were beat up and soaking wet, but that wasn't exactly hard evidence of a supernatural sea monster on the rampage.

Unless Kai could prove that something monstrous and powerful was coming, no one would believe his story. Maybe he would go back out later and look for proof, but right now, a storm was raging, dinner was about to be served, and there was nothing to do but take a quick shower, change his clothes, and eat.

CHAPTER 5

PLATES AND PLATO

PETER

Sophie had come back home while Peter showered and pulled his splinters out. One, a piece of wood two inches long, still made him queasy to think about.

When he went downstairs, there was his sister, jeans soaked to the knee, holding a bag of reject taffy. "Hey, hey, hey!" she called in a TV announcer's voice. "It's time for another round of 'What Flavor Was *This* Supposed to Be?'" She handed him a golden-colored piece of taffy. And then she stopped, examining his face. "What's wrong? What happened?"

"Nothing. Don't worry about it." Peter stuck the taffy, which tasted like green apple, into his mouth and hurried off to dinner.

Sophie didn't need to know, because it was over. So he and Kai maybe, *maybe*, raised some kind of sea monster. They tried to tell their dad, and maybe Peter could have pushed harder like Kai wanted, but if he had, what if Dad lost his temper and grounded them for lying? It would have been a mistake. No, they'd done all they could. Now, it was out of their hands. Let someone else handle this problem.

Kai, on the other hand, was a morose mess at dinner. He pushed his spaghetti around his plate, only ate one piece of garlic bread, and didn't even smile when Grandma referred to a Revolutionary War–era musket as "modern technology."

After dinner, Sophie brought down her laptop (the only computer in the house) for their video call with Mom.

As the computer started, Peter whispered to Kai, "Come on. Just act normal tonight. It's not like Mom can help us with the monster."

"You don't know that. Maybe she could," Kai said, but there was no fight in it. Peter knew Kai would keep his mouth shut. After all, Mom was on a dig in the Mediterranean, far away from all of this. What could she say or do to help?

It took a few moments to make the connection to Mom's laptop, even though Mom was expecting their call. Though they could call whenever they wanted, they always called every Tuesday and Friday, right on time, and Peter looked forward to seeing his mother through the screen.

Tonight, when the image did appear, it was more pixelated than usual. Their mom looked fuzzy, and when she moved, the image would freeze and turn green in terrifying flashes that reminded Peter of the creature's rise from the sea.

But still, he could see her eyes crinkle and her mouth turn up in a smile. The laptop's glow lit her face, tingeing her golden skin bluish white, as she sat in her tiny cabin on the boat the expedition used.

"Hey," their mom said, her voice buzzing through the bad connection. "How are you all doing?"

"Hello, Thera!" Grandma said. "It's good to see you."

"How are *you*?" Dad said. "It looks like your boat needs a new router."

Their mother shook her head and smiled. "The router is fine. It's just this storm. It's giving us some interference. Don't worry. Sam says it should even out soon."

"A storm?" Kai asked, and he and Peter glanced at each other.

Peter shook his head. *Don't. Don't you dare tell Mom.*

But if Kai was about to speak up, he lost his chance. Dad touched Kai's shoulder and said, "We're getting hit pretty hard here. A real nasty nor'easter storm. In fact, the boys experienced a pretty nasty wave."

"What?" Mom pushed a dark curl out of her eyes and peered at the boys. "Are you okay?"

"We're fine. But we're surprised you're getting a storm, too," Kai said. "At the same time."

He shot a glance back at Peter, which Peter read easily. *Two storms? At once? It has to be connected.*

Peter scowled but ignored Kai. They didn't need to tell Mom, because it wasn't their *problem*.

Their mom frowned. "Oh. Well. Storms are common here. But I have to admit, this one does seem a little . . . angrier than usual."

Kai nudged Peter, and Peter kicked him under the table. "No," he whispered.

But Kai didn't listen. "Angrier? Like a monster?"

As Peter and Dad sighed, Grandma said, "A storm *can* be a monster. Especially on the sea."

Mom smiled wryly. "If the sea's angry, I'm sorry. Sam's been saying it's because we brought *this* out of the ocean. The sea wants it back."

She tugged on some gloves and lifted something that Peter could barely see. It looked like metal.

"Turn it this way," Dad said, and readjusted the monitor so they could all huddle and peer through the pixelation to see what their mother had found.

"We uncovered it just this morning," Mom said.

It was a gray metal plate, about the size of his math textbook, though much thinner. Peter squinted. It looked like there was a figure of some kind engraved on it, and small images all around it.

Not figures. More like hieroglyphs.

"It's hard to see," he said.

"Maybe I can fix that," their mom said. She lowered the plate and fiddled with her computer for a few minutes, with Sophie providing advice. The video quality improved sharply, and their mother laughed.

"I probably shouldn't be showing you this. This dig is hush-hush. But you won't tell anyone, will you?"

She held up the plate again, right against the camera, and Peter's blood drained to his feet.

That figure in the middle was the creature from the beach! The same wide-set eyes, the same snaky body and fishy face. Powerful, it held a trident in one hand as waves curled beneath it. In those waves, Peter saw a crocodile.

How? How could Mom have found a picture of the sea monster in the Mediterranean?

He turned to see how Kai was handling it. Not surprisingly, Kai had blanched. His eyes flicked back and forth over the screen, and his lips fluttered.

"How old is it?" Grandma asked.

"At least a millennium," Mom said. She let them stare into the face of the sea monster for another few seconds before pulling it back. Looking at the plate's front, she said, "We have our guesses about who this ugly guy here is, but so far they're just guesses."

"Well, isn't it Poseidon?" Dad asked. "I mean, look at that trident."

"And aren't you in the Mediterranean? Who else would it be?" Peter asked.

Mom coughed and bit her lip. "It's not Poseidon," she said slowly. "This tablet *predates* Greece. It's truly fascinating. What I wouldn't give to know what this inscription says!" She tapped the hieroglyphs.

Kai cleared his throat. "It says, 'Hail to the Sea, which gives and takes as waves ebb and flow, with salt like blood and sand like gold, that surges land and water with earthquake.'"

Peter slowly turned to face Kai, as did everyone else in the family. Kai slumped his shoulders, but finished. "'We, the isle of your care, united in our devotion, honor and revere you, with light and with sacred metal.' Um, that's what it says, but it's not an exact translation. Some of the words have multiple meanings that don't work well in English."

The only sound was the whirring of the laptop's fan. The adults stared at Kai, who refused to look up.

Dad chuckled. "Nice one, Kai."

Peter relaxed. Of course it was just a prank.

"I'm not joking!" Kai said. "I can read it."

Sophie rolled her eyes. "Of course you'd say that when we can't prove you're kidding." She reached across the table and pulled over the French book she'd been studying with her tutor earlier. "Now, if you said you could read *this*—"

Kai leaned over. "I can!"

He pulled the book closer and ran a finger under the words. "'While many believe that the Louvre is the sole museum to visit while in Paris, one not worth overlooking is the Musée d'Orsay, where one can find great works of art produced by the Impressionists—'"

Sophie snatched it back and read the passage. "He's right."

"French is one thing," Mom said. She scribbled out a few words on a piece of paper and held them up to the camera. "I know you never learned Greek."

Kai could read that, too. And Cantonese, and Danish, and Russian. One language might be explained, but every language?

"How are you doing this?" Dad asked Kai.

"I—I don't know," Kai said, hands trembling. They were all in shock, but Kai was in the center of it.

After a while, all eyes turned back to the tablet in Mom's hands. "What did this one say again, Kai?" Mom asked.

"I've got to read it again."

As their mother held up the tablet, Peter watched his twin read the same words aloud, again. Because Kai was *reading* the tablet. Peter noticed his eyes moving from right to left, reading the symbols backward. Then, the eyes tracked up and down, reading in columns. It was bizarre.

Chills rippled over Peter's skin. His brother had become some kind of polyglot, able to read and interpret any language. How had this happened?

"I don't know how I know what it's saying, but I do," Kai said, once he finished.

"I believe you," Mom said quietly. She set the tablet down and looked at Kai, not saying anything for an uncomfortable minute. Then, she glanced at Dad. "Alex, I think we should tell them."

Dad leaned back. "Yes," he said. "All things considered."

"Tell us what?" Kai asked.

Mom looked at each of them. "I'm not in the Mediterranean," she said. "I'm in the North Sea, near Norway."

Peter sat up. "Why?"

"And why didn't you tell us?" Kai added.

"I suppose I was a little embarrassed," Mom said. "Though, the truth is, this expedition *is* related to Greece, in a way."

Dad winked at the boys. "It does if you *sea* things from a different perspective."

Peter groaned. Leave it to Dad to make puns about this.

Kai piped up. "So it is Poseidon, then. On the tablet."

Mom shook her head. "No. We're certain of that. Yes, it has the trident, but the crocodile is an Egyptian water deity symbol, not Greek. There are symbols and references on this tablet to ocean gods from many different cultures. Including the Norse, which is why I'm in the North Sea. Our best guess is this is supposed to be some kind of depiction of the *actual* ocean, but embodied and possibly sentient. Alive."

Kai scoffed. "The *ocean* come to life? That's not possible."

"Says the boy who seemingly conquered the Tower of Babel and can read any language," Grandma replied.

"Fair point," Kai said, and nudged Sophie's French book closer, eyes wide.

"How is the North Sea related at all to Greece?" Peter asked. He missed how he felt earlier that morning, when everything made sense.

"It's a long story. But it starts with Ric studying Plato and getting ideas. Since Plato was a Greek philosopher, Ric invited me because he knows I have a background in Greek antiquities."

Mom bit her lip again and continued. "Plato wrote about an island. An ancient island with a magnificent, enlightened civilization. An island no one has been able to find. Ric and Sam decided to cross-reference weather patterns with stories about lost islands, and turned up enough connections in the North Sea to get funding. It was a long shot, but then we found this tablet, which only seems to confirm that we're in the right place."

Peter sat back, putting the pieces together. With a Greek archeologist for a mom and an English teacher for a dad, he knew what they were talking about. But who didn't know the story about an ancient city that was a marvel of politics and engineering, medicine and arts, until it fell, and was destroyed in a single day and night, sinking beneath the sea?

"Are you saying that you've been out searching for—" Peter's throat closed up.

Mom nodded. "Atlantis. We came out here to find the lost island of Atlantis. And now, thanks to Kai's translation, I know we've found it."

CHAPTER 6

SOLVING THE PATTERN

KAI

Atlantis.

It was a couple of days since the incident, and still his mind reeled.

The island of Atlantis was real. It felt like destiny—Mom was Greek, and now Kai and his family were wrapped up in Greek mythology, like fate had chosen them.

And fate had also gifted Kai with powers. He could read any language, understanding them like they were written in English. Although he couldn't understand them spoken (Mom and Sophie both checked) that was still pretty cool.

Though, the Actual Ocean Come to Life, or whatever it was, had attacked Kai and Peter and was only escalating its attack. That wasn't as cool.

The rain that started when the sea creature first appeared had continued for about a day before dwindling to a gentle but consistent patter. At first, nothing seemed too bad. The rain was a constant reminder of the event at the Point, but not dangerous. And sure, the jellyfish that filled the sea off the coast and beached on the sand, melting like jelly, were unnerving, but easily explained away.

But then it got worse the next night.

An eerie blue light that Grandma called Saint Elmo's fire appeared around the Seaspire lighthouse. The wind howled words into people's ears, causing police to prowl the streets, causing Sophie to come home early from work, white faced and clutching her ears. Nothing anyone said could convince her to reveal what she heard.

Finally, and worst of all, an underground surge flooded the church graveyard, making coffins float to the surface.

The next morning, Grandma had gone with her community committee to help clean the mess up, and came home that evening muddy and silent. She refused to tell them what she saw at the cemetery, instead saying, "We need to figure out what happened to you boys on the Point."

Kai agreed. They were clearly involved now, and he knew things would only get worse. That's how all adventures went.

So, that night, they called Mom again and tried to figure out how and why the creature rose.

Peter began by explaining, again, what the boys had experienced on the Point.

"We barely got back alive," he finished. "And it was that creature."

"And now we have a tablet that was from Atlantis, and Kai can read Atlantean," Mom said.

Kai jumped in. "It's connected. It has to be."

Dad had printed out a scan of Mom's stone tablet, and Kai

couldn't stop examining it. The hieroglyphs carved there flared in Kai's mind, every one of them making sense. How? Last he checked, they didn't teach Atlantean writing at school. He shouldn't be able to look at the symbol of a circle with a vertical wavy line through it and think, *That's what the letter* A *looks like.*

Though that's *not* how it worked. That symbol meant "sea," but it also meant so much more. It was related to the word for life, for power, and, oddly, the word for twin. He understood every meaning of that symbol, and how it interacted with the symbols around it. He knew that writing as well as he knew English.

It was all a pattern. The hieroglyphs, sure, the way they created meaning together. But the monster rising, the tablet, and the writing—it was also a pattern.

"I think I can read Atlantean because we let that creature loose," Kai said.

Mom frowned. "Let it loose?"

"It," Peter said. "The . . . Sea, or whatever we want to call it."

"The Sea works for me," Kai said.

"Okay, that," Peter said. "*The Sea* said we released it from some binding. But we didn't do anything. We just went to the beach."

"You must have done something," Dad said. Kai noticed his father's hands were shaking.

Peter shook his head. "We didn't do any ritual, if that's what you mean."

"Maybe you did one and didn't know about it," Mom said.

Grandma's eyes lit up. "Your mother's right. Rituals are just actions with meaning, set in an order. Without the context of that meaning and order, you may have thought you just did random actions. Tell me. Was there any blood when you went to the beach? Before the creature showed up?"

Kai touched his nose. "I got hit in the face playing Frisbee. My nose started bleeding. It stopped, but it started again when we were at the Point."

Grandma nodded. "Lots of rituals involve blood."

"And special locations," Mom added. "Is that Point a place of power, maybe even considered sacred?"

Kai and Peter glanced at each other. "It's supposed to be haunted," Kai said.

Dad leaned over the table. "Walk us through what you did. *Exactly* what you did."

So Kai and Peter explained everything. How they played Frisbee and how Kai got hit. What Todd said about the lighthouse. How they got hot dogs and went to the Point. Embarrassed, Kai mentioned how Peter wiped his sweaty face on the hot dog and how Kai sneezed blood on it, and how they tossed it into the ocean.

At this, their dad hissed. "An offering," he said.

Kai shook his head. "It was just a gross hot dog," he said. "Who'd want that?"

"A gross hot dog covered with your blood and sweat," Dad said. "Blood and salt have power in a lot of folklore."

"Besides," Grandma added. "You'd be surprised what passes as an offering. In ancient Greece, the people would offer bones and fat, the leftovers of the animals they ate." She smiled. "It makes sense if Poseidon is who you summoned. I suppose a hot dog is basically the unwanted parts of a pig."

Kai decided he would never eat a hot dog again.

"And bread, like a hot dog bun, is also a common ritual element," Mom added.

Was that all that happened? Surely people got cuts and tossed food in the ocean. What made their "ritual" different?

"So we went to a place of power and made an offering that included blood," Peter said. "But don't rituals need, like, words? A spoken spell, or something?"

Peter had a point. They may have made an offering, but they hadn't recited some magic words.

"What did you say? Repeat everything," Mom said.

As Peter struggled to remember and recite what he and Kai had been saying at the Point, Kai scanned back over the day. He stuck on the little girls jumping rope. *One poor sailor dressed in red, brought some pork and brought some bread.* They weren't wearing red, but that could mean the blood. Pork and bread? The hot dog. But did the girls mention any kind of summoning words? He couldn't remember.

"Grandma, have you ever heard of a jump rope rhyme that talks about a sailor dressed in red?" Kai asked.

Grandma stopped interrogating Peter. "A little. We used to jump to it when I was a girl. I think I can remember it:

"*One poor sailor dressed in red,*" she said, tapping her foot.
"*Brought some pork and brought some bread.*
Fell asleep out on the stone,
When he woke up, not alone.
Made a new friend, and then,
Had to do it over again!"

Dad leaned back. "That does sound like our ritual. But it's not complete. It does remind me of . . . something." He turned to Grandma. "Isn't there an old chantey from Seaspire? Something about the ocean rising?"

She nodded and started to sing, and Dad joined in:

> *Rise, the ocean rise,*
> *Rise and greet the shore.*
> *With red and bread, he feeds on the dead,*
> *And meets you at the door.*

"I always thought that song was nonsense," Dad said. "I mean, isn't there a verse about the sailor coming to the point with 'his own sorry self by his side'? How could that even be possible?"

Kai sat up. "His own self? You mean, like an identical twin?"

As Dad and Grandma fell silent, Kai watched the pattern form. It was coming together. Somehow, he and Peter, being twins, had fulfilled part of the ritual's requirements. They'd used blood and salt and bread and meat and made an offering to some sea creature. But was that all it took? How would the creature know what they wanted?

"Rise, ocean," Peter said suddenly. Kai looked at him, and Peter said, "That song. It tells the ocean to rise. I told you to get up, Kai. I used your name."

Kai felt numb. "My name means 'ocean.'" He ran his tongue over his chipped tooth. "It was an accident. We didn't mean to raise that thing."

Peter was scowling. "Why twins?" he asked. "Why was that part of the ritual?"

Shrugs all around. No one knew.

Dad had more pressing questions. "Why's it attacking? You did *nothing* to it. If anything, you helped it."

Kai felt chilled. "I don't know."

Why was it attacking them? It had seemed calm, even disoriented, when it first arrived, but it became angry so quickly. Kai had no idea why it was causing rainstorms and Saint Elmo's fire and graves to float out of the ground.

But the *why* didn't matter. "It's attacking us," Kai said. "That's what matters. And we need to make it stop."

"At this rate, it's just going to get worse." Sophie's arms were tucked against her chest. She stared past the computer screen.

With a jolt, Kai remembered. It *was* going to get worse. "That thing said he'd flood the land when the moon lent him her strength." The moon. Didn't it create tides? Again, a pattern was emerging. "When's the next full moon?"

"In one week," Grandma said. She squeezed her sword cane.

Peter slumped in his chair. "We brought back a sea monster, and in one week the world will flood. Because of us."

Kai felt like he'd been pounded in the stomach by a tidal wave.

Mom's image flickered, and the laptop let out an electronic shriek. "Sorry," she said, her voice crackling. "The storm is getting worse. I have to get off tonight. Kai, Peter, it's going to be okay. I'll do some research, and we'll figure it out. It's going to be o—"

Mom vanished.

The kitchen was quiet except for the return of the pounding rain. Then Dad turned and ran out the door.

Did he just do that? Kai looked at Peter, and then back at the door. "Come on," he said to Peter, grabbing his arm. When Peter resisted, Kai added, "We can't let him be alone out there!"

Groaning, Peter followed Kai into the storm.

The gentle rain had once again turned into a downpour the boys had to blink out of their eyes. Kai splashed through the flooded street, searching for his dad and hoping he wouldn't see a corpse boating down in a floating coffin.

"There!" Peter yelled. Dad was sloshing toward the beach.

"Oh no!" Still towing Peter, Kai charged after their dad. "Dad! Stop!"

Their dad couldn't hear them. The rain drummed and thunder rolled as he ran onto the beach and to the edge of the gnawing waves. "Hey!" Kai heard him yell. "You! The sentient embodiment of the Sea or whatever you are! Come out if you're really there."

The sea roared like a tiger. Waves leaped higher, forming the shape of the creature. One, like a tentacle, surged across the sand, knocking Dad off-balance.

Kai raced toward his father and grabbed his arm. Peter did the same. Another wave came, and this time, in the roar, Kai heard, *You can't stop me.*

Another wave washed out the sand under Kai's feet, knocking him into the surf. Peter yelled as another white, foaming wave tumbled him to the ground. They were caught in a current as strong as chains, being dragged toward the raging ocean.

Toward a monster.

Dad acted quickly. Dropping to his knees, he grabbed their arms and hauled them out from the creature's control. Kai groaned. The ocean's pull was as strong as iron.

But Dad won. He towed Kai and Peter away as waves continued

to lash the shore, trying to capture them in its tides again. He didn't stop until they were back on the street.

"I'm sorry," Dad gasped. "I'm sorry."

"It's fine," Kai said. His legs had been scraped raw by the sand. So had Peter's.

"No, it's not." Dad, shaking, hugged both boys and pulled them up. "You could have been dragged out to sea. It's my fault. I shouldn't have . . . let's go home, where it's safe. Now."

Dad steered Kai and Peter back through the flood toward Grandma's house. Kai threw a glance over his shoulder at the ocean. Its surges roared with anger, baring white-capped waves like teeth. Home might be safe *now*, but Kai knew that, for him and Peter, no place would be safe.

And at the next full moon, nowhere on land would be, for anyone.

CHAPTER 7

STORM TRACKING

PETER

The next morning, Sophie was waiting at the breakfast table wearing her pink work shirt. A dirty dish, her laptop, and an open textbook sat next to her. "Raise any more monsters last night?" she teased as Peter trudged past on his way to the cupboard.

"Yep, and they caught me and ate me. Now I'm a ghost. Can't you tell?"

Peter hadn't slept well. All night, his dreams had been filled with slimy undersea creatures and waves flooding through the streets of Seaspire. They may as well have been more monsters raised from the deep. And he wasn't in the mood to banter with Sophie, especially not when he still felt guilty.

"It's going to be all right," Sophie said. "Of course it will." She returned to outlining her chemistry lesson, but only typed a few lines before slamming the laptop shut.

Peter grabbed a box of frosted cornflakes and wandered to the bowl cupboard.

"Sweetie, don't bother," Grandma said. She was by the stove, loading eggs into the copper shield-plate. A stack of bacon was already beside it. "Cereal won't be enough, not for the big day you have ahead of you."

"Big day?" It was Kai, swooping into the kitchen. "Hey, those smell great!"

As Kai scooped a pile of eggs and bacon, Peter frowned at his grandmother.

She limped over to the table, leaving her cane at the counter. "You'll need to stop that sea creature before he floods Seaspire," she said. "Well, the storm has passed, so today's the best time to start."

"Start?" Sophie tapped the closed laptop. "You mean, today? Right now?"

"No better time," Grandma said. "The signs seem to be clear. Why wait?"

Dad came into the kitchen. When he saw the heaping shield, he groaned. "Mom, why?"

"The real question, as always, is why not? The shield works beautifully as a platter." Grandma waved something that might have been a spatula, but, with her, you never could tell. "Kai, honey, get your brother and father something to eat."

Kai rolled his eyes, but loaded up a couple of more plates. "You don't want to start now?" he asked Sophie.

Sophie tilted her head. "I don't know. I just think we're rushing into this. Why not hang back and look at our options?"

"Such as?" Dad asked.

Sophie squirmed. "I'm just saying there's a lot we don't know. How are we supposed to stop this thing? If it really is some all-powerful sea entity there's no way we have a chance." She ran a finger along the side of her plate. In a quieter voice, she said, "Maybe we should just get out of town while we still can."

"Sophie has a point," Peter said.

Kai glared at Peter. "There's got to be some clue we can follow. I mean, I can read any language, including Atlantean. Why would I get that power if we were all doomed to drown?"

"Maybe it was just a side effect," Sophie muttered, and then stood to take her plate to the sink.

Peter didn't know. In fact, there was so much they didn't know. How could they get started, like Grandma wanted to, when they didn't even have enough info to make a plan?

"Look," he piped up. "Maybe all we can do is leave the coast. I mean, there's a lot of land. I'm sure this creature can't flood it all."

Kai scowled at him. "So you want people to drown?"

"No, that's not what I meant." Peter stopped and strung together his thoughts. "I'm just saying that we have no direction. We don't know why the creature was so angry at us, just that it was and it attacked our town."

Peter's arms felt heavy. It had been made abundantly clear that he and Kai were responsible for all this trouble, by raising the monster. And now that Kai could read Atlantean, it was also clear that they were *still* involved, no matter what Peter thought about the subject. No doubt his family blamed them for taking a nice family vacation and turning it into a nightmare.

But his family wasn't looking at him with blame. Even Kai had gone thoughtful. "I wonder where the storm went," he said. "It hit us, because the Sea was mad at us, sure, but it also hit Mom on the North Sea. Where Atlantis used to be."

"Maybe the storm is hitting places that were important to it," Grandma said.

Peter caught on. "Do you think it attacked anywhere else?"

"Let's find out."

Silently, Sophie opened her laptop and pulled up local weather reports. It didn't take long to discover that when the storm that struck Seaspire had lulled, it traveled down the coast and hit another location, raging with violence that made the rainfall in Seaspire look tame.

Peter looked at the location. "What's Dogtown?"

"Dogtown?" Kai looked at his dad. "Is the sheriff a German shepherd?"

"No, but he's great at sniffing out crime," Dad responded.

"Boys, please." Grandma snatched up Sophie's laptop and after a few moments, turned it to face the boys.

Peter looked at the screen. He saw old photos of huge boulders with phrases like KINDNESS and BE ON TIME carved into their sides, but also newer pictures, from the local news, of trees cracked and toppled, covered with what looked like seaweed.

Their new friend had been there, all right.

"Doesn't look like any dogs I've ever seen," Kai said.

"Dogtown is on Cape Ann, Massachusetts," Grandma said. "And it's not a town for dogs, Kai, for crying out loud. It's an old, abandoned settlement."

"So no one was hurt in the storm if it's abandoned," Peter said as Kai muttered something about "just trying to be funny."

Dad pushed his eggs around his plate, and Peter's stomach twisted. He imagined Dad falling into the water. What if the creature had wanted to carry Dad out to sea? What if Dad had been lost, because of Peter and Kai?

"We're sorry," he said. "We didn't mean to start all of this."

"You have nothing to be sorry for," Dad said. "You or Kai. If anyone knew that you could raise an ancient sea god by throwing a hot dog into the water by the Spire, they didn't tell anyone. You couldn't have known."

Grandma nodded. "And you *didn't* start this, boys. The Atlanteans did when they sealed the Sea up at the Point. You won't have to end it alone. We'll be with you. Starting with Dogtown." Grandma shook her head at the news images of the storm-wrecked Dogtown. "It's a shame you'll see it in this state. It's an interesting piece of local history. Apparently the town was thought to be a haven for witches."

Kai looked up. "Witches?"

"No such thing," Sophie said.

"Would have said the same thing about sea monsters yesterday, but here we are," Dad said.

Interesting, Peter thought, *that a place with a strange history would be attacked by the monster, specifically. What was hiding there?*

"Well, either way, Dogtown was abandoned," Grandma added.

Kai grabbed the laptop and did a quick search. "Apparently, decades later, a guy named Roger Babson had these boulders carved with moral statements."

"Maybe he sensed something spooky about that place," Peter said.

"And now spooky things are happening there again," Kai added. "If that creature is creating the storms, then maybe there's something at Dogtown it really doesn't like."

"Or *does* like." Grandma sat down with her own heaping plate. "Which is why we need our strength if we're going to visit Dogtown today and get some answers."

What?

"I don't think that's a good idea," Peter said. They had no plan. They'd already set this mess in motion without even realizing it. What if this time, one of them got hurt worse?

"I second that," Dad said. "The boys already survived one encounter with that thing. We can't drag them into another. I'll go, alone. You all stay here."

Kai raised his arms. "We're involved! That thing knows what we look like. Besides, what if there's an inscription written in Atlantean? Or in any other language. Unless one of you got a crash course overnight, you'll need me."

As Dad searched for a way to counter Kai's logic, Sophie jumped in. "Well, count me out."

Peter stared. It was unlike Sophie to stay home when something big was happening.

Kai noticed, too. "Why?"

Sophie leaned against the wall, her gaze slipping to the floor. "I have too much to do," she mumbled. "And you won't need me. Not if you're all going."

"But we'd want you there."

Sophie paled. "I just can't do it today. You know, with the tutoring and the job and everything."

Kai scowled. "And that's more important than saving the world?"

Sophie raised her hands. "No, it's just—you don't know that you'll find anything. Someone should stay home. Hold down the fort, right?"

Something was up with Sophie. But Peter couldn't tell what, exactly.

"Fine," Kai said. "But we're taking your drone."

"What?" Sophie's drone was one of her most precious possessions. It had a camera and everything.

"We could use eyes in the sky," Dad said, sounding tired. "We'll need it, Sophie." After Sophie, just as weary, agreed, Dad continued, "Okay, Kai, you boys are coming. But at my word, we leave. Got it?"

Grandma stood up, rubbing her hands. "I'd better get the Damascus dagger. It won't want to stay home for this."

"Mom, your leg. And won't the Cleanup Committee need you?"

"My leg is strong enough for this, and the girls can manage the park without me," Grandma said. Her face softened into somberness. "Seaspire needs this more."

"I don't mind staying home with Sophie," Peter said as Grandma hurried out of the room. After all, he couldn't read Atlantean, and the sea creature didn't seem to notice a difference between him and Kai. There was no point in his going to Dogtown, and if he stayed home, he couldn't make a mistake and accidentally cause more harm.

On the other hand, Peter realized they didn't know much about this thing. Sure, Dad seemed to think of it as some nature god, but Peter wasn't sure. Could a god be sealed away like that, and summoned with nothing but a hot dog?

And if it was the godlike embodiment of the ocean, why was it here in Massachusetts? Sure, the Sea's prison was at the Point next to the lighthouse, but why, if Atlantis used to be in the North Sea? Plus, why did the creature care about another Massachusetts location like Dogtown? Despite absolutely not wanting to get involved, Peter found himself interested. There was something more to this creature, and he might notice another piece of the puzzle at Dogtown—or at the very least, he could keep Kai out of trouble.

"Okay, never mind," he said, standing. "I'm coming."

Dad rolled his eyes. "You know, when I said this vacation would be an adventure, this isn't exactly what I had in mind."

CHAPTER 8

DOGTOWN

KAI

The drive to Dogtown wasn't too long, just an hour or so. That gave Kai plenty of time to steal his dad's phone and find out more about the place. It had been a town, but the last building was destroyed in 1845, and now it was simply a densely wooded Massachusetts historical site, where you could go and hike a trail past all the Babson Boulders with their inspiring messages.

"I did it once when I first moved here," Grandma said when Kai asked about it. "But you walk it once, you see it all, and boulders aren't much compared to a good blade."

With that, Grandma began checking her dagger's sharpness. The silver swirls gleamed in the sunlight.

Peter held Sophie's borrowed drone on his lap. He was mainly silent during the ride, but once, while Dad and Grandma discussed which route to take, he whispered to Kai, "Hey, do you think something weird is going on with Sophie?"

Kai thought back. Yeah, she had been weird at dinner. If there was one member of the family Kai thought would be right behind them on this adventure . . . well, it was Grandma. But Sophie was a close second.

He thought about the way she'd acted, what she said at breakfast. *You don't know that you'll find anything.*

"Maybe she doesn't really believe us," Kai said.

"After everything we've seen?" Peter asked.

Kai shrugged, closed his eyes, and tried to remember the Atlantean symbols he'd read.

They came back. It was so strange—he remembered some of them, and as he thought of them, their meanings became clear. Some symbols meant full words as well as sounds, and others had multiple meanings. English didn't always have a perfect match.

There was one meaning of the "ocean" symbol that Kai couldn't figure out. It was related to the meaning for twin, but it wasn't clear. Maybe if he thought harder, it would come to him. Or maybe if he read a little more Atlantean and got a better feel for the language.

"All right," Dad said. "We're here."

He pulled into a small parking area in the middle of a forest. It was just off the road, next to a wooden sign, the kind that you see at the beginning of trails. Kai was surprised Dad had found it. And when he looked around, he was surprised that Dad had been able to drive here at all.

Kai had seen pictures of the forests around Mount Saint Helens after it erupted in 1980. All the trees on the ground, bowled over by massive, heavy clouds of volcanic ash. Well, these trees were wet, not ashy, but the overall effect was the same. Only some trees remained standing. Many others had splintered and fallen, or had been ripped out at the roots. They lay as even as floorboards, like the blow had come from the same direction.

It was a far cry from the lush forest they'd expected.

"Who flattened this place?" Kai said, climbing out of the car.

Peter looked at him. "Who do you think?"

"Right. Poseidon." Feeling silly, he stomped his foot, enjoying how the dust puffed up before falling into a circle around it.

"The good news is we'll have the place to ourselves," Dad said. "No tourists. As long as we're gone before cleanup crews come in, we can do whatever we want." He shivered. "Let's be quick."

Grandma emerged, with her knife strapped to her side in a sheath and her sword cane in hand. She wore a backpack. "I have sandwiches, bottled lemonade, and obsidian knives in case of emergency." When Dad glared at her, she said, "They were made this century, Alex. I promise."

"That's not—never mind. We should get going."

For a moment, the family surveyed the wreckage. "Go where?" Peter asked.

"I guess we should hike the trail?" Kai said. "Or where the trail used to be."

Peter stared at the woods. "Yeah," he said. "It's hard to tell, but I think the damage gets worse that way."

Dad shrugged. "It's a start. And if all this began at the Spire, maybe the in*spire*-ing boulders are the way to go."

Kai snorted, and Peter held out the drone.

Dad pulled out his phone. "I'll let you know if the camera sees anything strange," he said. A moment later, the drone was airborne.

And the family was on its way. The going was not easy since the trail was covered with fallen trees and bracken. The air smelled like wet dirt and seaweed, with a fishy odor under it all that made Kai shudder. That creature had been here. But why?

The morning air was hot and humid, and Grandma had already opened her bottle of lemonade. She was limping worse, but never responded if anyone commented or asked if she wanted to slow down. Dad panted, climbing over another fallen tree. The trees, though still aligned with one another, had fallen in a new direction compared to how they'd fallen closer to the parking lot. So maybe whatever flattened them had come from multiple directions?

Interesting. Why would it do that, when the ocean was east?

Kai fell into step next to Peter. "What do you think we'll find?"

Peter shrugged. "Hopefully nothing. But I don't know. Why do you think the sea creature cared about this place? This isn't the ocean. It's a forest."

Good point. "I guess we'll find out," Kai said. They reached the first engraved boulder, and Kai pointed at it. "'Get a job,'" he read.

"I tried," Peter said. "No one would take me. They all thought I was you."

The boys laughed and raced ahead to be the first to find the next boulders.

HELP MOTHER

SAVE

TRUTH

WORK

COURAGE

Shortly after the COURAGE boulder, Kai felt something like bony fingers grab his ankle. Yelping, he looked down, but saw nothing but twigs. His foot must have caught on another fallen branch.

But it had felt like fingers, gripping him tight.

A moment later, Sophie's drone plummeted from the sky.

It crashed into a pile of seaweed hanging off a fallen pine, sending a crab scuttling to safety. Sophie would kill them all if her precious drone was broken.

Dad gathered it up, searching for damage. "It seems all right. Maybe it's just the battery," he said. "Though Sophie said it should be good for hours."

Peter stiffened. "I don't think it's the battery. Listen."

Rustling, all around. Trees creaking and moving as if in high wind. But there was only a gentle breeze that couldn't account for the goose bumps forming on Kai's neck.

Dad grabbed Kai's and Peter's shoulders. "Get back to the car. Now."

They turned around and headed back toward the car. The sparse, bleak forest was starting to give Kai the creeps. So many of the trees lay across the path, the leaves still clinging to their stripped branches beginning to wither and die. The ones that remained standing seemed to judge the family as they picked their way through the woods.

After what felt like hours, Kai was still looking at that ruined landscape and not the parking lot.

"I think we missed it," Kai said.

"We couldn't have," Dad said. "We're still on the path. I've minded the way."

Peter pointed. "Please tell me your mind wandered."

They were standing in front of a boulder. GET A JOB. The first one they'd passed.

"There's no way," Dad said, circling the boulder. "We couldn't have walked that long."

"We didn't," Peter said.

Beside them, Grandma unsheathed her knife, a gleam in her eye.

Dad turned red. "Put that away, Mom. We're close to the car. It was this way. I remember."

Dad started walking as Grandma ignored him and kept the knife out. Silently, she took out a ball of yarn and tied one end to a branch.

They pressed on. The forest seemed to watch them, and after only a moment, Kai jumped.

"Something just touched my leg," he said.

"Just a stick," Dad said, but he bit his lip and pushed on faster.

They hadn't gone far when a branch tangled around Peter's legs, making him fall. Grandma hacked it off him with her knife, but before they could take another step, Kai's shirt caught on a tree. Or had the tree caught him?

Kai tugged, tearing the fabric. He wrapped his fingers around his arms and tried to avoid thinking about the trees. But it was hard, as that rustling grew.

They turned a corner and found another boulder.

NEVER TRY NEVER WIN

"We never passed that one before," Peter said.

"That's because it's the last one on the trail," Grandma said. "I always thought it should be earlier, more as an inspiration for people about to make the hike."

"The end of the trail? Then what's that?" Peter pointed at a boulder just yards away.

GET A JOB

"We're going in circles," Peter said.

Kai's skin crawled. "No," he said. "The forest is circling *us*."

Grandma pulled on the yarn. Its end came back quickly, severed.

The rustling turned to creaking and shrieking as all chaos broke loose.

Though the sun was shining, the few standing trees whipped around like in a storm. The fallen trees rumbled and creaked, quaking and rolling. Kai, Peter, and Dad stumbled, and Grandma would have fallen if Dad hadn't grabbed her. The fishy smell in the air was chased away by the sawdust scent of freshly cut wood, as the trees twisted, damaging themselves just to reach the family.

Twigs clawed at Peter and Kai, and Dad yelled, "Get down!" as a thick branch swung at them. He dropped to the ground, and yelled as the branches of the trees he'd landed on stretched up, binding his arms and legs.

"I've got you!" Grandma sliced at the branches and pulled Dad free. Her eyebrow was bleeding, but she looked excited. "I knew this knife was the right choice."

"Peter, Kai," Dad said, fighting off another branch that had come up, groaning, from one of the fallen trees. "Run. Find the car. Now. We'll hold them off."

"We're staying," Kai said.

"No, you're not! Go!"

Peter screamed as a branch the size of a python wrapped around his ankles and pulled him down, dragging him away from the group.

"Peter!" Kai leaped on the branch. It was like wrestling a mad fire hose, only one that could simultaneously blind you with wads of drying leaves. When he finally beat them off and looked up, expecting Dad to come help, he saw his father busy fighting branches that were snatching at his hair and clothes, pulling him down to the ground. Grandma was cutting them back as fast as she could, but how long could she hold out?

So Kai did the only thing he could think of: He bit the branch on Peter.

It writhed and released Peter, who scrambled away. Kai checked to make sure he hadn't chipped another tooth. All good.

"Boys!" Dad again. "Get out of here!"

"This way!" Peter called, waving Kai away from the fight.

But Kai didn't move. All around him, the forest was a maelstrom of wood and leaves, creaking and rustling as they fought. Why? Because of them.

They'd arrived. He and Peter, the ones who woke the sea creature. He'd arrived, the one who could read Atlantean. Leaving the forest wouldn't help Dad and Grandma.

"No," Kai said. "This way!"

He charged deeper into the forest, away from Dad, Grandma, and the safety of the car.

"Kai, stop!" Dad called. Kai didn't stop.

Peter complained, but Kai heard his brother running after him.

"We need to get to safety," Peter said.

"There's no safety here. Not for us."

Peter groaned. "Is the sea creature doing this?"

"I don't think so. Ow!" Another branch hit Kai's shoulder. "It already attacked this place. This is different."

Another boulder marked the path: USE YOUR HEAD.

Good advice.

Why would the forest attack them now instead of when they first entered the woods?

We must be nearing it. Whatever it was that the sea creature had come here for.

But how to find it?

Look for the pattern. Kai looked at the ground. Pattern.

The fallen trees.

Of course! There was a pattern here. The trees were neatly lying side by side. But not in a straight line. They changed direction.

They looked like a boardwalk. Or a path, curving through the trees. Curving to the left.

Always left.

A circle.

The blast hadn't come from the ocean! Like water rippling away from a stone dropped in a pond, the trees had fallen *away* from where he and Peter needed to go.

As Kai dodged another blow, he pointed at the trees. "Peter, we have to go that way! To the center of the circle!"

For the first time in a while, Peter didn't argue. He followed.

Kai leaped from fallen tree to fallen tree, forcing his way through the still-leafy branches. It wasn't easy going. The forest closed in tighter, and Kai still had to dodge attacks. But the fallen trees didn't fail. Every one of them lay in pattern, a circle around some central blast site.

The forest's attacks grew. Kai heard grunts as Peter took hits. He hoped that, now that he and Peter had left, Dad and Grandma were okay.

A huge branch, like a swinging fist, rose and struck Kai in the stomach, knocking the wind out of him. He slipped on mildewed wood. Gasping, he crawled forward.

The roar stopped.

Still wheezing, Kai let Peter lift him up. "It stopped," Peter said.

"W-why?" Kai asked.

Peter shrugged. Kai looked around. The circle of fallen trees had led them to a clearing.

"What do we do now?" Peter said, looking around. "Is this what we're looking for?"

Kai squinted at the clearing. There was another boulder here that read IDEAS. *Perfect.*

Kai climbed on the boulder and looked over the clearing. It wasn't as clear as he'd first thought; at the center of the clearing lay a small pile of fallen trees. They looked like they'd been young trees, little more than shrubs. But their size wasn't what made them interesting.

Somehow, their trunks and branches had fallen to form an Atlantean hieroglyph. Kai wasn't up that high, but if he squinted and concentrated, he could see it. Like one of those optical illusions where you have to hold the paper at eye level to read it, or a stretched-out warning painted on a road.

A single hieroglyph that represented a word.

Peter was looking around. "There's no seaweed here."

He was right. This was the only part of the forest that hadn't been marked by the sea. So what did that mean?

Maybe the Atlantean hieroglyph would explain it. Kai peered at it, and a moment later, a smile began to stretch over his face. "'Binding' or 'seal.'"

As Kai climbed down from the boulder, Peter rubbed his arm. "What do you mean, binding?"

"See those trees at the middle? They form the Atlantean symbol for 'binding' or 'seal.' That must be why our friend attacked this place," Kai said. "He didn't want anyone binding him again."

"I don't blame him," Peter said. He looked back into the trees. "Think Dad and Grandma are all right?"

But Kai wasn't thinking about the adults. They could end this right now! He loped toward the clearing and the huge symbol he'd read. "Let's activate it."

"Activate it?"

"It's like a giant button, right? It says 'seal,' so it must be a seal. If we activate it, we can send Poseidon back to his lair. We can win, right now!"

"Yeah, and how are we supposed to activate a pile of trees? And am I the only one wondering why there would be a seal to bind a powerful Atlantean entity in Massachusetts?"

But Kai wasn't listening. The seal was his. He found it, read it, and now it waited for him to activate it. So Kai, grinning, raced over to finish this once and for all.

Kai hit a wall.

Not a real wall, but right on the edge of the small cluster of trees that created the symbol, he couldn't take another step. He reached out, trying to touch it, but he couldn't.

"I can't touch it," he called back.

Then Peter wandered over, frowning like he had thought of something he still couldn't quite wrap his mind around. Once he reached Kai, he put out his hand and took one more step. The invisible wall holding Kai didn't stop him.

Peter kneeled beside the cluster of trees and looked back at Kai.

Then, turning back to the symbol, he extended his hand over the binding word. He hovered, as if waiting for permission. Then he placed his palm on the closest tree.

At first, nothing happened. But then Peter jumped back as smoke wafted up from the symbol.

"Kai! Rocky!" It was Dad, arm around Grandma, as they both hobbled toward the clearing. Dad's jeans were stained with seaweed, and Grandma had lost her bag, though still carried both knife and cane.

"Are you boys all right?" Dad asked, approaching them at the center of the clearing. "Don't run off like that. I had no idea—" He stopped, looking past Kai to the small trees and Peter. "What did you do?"

Kai turned. *Oh no.* It was more than smoke now. Orange tongues of fire had begun to blacken the trees that made up the binding word.

"Peter!" Kai yelled. "Let's go!"

Peter rubbed his forehead, but he didn't move away from the fire. So Kai reached in and grabbed his arm. "Come on!"

Peter stumbled, but soon found his footing. Dad and Grandma reached out for them, and without looking back, they ran into the forest.

The rustling and creaking had stopped, and the trees lay lifeless and broken once more. Kai's heart leaped. They'd succeeded in doing what they'd come here for.

But there was still the fire. As flames spread across the ground to the fallen trees, the family didn't stop until they reached their car. As they drove back to Seaspire, fire trucks passed them, sirens wailing, on their way to save Dogtown.

CHAPTER 9

SEVEN SEALS

PETER

Peter's hand itched since he'd touched that binding. Or maybe he was just imagining it.

As they pulled into Grandma's driveway, Peter wondered what had possessed him to touch the symbol. After all, they had no idea that the word even was a binding, let alone something a touch would activate. Maybe, he figured, if Kai had gained a special ability from interacting with the sea monster, then Peter did, too. Maybe something about it called to him.

Right after he'd touched the symbol, it was like the fire started in his own mind, also. He saw a burst of reddish gold and felt a release, like he'd completed a chore he had dreaded. It was dizzying. If Kai hadn't pulled him away, he wouldn't have noticed how the fire around him was spreading.

Still, why did the sea monster's attack only write the symbol in a clump of fallen trees? If it was trying to destroy the seal, it failed so badly that it actually *helped* them find it.

There had to be more going on here than what it seemed.

Once inside, the family collapsed on various couches and chairs, except for Kai, who claimed the floor.

"That hurt," he moaned.

Grandma waved an arm at the kitchen. "I have disinfectants and bandages in there. Give me a moment."

"I got it," Dad said, and, groaning, stood. A few moments later, the twins, Dad, and Grandma had slathered on antibacterial cream and were dotted with brightly colored bandages.

Sophie wandered in, smelling like caramel. "Whoa," she said, looking them over. "What happened to you?"

"The forest attacked us," Kai said.

"The forest . . . ?" Sophie trailed off. Then she shook her head and raised a bag. "I brought home peanut butter fudge. Help yourself."

"Don't you want to know what happened?" Kai asked.

"Um, no, not really. I—I did some research on various sea deities that could be related to the Sea, but honestly, it seems like a dead end. Sorry. My notes are on the kitchen table if you want to look them over."

Peter frowned, watching his sister. This wasn't the same girl who came to their rescue at the cemetery. What was wrong with Sophie? Staying behind, not interested in what happened, not dripping with optimism? Sophie wouldn't act against her family, but maybe she really didn't believe this was all real.

To be honest, sometimes *Peter* had a hard time believing it all.

Sophie spoke up. "But was my drone helpful?"

"Kind of," Dad said. He handed her the depleted drone. "It just ran out of batteries," he said. "It's fine. But it fell out of the air when things started getting really weird."

"So it was kind of an early warning signal," Peter said.

Sophie nodded. "That's good, I guess. I should . . . see if Mom emailed us anything. Enjoy the fudge."

She handed the fudge to Dad and left.

Dad watched her go. "I'm worried about her," he said, then shook his head, looked at the boys, and added, "One crisis at a time."

"So was that it?" Peter asked after Dad sat down, "The word said 'binding.' Did we seal the sea monster away again?"

That would be wonderful. After hard work and a terrifying walk through a moving forest, they'd reactivated the seal that they'd broken when they threw the hot dog into the sea. The job was done, and Peter could go back to just enjoying the summer.

"Maybe," Kai said. He beamed at Peter. "You got a superpower, too! I read the words, and you closed the gate. Nice teamwork, twin."

Peter smiled, causing a scratch on his face to sting.

Grandma moved to grab some fudge from Dad, who pulled the box away without taking his eyes from the window.

"I don't think we're done yet," he said. "Look at the ocean."

Together, Peter and Kai went to the window.

A news van was parked on the beach, along with a small group of spectators. All were watching a dark cloud shadow the ocean. Waves rose higher than Peter had ever seen them, under that dark patch, and crashed back to the sea, though all around the shadow the sea was calm. It was a small tempest, brewing in their backyard.

"That doesn't look natural," Kai said.

"And now we've established the obvious." Peter groaned. "It's not over. What did we even *do* today if it's not over?"

"Hey, it's okay," Grandma said, hobbling to her feet. She put an arm around Peter. "I'm sure it wasn't in vain. Maybe tomorrow we can go back to Dogtown."

"We are *not* going back there," Dad said. "Not after today."

"Then let's see what we remember," Grandma said. "Alex, get your camera now and let's make a permanent memory."

Dad pulled out his phone. "Battery is dead, just like the drone."

Peter shivered.

So Dad got a pad of paper and a pencil and the family recounted the day, from figuring out it was Dogtown to leaving the forest behind. Peter explained what it felt like breaking the seal, and Kai interrupted, "You mean activating it. We already broke the seal. Whatever we did today was a rebinding."

"*Activating* it," Peter corrected.

"How did you know where to go?" Dad asked Kai.

Kai shrugged. "The trees fell for a reason. I figured something powerful knocked them over, so I followed them to the center."

"Disobeying me."

"But it worked out great!"

Peter watched his dad. "You okay, Dad?"

Dad was chewing his cheek, not fudge, and his fingers kept flexing. "Huh? Oh, yeah. I just ... Okay, trees laying a path, of sorts. It sounds kind of familiar." He rubbed his face and yelped as he touched a splinter. "I'd better deal with this."

Dad stood and left.

"If it's not over," Peter asked, "then what do we do now? Was there anywhere else in the world that the Sea attacked?"

Kai and Grandma didn't answer. Then Grandma, leaning heavily on her cane, swooped down on the fudge box. "Let's give it a rest and pick it up when we feel more refreshed. How about you boys help me eat this and sort through my collection? Next time, we'll need to be better prepared."

"Next time." Because there would be a next time. Because this nightmare Peter never meant to sign up for wasn't over yet.

There was still a chance to fail.

But he and Kai, who looked thrilled, followed Grandma to her weapons closet and helped her categorize her collection based on resiliency and how capable each blade was at fighting monster trees.

———— • ● • ————

A couple of hours later, as Peter was hefting a medieval ax ("Leave that one, dear, it was made for executioners," Grandma said), he heard Dad and Sophie talking in the hall.

As Kai picked up a flail, Peter sneaked to the door.

"I wish we'd brought my laptop instead of yours," Dad was saying. "It's old and slow, but I have access to scholarly databases that might have given you more than *this*."

"I know. I tried. I thought I'd start by looking into Poseidon, but . . . then I looked into Aegir, and Lir, and Oceanus, and there are so many stories about them. If even half of them are just exaggerations of the truth about this thing attacking the boys, then we're in trouble."

"They're just stories, Soph. At the end of the day, this thing is just the ocean with a face."

"Isn't that bad enough?" Sophie asked.

Dad was silent for a moment. "Is this about those voices you heard?"

"No, of course not," Sophie said quickly.

"You can tell me if it is. It's okay to be scared. This *is* scary."

She let out a half-hearted laugh. "Me? Scared? You know me better than that." Both were silent for a while. "Here," Sophie said. "You can take the laptop and do whatever research you can. I . . . I gotta go clear my head."

"Okay. Be safe," Dad said.

What was going on with Sophie?

Dad sighed, and knocked on the door. Peter opened it to see his dad, looking tired but in possession of the laptop.

"Let's figure out what we're dealing with," Dad said. He handed the laptop to Kai.

Kai sat with the laptop open in front of him. "Weather patterns, anyone?"

Grandma nodded, and Kai did a quick search, then pushed the laptop away in disgust. "Anomalies here and over the North Sea. Nothing new."

Peter leaned back. "Dad, didn't you say the path of trees sounded familiar to you?"

Dad frowned. "Yeah, it did. I don't know from where. A song, maybe? Or a poem?"

Kai got to searching again. "'Path of trees . . . song or poem . . .'"

Peter watched as Kai picked an entry written in German and began to read it quietly. "Um, Dad? You know poets. Who's Roger MacHale?"

Dad stood up and paced, staring into space. "It's familiar. I've heard that name."

"Me too," Peter said. When the family looked at him, he said, "It's that guy who lived at the lighthouse. Todd told us about him. He left because he thought it was haunted."

Dad snapped his fingers. "That's it! Kai, search for his poems."

Kai did, pulling up a page of seven small verses, in English this time. Reading the introduction, Kai said, "This says Roger MacHale would wake up from nightmares and find himself sitting at his desk, having written a series of cryptic poems in his sleep. That was the final straw, and he left the lighthouse."

Peter wondered, for a moment, if MacHale had the same kind of nightmares he had been having. Seaspire flooding, sunken cities, terrible storms. If so, he didn't blame the man for running away.

Kai continued, "He gave the poems to his sister and then packed up the lighthouse and moved. She published the poems." He laughed. "There are a lot of comments under the post arguing whether this is a hoax or a scary online story like a creepypasta, or if it really happened. The consensus seems to be creepypasta."

"But we know better," Peter said. "The lighthouse was built right by the gate to the Sea's prison."

"Maybe ground there *is* cursed," Grandma said. "Maybe something spoke to MacHale while he was sleeping and he wrote those hidden truths into poems."

"They sell pamphlets of those poems at the Seaspire Tourism Center," Dad said. "That's where I heard of him."

"Look at the first poem." Peter pointed.

Peter looked as Kai started reading out loud:

> "1.
>
> *If land in common meets the sea,*
> *And find ye path of trunk and tree,*
> *What man has built, Mother sets free.*
> *Inspired past and future see:*
> *Mongrel town, lost history.*
> *'Neath pine and boulder find the key*
> *Then fire burn, and seeker flee."*

Peter sat up. "That sounds familiar," he said.

Kai frowned. "Land in common?"

Dad nodded. "Doesn't make a lot of sense, does it? I doubt MacHale himself had any idea what it meant. But we do. 'Mongrel town.' Dogtown, anyone? And the place is known as Dogtown *Commons.*"

"Path of trunk and tree," Kai said. "That's what we found."

"And boulders with inspiring phrases carved on them," Grandma said. "'Inspired past and future.' Words carved in stone, meant to last."

Fire burn. Peter looked down at his hand, which had stopped itching. "The poem even knew about what happened when the binding was activated." He looked at the verses. "But there are seven of them."

Kai frowned. "The first one was about the seal at Dogtown. What if the rest are about other seals?"

"Seven is a good ritual number," Grandma said. "It's the number of magic."

Peter groaned. *Seven.* So it wasn't even *sort of* over. Six more to go, and less than a week to track down the others and activate them, too. And if the first one had vicious trees guarding it, what protections would the others have? Peter's stomach felt full of wet sand.

Kai, however, saw it differently. "Okay, great! We've already got one of them, and we have the poems. We can find the next one now, no problem. MacHale must have seen the seals in his nightmares and gave us these clues. Maybe the rest are in Massachusetts, too. Dogtown's was."

"What do the other poems say?" Peter asked.

Together, they read the next six poems:

2.

Where sailors return with fishy tale
To sun's shore from sacred wave,
Where crest glitters with golden scale,
And Charles Curtis failed to save,
Upon spectral boards and under sail
A song reverbs from watery grave
Let ocean roar, and woodwork fail.

3.

In darkness deep beneath the stone
The dead still plead for breath.
In metal ground is flood of flame,

And in dust destruction's crop is sown.
Pits run deep with blood of death
And walls are traced with like and same,
So sense by scents and rock is blown.

4.

Devils play in stonework grim,
As righteous folk to monsters turn.
Mirror and egg, a simple trick
Returned stony press and the water's test.
Then voices taunt and needles prick,
And visions, both wicked and stern,
With twisted words the mind bedim.

5.

Fear the holy land of death,
Where spirits roam and devils dwell.
Within this land inscription strange,
Words of power, lost to time:
Island mineral may river's path stay.
Marvel at what time doth not change
And dread the light beautiful and fell.

6.

What unhallowed beasts dwell in mire!
What deception lurks 'neath noxious ground!
Brambles trap or earth's mouth gapes,
And serpent and hound stalk every step.
Their master walks with mammoth tread.

Mind, though solid become sand without whole spring,
The dark is only dispelled by fire.

7.

Six must fall before the last appear.
The prize is at hand, the curse at heart.
A dream turns nightmare with revealed price,
For who can pay that which asks for all?
Will you reach for peace or truth?
I set down my pen, the choice is yours:
Once land may grow, but, too, more sea.

Peter listened, heart pounding. The poems felt like his dream the night before: unearthly, twisted, impossible to understand.

When Kai finished reading, Peter said, "Is it just me, or did those poems mention death and curses an awful lot?"

No one answered him. They all seemed to be thinking the same thing, though. Dad shifted and opened his mouth to say something.

Kai didn't let him. "Did anyone else notice the rhymes change?" he said, waving the paper.

Dad brightened. "Yes! The first poem has only one rhyme used seven times, the second two, and so on until the last has seven unrhymed lines."

"Why does he do that, English teacher?"

Dad's good mood left. "No idea. It's not a common meter or poetic form. MacHale must have come up with it on his own. I'd say it's a sign he didn't know what he was doing, but—"

"But there's a pattern," Kai said, looking at the screen.

"Well," Grandma said, picking up the laptop. "We're wasting time. Let's figure out our second riddle. *Where sailors return with fishy tale.* That's easy. Massachusetts has many harbors and fishermen. We're going to the ocean next."

"The ocean?" That's where the monster lived!

As if sensing Peter's thoughts, thunder boomed outside. The tiny, contained storm at sea had finally crashed on shore. Heavy rain pattered on the roof, and Kai and Peter glanced at each other.

"If we want to stop this thing and save Seaspire," Grandma said, looking at torrents beyond the window, "then yes."

Seaspire. Right. Kai's eyes gleamed, but Peter just felt heavier.

"Okay, the ocean," he said. "There's a lot of that around here."

"*Crest glitters with golden scale,*" Dad muttered. "Significant?"

"We'll all get rich," Kai said. When they stared at him, he explained, "Golden scale. Could be gold."

"Or a gold fish," Dad added. "*Golden scale.*"

"*Charles Curtis failed to save,*" Peter muttered. "That's a really specific detail."

Failed.

"Maybe that's our key," Kai said. "Who's Charles Curtis?"

No one answered.

"Grandma?" Kai asked.

Grandma shook her head.

Dad picked up the laptop. "Okay. Let's see what I can find online."

Peter closed his eyes. He sat, deep in thought. "*Charles Curtis failed to save,*" he said out loud. "*Charles Curtis failed to save. Charles*"—he stopped for breath—"*Curtis failed to save. Charles*—"

"Wait." Kai grabbed his arm. "Say that again. That last part."

Peter frowned, then his jaw dropped as he understood. "*Curtis failed to save Charles.*"

"It's in that backward poetic speech!" Kai said. "We're looking for a guy named Curtis who failed to save a guy named Charles."

Dad stopped typing. "Not a *guy* named Charles. A boat." He showed them what he'd found.

Grandma snapped her fingers. "Of course! The *Charles Haskell.* The next seal is in Gloucester Harbor."

CHAPTER 10

A DANGEROUS SEA

KAI

Kai turned to Grandma. "Gloucester Harbor?"

Grandma nodded. "Gloucester Harbor isn't far from Dogtown, and it also has some strange stories. One is about a sea serpent that lives in the harbor."

Crest glitters with golden scale. Kai couldn't help grinning as he imagined a huge, golden snake swimming through the dark waves. This adventure was just getting cooler by the minute!

Grandma went on, the history professor inside her taking over. "The *Charles Haskell* was a fishing boat. When it was built in 1869, a workman was killed during construction. The boat was captained by a man named Curtis, and only a few days into captaining the ship, a storm hit. Captain Curtis ordered anchor lines cut so they could escape the storm, but that resulted in the *Haskell* hitting the *Andrew Johnson*. The *Johnson*'s crew was doomed."

Grandma fell silent. Kai piped up, "But it sounds like Curtis did save the *Charles Haskell*. Maybe the poem refers to something else?"

Grandma shook her head. "He didn't know it, but he doomed the ship. The next year, when the crew went out, two dozen ghostly sailors climbed over the sides and began to work alongside the living crew. This frightened the crew so much that Curtis had to bring the ship back to port. The ghost crews kept coming, and sailors kept refusing to sail, until the *Haskell* was no good for work because she could keep no crew. She either sank in Gloucester Harbor or rotted at the wharf years later."

"Oh. Great. Ghosts." Peter looked down.

Kai read the poem again. *Spectral boards.* Sure sounded like a ghost ship to him.

Kai's grin expanded. A sea serpent *and* ghosts? Even better! And ghosts weren't dangerous. How could something without a body hurt anyone? The sea serpent seemed like the bigger threat. He'd have to pack one of Grandma's weapons.

For a moment, Kai imagined himself as a knight in armor, carrying a sword. He battled a gold-scaled serpent for glory and to save the world. Actually, that *was* what he was doing.

"So we go to Gloucester Harbor tomorrow," Kai said. "All of us."

Grandma's eyes gleamed. "Well, boys, you won't find me hiding at home when there's a ghost ship and sea serpent to find. We'll leave bright and early tomorrow. That sea demon won't know what hit him, not with us as a team. Now, where did I put my harpoon?"

Kai grinned. He had the best grandmother in the world.

"No, no, no!" Dad had set down the laptop and was waving his arms. "None of you is going anywhere. You," he said to Grandma, "have a meeting with the Cleanup Committee tomorrow. Remember?"

Grandma shrugged. "They can manage without me."

"But it's better if you're there, right?" Dad looked desperate. Kai saw him glance at Grandma's cane.

Then Dad turned to the boys. "And you. Today was dangerous. We went in without a plan. Tomorrow, we're going to stay inside and look at the poems. Maybe they'll give us more information, so we can end this without getting attacked by any more forests."

Kai stood. "Dad, come on! We have less than a week. We have to go."

"No, you don't. I won't drive you anywhere tomorrow."

Kai's heart sank. They could try to take a bus, but buses didn't run until late morning, and by then Dad would be awake to make sure neither he nor Peter left the house. Looked like they'd have to spend a day deciphering poems. As much as he enjoyed solving puzzles, it wasn't fighting a sea serpent for the fate of the world.

Thunder boomed. The freak storm still raged.

"We have to go," Kai said, trying again. "Come on, Peter. Back me up."

But Peter didn't say anything. He just looked at Grandma's weapons closet like it was an exhibit at the zoo.

"Peter!"

"Look, maybe Dad has a point. If we just take a day to prepare, we could make better progress when we get back to the hunt."

Dad beamed. "Great minds think alike, Rocky."

Kai turned away, disgusted. Leave Peter to back Dad up when Dad was being unreasonable. Good thing he had another adult to appeal to. Kai turned to Grandma.

But Grandma just smiled. "Listen to your father." Before Kai could protest, she stood. "It's getting late, and I'm sure you're hungry. Kai, Peter, come help me make stir-fry."

Fine. Kai went to the kitchen, where he helped chop vegetables but did not say another word to Passive Peter, even during the meal. He meant to hold a grudge against Grandma, too, but then she started telling stories about Roman legionnaires and Kai couldn't resist forgiving her.

After dinner, while Dad and Sophie did the dishes, Kai printed out the poems to study. It was the only thing he was *allowed* to do to fight the sea creature. And hey, if he solved them tonight, Dad had no reason to keep them back from Gloucester Harbor the next morning.

Sifting through the old verses, he found them fascinating. The changing rhyme scheme, and the subtle clues woven through them. Had Roger MacHale really written these while asleep? And the haunting of the *Charles Haskell* hadn't happened before MacHale wrote these. How had he known it would?

What if these riddles had gone unsolved for so long because things mentioned in them were in MacHale's future? What if they needed to be read *now*, at this time, to understand them? Like, by a special, chosen hero? Like Kai and Peter.

That unique rhyme scheme . . . how clever, though Kai didn't know why. There was a pattern to it he couldn't see. Something MacHale had done on purpose, if he could have done *anything* on purpose while asleep. Even if it meant nothing to their quest, Kai wanted to know what it was.

Before he could figure it out, he found himself yawning deeply. It was late. So Kai and Peter trudged upstairs and went to bed.

In the dark, as the storm raged outside, Kai whispered, "Isn't this exciting?"

A grunt. "I'm not sure 'exciting' is the word I'd use. We could have died today." Silence for a moment. "Dad's right. This is dangerous," Peter said.

"But we didn't. Die, I mean." Kai stared at the ceiling. "I think we're part of something bigger than we know. We're . . . heroes."

Peter laughed. "You *would* think of yourself as a hero. Just don't think of how many so-called heroes don't survive their quests."

"Nah." Kai rolled over. He wouldn't let Peter's pessimism get to him. There was a pattern here, too. Heroes were chosen. They fought. They won, and came home shining with glory. And so would he and Peter.

With that determined thought, Kai drifted off to sleep.

He found himself standing on a windswept beach. Flying sand burned his legs, and cold water sprayed from dark, crashing waves. Kai touched the drops where they struck his face. Wet, and cold. Like real water.

But I'm dreaming. I know this is a dream, but I can't wake up.

The beach was not Seaspire's shore. The sand was dark and reddish, like dried blood. A blue crab huddled beside a rock. When Kai turned around, he saw stone buildings nestled in a lush forest. Even under the cloudy sky, the buildings gleamed with gold and copper.

But there were no people. At least, none that Kai could see.

Maybe it's because of the storm. They're taking shelter.

Kai closed his eyes and tried, one more time, to wake up. It didn't work.

"You shut out what you came to see, little human?"

Kai's eyes opened with a snap. Spinning around, facing the ocean again, he saw the sea monster. Its slitted eyes stared into his.

This was only a dream. Kai was in no danger. But then again, two days ago he would have thought he was in no danger from violent forests and ancient sea gods, so what did he know?

Time to hero up. "Did I come to see this? Or did you bring me here?" He could afford a small risk. "What name should I call you?"

The creature grinned, baring its needle teeth. It snaked closer to Kai through the water. "I have had many. Each people that knew me chose their favorite aspects of me and gave them a name. Aegir, Lir, Sobek, all fragments of a whole. This people called me Oceanus, when they lived and breathed above the waves." He gestured at the city behind Kai. "Now they live and breathe no more."

Kai looked over his shoulder. "So this is Atlantis."

"If that is what your people call it. They, too, had their own name." The sea creature was almost at the shore, but it stopped. It dipped a hand into the water beside it, calming the churning waves, and then sending them higher and stronger than before. "I have many names," it repeated. "But they all mean the same thing. I am the Sea, and the Sea is mine."

"Well, good," Kai said. "You keep it, and we'll keep the land."

The water swirled in a tight cyclone. The Sea's eyes narrowed, and its fist clenched. "You dare insult me? I am the Sea!" it bellowed with the roar of a hurricane. Kai covered his ears as the wind pushed him back, sliding through the sand.

"Land is nothing compared to me, and it will feel my wrath!" With that, the Sea sent the water at Kai's chest.

It struck Kai like a pro boxer's fist, driving him back. The water swelled around him, flooding the city. Muffled screaming wavered from the gold-and-copper-decorated buildings, and the island itself seemed to buck and sway as the water drowned it, dragging tree and city and Kai down, down, down—

Kai woke up in his own bed, soaking wet and gasping. The roof had sprung a leak over his pillow. Rainwater from the storm violently raging outside trickled down over his chest and face.

And that wasn't all. Rubbing his chest, Kai felt the grit of sand. A tiny turquoise crab skittered across his shirt. Kai seized it and threw it across the room.

Still choking on water, Kai rolled out of bed. He knelt beside his soaking pillow and breathed, deep and heavy. Whatever had happened was over. The important thing was to see to the leak.

The bed was now too wet to sleep in, so Kai wandered through the dark house to the living room and kitchen area. He grabbed a helmet that doubled as a bucket and a spare blanket. Once back in his room, he put the helmet under the leak and looked for a dry area on the floor to sleep for the rest of the night.

After he lay down in a space by the closet, Peter started thrashing.

Kai scrambled to his feet and ran over. Peter's eyes rolled back in his head, and he gasped and kicked and fought.

Like he was drowning.

Kai reached out to Peter. As soon as he touched him, the window burst open. Wind howled and rain spit at both boys. Once again, Kai felt sand in the water that blasted against his skin. But Kai didn't let go. "Wake up!" he yelled.

With a deep, shuddering breath, Peter sat up. His eyes darted around the room, before landing first on Kai and then on the open window. "Come on," he said, sliding out of bed.

Together they forced the window closed. Kai latched it, and Peter placed Grandma's Viking hammer against it so it couldn't open again.

Breathing heavily, the brothers looked at each other. Kai searched Peter for any damage. If anything happened to his brother, he was going to take Grandma's sharpest sword down to the beach and issue a challenge to that creature.

The Sea.

Peter's breath slowed. He looked past Kai to the leak pattering into the helmet.

"Just a storm," he said, though Kai noticed his twin brushing sand off his arm. "Just some rain."

He lay back and rolled over. Kai muttered, "Good night," and went back to his patch of dry floor.

The little crab sidled past Kai, and Kai smashed at it with a book so it couldn't go back to its master to report. He was pretty sure he got it.

Had Peter had the same dream as Kai? It was possible; they were twins. They shared things all the time. It was easy to believe they shared this, too.

Now, Peter had to take this more seriously. No more of this passive waiting. Peter would have to take action to fight back.

Or at least, that's what Kai told himself.

CHAPTER 11

WHAT SWIMS BELOW

PETER

The next morning, Peter woke, damp and groggy, to Grandma shaking him at the crack of dawn. "Shh," she said. "Hurry and get dressed. We'll have breakfast on the way."

"The way?" Peter asked. He yawned, but rolled out of bed. Kai was already up and getting dressed.

"To Gloucester Harbor," Grandma said.

"But Dad said we couldn't go."

"He said he wouldn't drive you. But I will." Grandma turned her head, looking down the hall toward where Dad was still sleeping. "This needs to be done, and you two need to do it. Alex must learn to understand that, or . . ." She patted Peter's knee. "I'll be waiting at the car."

Kai beamed at Peter. "Best Grandma ever."

But Peter couldn't summon the excitement. He got dressed and ready, since that was expected, but he couldn't help but startle when he saw sand on the ground. When he closed his eyes, he saw the Sea.

He remembered standing on that dark beach, that gleaming city behind him. The creature appearing in front of him in the waves. The way it felt so real.

That's because of the storm. The water, hitting my sleeping face. But that didn't explain why the dream was so clear, especially in the strange way the creature that called itself the Sea ignored everything Peter said and answered different questions.

When Peter told the creature to back off, it made a comment about its name. When, curious, Peter asked about the name, it started talking about the island. And, finally, when Peter asked where everyone was, it named itself as the Sea (convenient, since that's what the Syracuses were calling it already) and threw some kind of tantrum. That's when he woke up, gasping for air.

It was like the dream was prerecorded, meant for someone else. And since Kai had been awake when Peter's dream ended, Peter had a suspicion that it was really Kai's dream, not his.

Not that that was a bad thing. It gave Peter a chance to watch and learn without having to actually interact with this sea creature. Let Kai handle the confrontations; Peter didn't want any part of it.

He wondered what stupid thing Kai said to make the creature so angry.

Peter wanted to suggest they wait at home and figure out what was really going on, like Dad wanted, but he couldn't. Not when Grandma was downstairs, car packed with the harpoon she'd been looking for, along with a couple of bronze daggers and her cane sword. Not when Kai acted like they were going to Disney World.

So Peter climbed into the car and placed his breakfast order when they went through a drive-through. He spent the ride wondering why it was so important to Kai that they take action *now* instead of waiting to make a plan.

A tiny blue crab had gotten into Grandma's car. Peter tossed pieces of ham at it to distract himself from thinking of all the ways they could fail and get hurt today.

Before too long, the car arrived at its destination. The large harbor was full of sailboats and fishing boats. Grandma hid the daggers inside an embroidered bag and, with a smile, said, "We'll come back for the harpoon if we need it. Let's get searching."

Peter scooped up the little crab and released it in the parking lot. It scrabbled sideways toward the sea. At least someone was where he wanted to be.

The day was overcast but pleasant. Peter and Kai followed Grandma to a busier area of the harbor, near a pier and a sandy beach to the left. A statue of a sailor, green with age, looked out over the harbor as he turned a ship's wheel.

Grandma noticed Peter looking at it. "The Fisherman's Memorial."

The *Charles Haskell* was a fishing ship. Peter followed the man's gaze over the water, but all he saw were boats and small islands decorated with lighthouses.

"I don't see anything," Peter said. "Kai?"

Kai shook his head. "There's no binding word in the ocean, if that's what you're asking."

Grandma shrugged. She pulled a camera out of her bag and snapped a picture of the statue. "In case we need it," she said, grinning. "Always bring a camera on an adventure." Then she tucked the camera away and said, "The harbor is big, and this is just one area. Let's get searching!"

As Grandma hitched her bag full of weapons higher on her shoulder and marched away with her sword cane clicking against the stone, Peter turned to Kai. "Do you think we'll get in trouble for coming here instead of staying home and making a plan to stop the Sea?"

"Grandma is Dad's mom. If anyone can tell him what to do, it's her," Kai said, then stopped. "Wait, did you just call it the Sea?"

"Yeah. I saw your dream last night."

"Why?"

"How should I know?"

Kai fell silent, thinking, and Peter ran ahead to where Grandma was singing a bouncy ditty to herself: "*It was Friday morn when we set sail. We were not far from the land. The captain he spied a mermaid so fair with a comb and a glass in her hand.*"

"That's a fun song, Grandma," Peter said. "What is it?"

"Hmm? Oh, just a sea chantey," Grandma said. "It's called 'The Mermaid,' and it's actually about a ship of sailors seeing a mermaid and knowing they were doomed. A mermaid was an omen of shipwreck, you see."

Huh. The Sea had a fishy, or snaky, tail. Maybe that was where the legend came from.

"Weren't chanteys sung by sailors?" Kai, just catching up, asked.

Grandma nodded. "They had strong beats to help synchronize work. Lots of sailing involved rope handling and rowing and other jobs that needed to be perfectly timed. Singing a song helped that timing. Then, like now, a team had to be perfectly united or they wouldn't succeed."

"But why sing about sinking?" asked Peter.

"Perhaps it was a way to whistle in the dark," Grandma said. "Sailing was a dangerous job, and maybe singing about danger made them feel more comfortable with it."

"Wait, doesn't Seaspire have a chantey about the Sea—I mean, the creature attacking us?" Peter remembered Grandma singing it.

Now Grandma looked a little uneasy. "Oh yes, that one."

"Can we hear it? It might be important."

"Perhaps," Grandma said. "All right. *A sailor came to the stony point, bringing his loaf of bread . . .*"

It was wild hearing a chantey about the ritual that raised Poseidon, or the Sea, as he preferred to be called. Especially one that was so catchy.

Grandma struck the ground with her cane in rhythm as she sang. The words' beats varied, with some lines having more syllables than others, but under it all a regular beat in sets of four and three kept the song thrumming like an even heartbeat. By the second verse, Kai joined in, singing with Grandma on the chorus. Peter found himself walking to the rhythm. No wonder sailors used the songs to stay in time with one another!

Once Grandma finished, Kai pushed her to sing it again, so he could learn it. Meanwhile, Peter listened for clues about the Sea and how to defeat it, but soon gave up when he realized the chantey was only about the ritual. It seemed MacHale's poems would be more useful now. So he just kept an eye on the harbor.

All seemed at peace. Kai was better at spotting patterns, but Peter would have noticed anything strange, and he didn't. Just the gently gray sky and the passersby talking and laughing.

Slow but sure, Grandma led them from end to end of the horseshoe-shaped harbor. Every so often, her phone would ring, but she'd silence it, smile at them, and say, "I'll deal with that later."

It was Dad. Peter was sure of it.

Ignoring the frequent phone calls, Grandma and the boys

explored, stopping at important sites like Hammond Castle. They even took a ferry out to Ten Pound Island to see its lighthouse. A salty breeze mussed Peter's hair, and he developed a small blister on his right heel. They walked all day, eating the sandwiches and chips that Grandma had packed, and searching the harbor for any kind of clue.

Gloucester Harbor seemed to be the place to spot marine wildlife; Peter hadn't seen these numbers of crabs at Seaspire's beach. Blue ones, that Grandma said were common.

But the shadows lengthened, and the sky turned grayish blue, and they'd found nothing. Grandma, Kai, and Peter returned to Eastern Point Lighthouse in one final sweep of the harbor and to sit with a takeout dinner of burgers and fries.

"Let's take our food over to the Dog Bar. That's it right there," Grandma said, gesturing to a long pierlike structure of gray stone. "Maybe we'll see something."

"We checked the Dog Bar this morning," Kai grumbled. "And again after lunch. We didn't see anything then. Why is everything in this area named after dogs, anyway?"

But they went, Grandma sighing with relief and rubbing her leg as they sat. It was quiet, all other visitors gone for the day. A crab clacked its claws at her. A few drops of light rain began to fall.

As Peter nibbled his burger, he couldn't help feeling a bit cheated. *No clues to the next seal found.* The thought surprised him. He didn't really want to find the seal and get deeper into this nightmare, did he?

If he did, it was only because he was curious. He wanted to know what was hiding beneath the layers of history and myth, whatever had made him able to activate the seals and Kai to read every language.

There was something *there*. He could feel, like, ripples in the harbor as something huge and scaly swam beneath the waves.

It took a moment for Peter to realize the metaphor hadn't come to him from thin air. Waves lapped against the stone of the bar, stirred by something Peter couldn't see. Peter crumpled his burger wrapper and stood up.

The boats had stopped coming back or going out for the night. But there, under the water, something was creating a wake.

Whatever was making that wake had to be at least fifty feet long. It curled and circled, as flexible as ribbon. Peter's neck broke out in goose bumps. Submarines and boats didn't move like that.

Was this their clue? Or was it the seal itself? Kai didn't see it, busy as he was peeling pickles off his burger.

This movement could be writing the binding word. After all, it wasn't like only Kai could *see* the hieroglyph. Peter searched the water, watching the movement. Was it creating an ancient symbol as it wrote a wake on the water?

How would he know? But it didn't matter. Touching it would either work, activating the seal and finishing their work for the day, or have no effect. Peter laid his palm against the harbor's surface.

The movement stopped, the waves healing the wake. And then, the wake grew, sharper and stronger, as the thing creating it charged straight at Peter.

Stumbling backward, Peter grabbed Kai and Grandma. "Run! Run!"

"Huh? What is it?" Kai asked.

Something huge thumped against the stone bar, shaking it.

Sea serpent. There's supposed to be one here.

Peter almost fell. Kai collapsed, dropping his burger. Grandma frowned. "I don't understand," she said. "From what I've heard, the serpent is supposed to be friendly, especially to children."

"Clearly it's not. Run!" Peter said. The waves on the sea side of the bar churned with action.

Kai scrambled to his feet and grabbed a knife Grandma offered. But he, like Peter, turned to run.

Water splashed across the bar, soaking their shoes, as the serpent rose.

In better light, it may have shone like gold. But under the gentle rain, at night, the serpent looked greenish. Gills extended from both sides of its huge, flat head. It rose, mouth gaping to reveal fangs as long as Peter's hand.

It and the Sea could be friends, or maybe even relatives.

"Go!" Kai said, pushing Peter.

Another wave washed over the stone, almost knocking Peter to the ground. But Grandma grabbed him under the arm and hauled him to his feet. "We need to get to land," she said. She started to run, but her limp slowed her pace.

Land seemed so far away. Would anyone from town even be able to see that they were being attacked by a sea serpent? And if they did, would anyone believe it?

The serpent hissed and crashed its tail against the bar, right behind them.

The giant snake sank back into the water. But it wasn't done. Peter could see it swimming beside the bar, a bronze glimmer under the dark water. It was fast.

It was faster than they were.

Grandma reached into her bag and grabbed a knife. She threw it at the snake. It bounced off scales below its head. The creature recoiled, hissing.

Grandma had bought them some time.

"Go ahead!" Grandma said. But Peter wouldn't. Not when Grandma's leg slowed her down. He stayed back with Kai, helping support Grandma, as water sloshed over the bar.

They'd almost reached the end of the bar, almost back to sturdy land, when the serpent, recovered, loomed ahead of them.

"Whoa!" Kai stopped, throwing out his knife arm in front of Peter. Good thing the blade was angled away from him.

Buckets of water splashed over the stone, but that was nothing compared to the scaly coils that slithered out of the ocean, looping back and forth on the path ahead of them.

The only path to land.

Grandma pointed. "The water. We have to swim for it. It's not far."

"No way!" Peter said. "That thing lives in the water."

"But it's on land now," Grandma said, wadding up the weapons bag.

Peter and Kai shared a look, but they followed their grandmother. All three dived into the water as the sea serpent roared ahead of them.

Peter's nose burned as salt water filled it. The freezing waves of the nighttime harbor seemed to grow as he swam with everything he had back to land.

Was the water churning more? Was the wind stronger? Why did it feel like he was swimming in a storm? And, even worse, was the serpent back in the water, pursuing them, when Peter didn't have time or energy to look back?

A loud hiss split the air. Peter, squeezing his eyes closed, poured all his attention into swimming. He paddled, sensing a giant snake behind him, knowing that any second now, he'd feel those fangs and that would be the end—

Someone grabbed him by the shirt and arms and pulled him up. Opening his eyes, Peter saw Grandma and Kai holding his arms, both soaking, both on land. Like he was.

The serpent's tail vanished into the water. In a moment, it was like it had never been there.

Cold seawater ran down Peter's neck and back and into his shoes. He shivered. "It worked. How?"

"I don't know," Kai said. "I stabbed at it, but I'm pretty sure I missed."

Peter frowned. It was like the serpent had just let them go. But why would it do that, when its prey was in easy reach?

Grandma sighed and opened her soaked bag. "I just lost a knife, and I'll have to clean the salt water off the others. Perhaps this was a mistake. We should go home. Regroup, and see if your dad has found anything."

Kai stomped a soggy foot. "We spent all day looking for a clue, and we just got one! We can't give up now."

A clue. Yes. Why did the serpent attack now? It was minding its own business until Peter tried to activate what he thought was the seal. The serpent struck then. So maybe it was protecting the seal?

Which meant the seal had to be here, or near here. The serpent let them go when they went back to land, so it would have to be on the sea, right?

Peter walked to the harbor mouth. The lighthouse flashed behind him, still working after more than a century. The beam illuminated the falling rain and the dark waves of the open ocean.

For a minute. And then, as Peter watched, the light flickered and died. The ocean was black with night.

A glow like moonlight appeared on the waves.

A ship.

A gently glowing, ghostly ship.

CHAPTER 12

THE *CHARLES HASKELL*

KAI

As Kai argued with Grandma, his twin stepped out to the beach.

"Look," Peter whispered, pointing.

Kai looked out over the water, as did Grandma. There was an old-fashioned ship there. And it was *glowing*.

"The *Charles Haskell*," Grandma breathed.

"That's it," Kai said. "That's what we came here for."

Grandma squeezed Kai's shoulder. "We need a boat," she said. "Stay here, and don't let the *Haskell* out of your sight. I'll be right back to pick you up."

Cane scratching at sand, Grandma hobbled down the beach. A few blue crabs scrabbled away as she passed them.

For several minutes, Kai and Peter didn't speak. They watched the ghostly ship out in the waves and listened to the rain fall on the sand. Every so often, though, Kai could have sworn he heard something else. Something like music, floating over the water.

A moment later, he jolted. "The boat's sailing away."

"Just spotted that, did you?" Peter was shivering.

"How long does it take to get a boat?" Probably a long time.

Grandma had to walk to town on her bad leg, find a boat rental open this late, and then get the boat out here. By the time she came back, the ship would be long gone.

They needed another ride out to the ship. And they had to remember to avoid the sea serpent.

Or did they? Kai had an idea.

A bad idea, but still, time was of the essence.

"Come here," he said, pulling Peter to the Dog Bar. They stopped just before stepping onto the stone pier.

"We were out here earlier, and the snake didn't attack," Kai said. "What changed?"

Peter sighed. "I touched the water. I thought maybe I could activate the seal."

Kai nodded. His heart thumped. "Do it again."

"What?" Peter looked at Kai like he just said hungry sharks made great swimming buddies.

"Do it again. Look. I think the serpent is protecting the boat. It's out there now. We can ride it there."

"It *attacked* us, Kai! It's a creature of the ocean."

"Which is why it will come back here if you touch the water. We can't let that ship get away!" Kai clenched his hand around Grandma's old dagger. "If you have a better plan, tell me now."

Peter muttered something about "wait for Grandma" and "not become snake food," but then he looked at the ship and sighed. He took one step onto the bar and, still muttering, put his hand on the water again.

The waves spiked as the snake returned. It rose out of the water and bared its fangs at the boys.

Kai pulled Peter off the bar, and they watched the serpent lose interest and turn, heading to open water.

"Now," Kai whispered.

As the long, golden body moved past him, Kai leaped onto it, wrapping his arms around the slick scales. Just behind him, Peter did the same.

Kai braced for the serpent to buck them off, but the snake had a different plan. It dived into the water, and Kai barely managed to hold his breath in time.

The water, choppy on the surface, calmed to a cold stillness beneath the waves, and the serpent dived deeper. *This might have been a mistake*, Kai thought as his lungs ached, then burned, then full-on screamed at him. He thought the serpent would carry them to the ship, but it looked like he was wrong. Maybe he should have planned this better.

Could Peter hold his breath long enough?

Kai held on until he couldn't take it anymore. Kicking Peter to get his attention, Kai let go of the snake and swam for the surface. When he reached it, he gulped for air. Peter surfaced next to him, doing the same.

"Great idea, Kai," Peter said, spitting out seawater. "I can't imagine why I ever thought letting Grandma bring a boat would be a better idea."

"Shh. Look." The ghost ship was only a short swim away. He *had* been right all along!

Peter looked impressed. "All right, let's go."

The blowing wind froze Kai's ears. The waves grew, filling the air with a rushing, roaring sound.

"Let's hurry. I don't think the Sea likes us being here," Kai said.

"Well, it does claim the water as its own," Peter said.

As the wind and waves grew, Kai and Peter struggled to catch the *Charles Haskell*. But, exhausted, Kai managed to get close enough to cling on to a trailing rope. It felt sturdy and real enough, even though it was glowing.

The boys used the rope to hoist themselves out of the stormy water. As soon as they left the sea, the water calmed.

Kai climbed, hand over hand, up the side of the ship, until he was able to clamber over the railing and onto the deck. Peter, soaking wet, dropped beside him.

The *Charles Haskell* glowed with an unearthly luster that resembled the light from a full moon, though it was still cloudy and raining. Water glazed the gleaming deck, and as the ocean rocked the ship, wooden beams creaked and sighed.

But those weren't the only sounds. Kai heard ropes and sails snapping tight. Heavy objects moving. Fish slapping against the wood. And voices. Men, calling to one another. Even singing.

The song seemed to echo in his own heartbeat.

Kai looked at Peter, who had a hand to his ear. "I hear it," Peter said.

"It really is a haunted ship." Running a hand along the railing, Kai walked around the deck, stepping carefully. What if he walked through a ghost? Would he even know if he had?

"That's not good," Peter said. "The trees attacked us in Dogtown. I don't want to know what ghosts we can't even *see* could do to us."

That was a good point. "Then let's get that seal and get out of here."

Peter nodded, and the boys moved together to the center of the ship.

The light dimmed. At first, Kai wondered if a cloud had passed over the moon, before he wiped the rain from his eyes and remembered there was no moon.

"Kai!" Peter grabbed on to him as Kai's foot reached the deck—and then kept going.

"Whoa!" Kai fell into Peter's arms, staring into the gaping hole that had appeared in front of him. Below, under the ship, the water rushed with the Sea's wrath.

All around, the ship's light dimmed and grew as patches of the ship disappeared and reappeared.

The boys hurried back to the edge of the boat and grasped the railing.

"It's fading," Kai whispered. "The ship is fading."

"It wasn't a real ship, anyway," Peter said, his eyes huge. "But what are we going to do?"

"Find the seal." But how?

Last time, at Dogtown, there was a pattern. The trees, all fallen the same way, led the way to finding the seal. Kai was certain there was a marker here, too. He just had to find it.

Kai spread his stance and held on to the railing. If a patch disappeared, he should still have enough stability to save himself. Now, to find a pattern.

The deck shimmered and danced as pieces appeared and disappeared. Kai searched. The floor vanished under Peter, who yelled and scrambled to grab Kai.

"Got you!" Kai reached, but he was too late. Peter's hand slipped past his as Peter fell through the missing deck toward the water below.

No, no, no!

Should he jump after Peter? He had to do something!

"Oof!"

Peter had landed on his back on a lower deck. A patch of the ship to Peter's left started to reappear, and Peter, frantic, rolled to it as the space under him vanished.

"I'm fine," Peter called up, and Kai sagged with relief.

Three seconds later, Peter had to roll back to the previous spot as the vanished patch switched places again.

The deck under Kai shifted at the same time, but this time, Kai let go and slid down the side of the ship to meet Peter below.

The floor under Kai opened up, revealing the sea, but Peter, now on his knees, grabbed Kai's shirt and pulled him to the side.

"Thanks." Kai and Peter scrambled to safety as the floor vanished again.

They were in a dark, slimy hold. Cold ghost light painted the space pale silver. Ethereal nets swung from the beams.

And the floor was disappearing. Patches phased in and out of existence, forcing the boys into an odd dance, leaping from patch to patch. Kai misjudged one jump and only Peter pulling him to the side saved him from dropping into the water, and Kai returned the favor when Peter moved a little too late.

Peter pointed. "Look."

The mast extended from the upper deck into the lower hold, and on it Kai saw the binding word, the same one from Dogtown. Right there in the center of the ship.

Past yards of disappearing boards.

The *Charles Haskell* was going back to where ghost ships usually docked, and it wasn't going to take them with it. Sooner or later, they'd be dumped into the sea.

Kai felt like the ghostly fishermen were right next to him, shouting in his ear. He couldn't understand the words, but the tune sounded familiar. That rhythmic beat pounded through him, reminding him of Grandma's cane as it tapped out the chantey's rhythm. *Bang, bang, bang, bang.*

And then the patch under the boys faded and they had to jump. *Bang, bang, bang*, and they jumped again.

It was like dancing, this side-to-side leaping with the beat pounding behind it. Kai almost smiled. *Bang, bang, bang, bang*, and jump again. Swing your partner round and round, avoid the water, don't fall and drown.

Wait a minute.

These patches. They all appeared and disappeared in *rhythm*. Four beats, jump. Three, jump again. Back and forth. Always back and forth. Under his breath, Kai began to sing the chantey Grandma taught him. The one about the Sea ritual.

"What are you doing?" Peter asked as they shifted spots again.

"It's on the beat!" Kai said. "Don't you hear it? It's that Sea-spire chantey. The ship is on the beat." He waited three beats until the patch in front of them appeared again. Then, pulling Peter, he stepped on it. "Come on."

"*A sailor came to the stony point,*" Kai sang, snapping his fingers in time with the four beats. He jumped to the next patch, a step closer to the mast. "*Bringing his loaf of bread.*"

They were almost too late. The floor opened up just as Kai and Peter jumped to the next patch.

Gasping, Kai continued, listening to the beats rather than the words themselves. "*With a heave and a throw he hurled it below.*" Four. "*And saw the ocean's mouth fed.*" Three.

The mast was just out of arm's reach now. Peter picked up on the pattern and sang along at the chorus: "*Rise, the ocean rise / Rise and greet the shore / With red and bread, he feeds on the dead / And meets you at the door.*"

Three, three, four, three.

It was working! The deck followed the music, which Kai and Peter could hear in the invisible bustle around them.

Soon, they reached the mast. Only three beats before the floor fell out from under them.

"Get it!" Kai yelled.

Peter wasted no time. He pressed his hand against the binding word.

Immediately, the seal glowed blue. Peter gasped and closed his eyes, and Kai grabbed his brother and the mast, waiting for the deck to vanish below them.

Instead, as Peter released the binding word, the symbol spewed water like a fire hose was hooked up to it. The salty blast struck Kai in the chest, driving him and Peter away from the mast.

Thankfully, the boards stopped fading. They were solid enough to stand on.

"We got it," Peter said. He tried to block the spray with his hands. "Now what?"

Kai wasn't sure. He didn't know if the sea serpent was near

enough to catch a ride. And the hold was filling with seawater, very fast. "Maybe they have a lifeboat we can borrow."

But the ghostly light blinked out, and Kai and Peter plummeted into the cold ocean below.

The icy water knocked the breath out of Kai, which was unfortunate, since he needed that air as he sank into the sea. Clawing, kicking, he fought for the surface.

He emerged to a hurricane. The *Charles Haskell*, having done its job, had vanished, and in its place was a storm that shrieked in Kai's ears and burned his exposed skin with vicious spray. Waves tossed him up and down, and it was all he could do to stay afloat.

"Peter!" he called, and choked on seawater. "P-Peter!"

Where was his brother? Kai spun, almost getting sucked underwater by another swell.

There! With a surge of relief, Kai spotted Peter, not too far away, desperately trying to tread water. He was staring farther out to sea, eyes wide.

Kai tried to swim over, but a wave forced him back. He tried to free one hand, to wave and call, but then he saw what Peter was staring at.

The Sea was there, in the water. It didn't say a word. It just smiled, and lowered its hand to the water beneath them.

Hundreds of claws clamped on to Kai's clothes. Crabs. Tons of blue crabs, but bigger than the one he'd seen in their bedroom.

Kai felt the crabs' weight, heavy as lead, tug on his legs and body. They covered him in a chitinous suit of armor, one too heavy to swim in.

"*Nnngh.*" Struggling to keep his head above water, Kai swiped at the crabs. A few broke away, pinching his hands in retaliation, but even more climbed onto him. Blue, jointed legs crawling over him, dragging him below.

Peter's arm rose over the surface, crabs clinging to it. He tried to say something to Kai, but choked on the water.

Peter! Kai tried to swim to his brother, but the crabs were too heavy. His head fell beneath the waves. *NO!* He fought the crabs, managing to get his face above the water, but there were so many of them.

Thunder boomed. The Sea spoke. "This ends now, little human."

Peter spluttered. "*Humans.*"

Waves slammed against Kai's face. His arms ached, and his lungs screamed. He couldn't keep this up for much longer.

Something gold and scaly snaked beneath Kai. *Oh no.*

The sea serpent reared over the boys. It hissed, shining fangs protruding from its mouth. Kai stared up at the snake. If it was going to strike, he was going to be brave and watch with his eyes open.

The snake attacked.

It flashed past Kai and Peter and attacked the *Sea.*

Coils of golden scales lashed the waves as that fanged mouth struck at the Sea, again and again.

Its golden tail thrashed, ramming into Kai. Crabs crunched and fell away. Kai swam over to Peter and started pulling crabs off his twin.

"Peter! Kai!" Kai looked up to see Grandma in a small motor-boat. She held her hand over the side toward Kai. Relieved and exhausted, Kai pushed Peter ahead of him. "Him first."

Grandma hoisted Peter out, blue crabs still clipped to his clothes.

Once Peter was safe, Grandma reached down to help Kai up. As the remaining crabs fell like rain onto the deck, Kai looked over the railing. The serpent had coiled around the Sea and was preparing another strike.

"Get him," Kai muttered.

The Sea looked past the snake, straight at Kai. It narrowed its eyes. There was a crash of water, and then the Sea was gone. The snake, finding its prey vanished, hissed and arced back into the water.

Grandma, her harpoon in hand, stood, watching the ocean. "Don't worry, boys," she said. "I'll protect you."

But no attack came. The waves calmed, and even the rain grew gentler. The snake had apparently gone back home to rest for the night.

A crab skittered over Kai's leg. Shuddering, he grabbed it and flung it back into the water. Both he and Peter, with Grandma's help, spent the next minute ridding the boat of every treacherous crab.

Grandma took a deep breath and turned to the boys. "Once we're back on shore, you can explain to me why you didn't wait, and your story had better have a happy ending."

"It does," Kai said. He slumped against the boat floor. "Two down."

"Good." Grandma handed him the harpoon and started the boat. The smell of gas overpowered the smell of the sea, and Kai sank down. He could finally relax.

"We did it," he said, and he and Peter bumped fists.

"Nice catch on the chantey," Peter said.

"And nice work on the seal. But we have to give some credit to the sea serpent."

Peter fell silent. Kai watched his brother, waiting.

Finally, Peter spoke. "Why did it help us?" He looked at Kai. "The serpent. It attacked us earlier. It's clearly a sea creature, just like the monster. So why did it save us now?"

It was a good question. Too bad Kai had no answer.

CHAPTER 13

A MIDNIGHT SNACK

KAI

The three drove home, stopping only once for more takeout. On the way, they discussed why the sea serpent had attacked and then helped them.

"The Gloucester Harbor serpent is supposed to have a soft spot for children," Grandma said. "I think it must have been tasked with protecting the seal, like the trees at Dogtown. But when you were in danger, it attacked the Sea to protect you."

"So it was protecting the seal, and then we broke the seal, so it protected us instead?" Peter grimaced. "My head hurts."

Kai felt a little bummed that the serpent hadn't been trying to hurt him, like the adventure hadn't been real. But then he remembered the ghost ship and the Sea trying to drown them with crabs, and he brightened.

When they got back, the storm from Gloucester Harbor had followed them home. Rain pounded and the church glowed with blue Saint Elmo's fire. Kai hoped the graves hadn't flooded again.

They reached Grandma's house well past midnight. However, Dad and Sophie were still awake.

Kai's stomach churned as Dad set a stack of papers down on his chair. They were in so much trouble.

Grandma stood up straight, hand on her cane. "Still awake, Alex?"

"You took them to the harbor," Dad said, voice tired. "Why?"

"Because it needed to be done, and you weren't going to do it."

Grandma and Dad stared at each other, and then Grandma said, "The boys are exhausted. They should get some rest."

"I agree." Dad nodded at the stairs. "Go to bed, boys."

Peter staggered upstairs. Kai hoped he'd at least check for crabs in his pockets before falling asleep.

Crabs. Kai didn't know if he'd ever be able to eat at a seafood restaurant again.

Or maybe he'd eat more crabs. As revenge. Who knew?

"Kai, you too," Dad said.

But Kai wasn't tired. The ghost ship and sea serpent sailed through his mind on repeat, as did the Sea trying to drown them under the weight of hundreds of blue crabs.

In all honesty, he didn't want to sleep. Last night, he'd come face-to-face with the Sea, and waking up to a leaking roof and a windstorm outside . . . it was too real. Too immediate. And now that they'd found the second seal and activated it, the Sea would only double its efforts.

That math seemed right to Kai.

What kind of twisted nightmare would he have to view tonight?

Would he have to see Peter drown? Peter, Kai's brother, his twin, his other half. He had protected Peter in the real ocean, but in the dream, the Sea would have total power.

Kai just couldn't do it.

Sophie was studying her textbook, but her laptop was next to her. "Can I borrow that?" Kai asked, pointing at it. "I want to call Mom."

Sophie pushed it toward him with a finger, and then closed her book and went upstairs.

Dad softened, too. "That's probably a good idea." He turned to Grandma. "Mom, can I talk to you?"

Dad and Grandma vanished into the office to argue in hushed voices while Kai took the laptop to the kitchen table and sent a video call request to his mom. As the connection formed, he spun the shield-platter on the table.

She might be busy. But she might be around to pick up.

The call connected, and Kai's mom appeared on the screen. She looked like she hadn't slept all night. "Hey," she said, cradling a mug of coffee. "How are you? Why aren't you in bed? It must be pretty late your time."

"Yeah," Kai said. "Me, Peter, and Grandma had a busy day."

Mom scooted closer to her screen. "Dad said something like that."

"He called you?"

"Not a call. More an email. He said you three were gone when he woke up this morning, and he figured you were trying to find and activate the second seal."

"So he told you about the seals?"

"Somewhat. He wasn't happy to find you gone. But you're here. I assume you found the second seal?"

Kai beamed. "Yeah, we did! We had to fight a sea serpent to get to it."

As Mom listened, Kai told her, in epic detail, about their adventures locating and activating the seals at Dogtown and on the *Charles Haskell*. "A ghost ship, Mom, a real ghost ship."

Kai finished, telling Mom all about the Sea's attack on them in the water, and how the sea serpent fought it off. "Grandma said it protects kids, which was good for us. Anyway, we're back now. Peter and I smell like seafood, but we're both okay. Which is good, since I need to read the Atlantean, and Peter is the only one who can activate the seals."

Mom leaned back. She exhaled and ran her hands through her hair. "I think I understand why your dad was so upset."

"We're fine, Mom." Kai spun the serving tray again.

"Yes, but this is dangerous. Your dad spent yesterday trying to solve the riddles. I think they only scared him more. Maybe it would be wise to take a step back."

"We can't do that! We have to act now or we'll run out of time. You should see this town. I'm tired of the rain and floods and the creepy blue lights."

"And I get that. But charging into danger without a plan could lead to a greater setback than you have time for. Or worse." Mom sighed. "I know you need to do this, and soon. But your dad and I just want you to make sure you're doing it as safely as you can."

Kai nodded, but still felt like Mom didn't really get it. So he changed the subject. "You haven't dug up anything else out there, have you? Any more Atlantean?"

"Right. Right, right, right." Mom fidgeted with papers on the table beside her. "We did, actually. Here. Can you see this?" She held up a photograph of a stone panel, maybe part of a wall.

Kai squinted at the screen. "Yeah, I can. It says, up at the top there, 'Glory to the Twins,' and I swear, I didn't make that up."

Mom laughed. "Until you said that, I believed you." When Kai started to protest, she raised a hand. "No, seriously. I trust you. Go on."

"Okay, so it says, 'Glory to the Twins,' and then it says, 'Here have we brought the gleam of the sea-waves and the brightness of the lily, the sun's own warmth. May two become one and may one bless us with bounty precious beyond compare.' Um, it may not be a perfect translation. Some of the words have multiple meanings."

"Like?"

"Well, 'lily' is some kind of day flower, but it might not mean an actual lily."

Kai spun the shield again. There was more than that. The word for "twin," again, seemed to have other meanings. And why even mention twins?

There was a pattern in here. The idea of twins kept repeating. But why?

"We found something else," Mom said. "It's on a metal plate. Hold on." She got up and came back a few minutes later with a bronze tablet. Green corrosion covered the surface. "It may be hard to read."

Kai squinted. "I'm only getting a few words here and there. Um, there's 'sacred' again, and I think I see something about 'heart' and

'life,' so that sounds serious, but I don't know exactly what it says."
He leaned forward, his nose touching the screen. "Um, that word
might be 'sea,' though. This could be important."

Mom nodded. "How about I clean it up and send you a better
image tomorrow?"

"Thanks! And could you send me pictures of everything else
you've found? I'll tell you what they say." Kai grinned. "Does the
rest of the team know you have such a talented translator?"

Mom snorted. "Don't let your head get too big. But sure, I'll
send you the rest. They may help you and Peter." Mom peered at
Kai. "Are you sure you're okay?"

"I'm fine," Kai said. "It's actually kind of cool. How many kids
can say they rode a sea serpent and a ghost ship in Gloucester Harbor?" He settled back. "But I don't know about Peter."

"Is Peter hurt?"

"No. He's fine. We're both fine." Kai tried to figure out how to
say what he meant. "Well, Peter's . . . acting scared. And he's gone
kind of quiet." Peter hadn't said a word on the drive home.

"Well, people react to challenges in different ways. This one
seems to enliven you, but maybe Peter feels overwhelmed."

Kai frowned. That didn't make sense. Peter was his identical
twin. Kai knew him better than anyone did. Shouldn't Kai have
noticed before if Peter was stressed-out?

Was this related to the distance between him and Peter?

In the end, he didn't say anything. It wasn't something Mom
would understand.

"Just take care of Peter," Mom said.

That's all he'd been trying to do. "I will."

"All right. Now, get some sleep. I'm sure tomorrow will be another busy day for you. Plus, I have a call I need to make."

Kai yawned. He'd put off sleep for too long. "Good night, Mom."

"Good night. I love you. Stay safe."

"I will. I'll keep us both safe. Good night. Or morning. Whatever."

Kai hung up. He trudged upstairs, sudden weariness dragging him down. His heart sank when he walked into the bedroom he shared with Peter and saw his twin had kicked off his covers and flailed like ants were biting him. Another nightmare waited for him.

But he needed his sleep. Tomorrow, he'd need his strength. So Kai climbed into bed, still dressed, and slipped into a nightmare where the Sea, just as Kai predicted, showed him visions of Seaspire, his family, and especially Peter, slipping beneath the waves.

———— • ● • ————

The next morning, Kai woke to Grandma shaking him awake again.

"What?" he said, and yawned. "Did you figure out the next riddle? Are we leaving?"

Grandma shook her head. "Your father is missing," she said, and left the room.

Kai sprang out of bed. Had the Sea taken Dad? Stopping only once to shove Peter into wakefulness, Kai chased after Grandma.

Sophie was still snoring in her room, but Dad was gone. Kai and Peter found Grandma on her driveway. Her car was gone.

"He's probably getting doughnuts," Peter said.

Grandma frowned. "Go upstairs and clean up," she said.

"Shower. You need to wash off the smell of the ocean. I'll try to contact your father."

Peter claimed first shower, so Kai woke Sophie to ask if Mom had sent them any emails.

"Yeah, she did." Sophie looked at the clock. "Oh, good. Still time before I have to go to work." She fell back into bed.

Kai took the laptop and had just enough time to print out Mom's scans before Peter came to tell him the bathroom was free.

When Kai got out of the shower, Dad was still gone. Grandma was cooking pancakes, using a broken sword as a spatula.

"I can't reach your father," she said. "He won't pick up his phone." She shook her head. "He learns too much from me."

Kai grabbed a fork. It reminded him of a trident. Poseidon. The Sea. Could the Sea possess his dad and convince him to come down to the beach? Was Dad already underwater, never to resurface?

The fork quaked. Kai set it down.

No. Heroes won the day. That was the pattern. They just needed to take action. "Where would he be?"

"Possibly the library," Grandma said. She handed Kai a plate of pancakes, her eyes soft. "I'm sure he's fine. Probably out researching, like he said he wanted to. Eat."

Kai took the plate into the living room, where Peter was sitting on the floor, watching the news. His own plate, empty of everything but smeared syrup, lay in front of him. "Look at this," Peter said. "The weather says there's a big storm brewing over the Atlantic. Barometers are dropping, fronts are closing in, that kind of thing. All next to Seaspire."

"What made you check the news?" Kai asked. He sat on the couch and took a bite of pancake.

Peter shrugged, which Kai took to mean that they *did* have the same nightmare about the water rising. "They're projecting that it will reach full power and hit land in five days."

"The full moon," Kai said. So they knew their deadline. To find five more seals.

And Dad.

"Where do you think Dad is?" Kai asked.

Peter shrugged again. He stared at the TV until Kai turned it off. "Maybe researching, like Grandma says. It's a good idea. We should have done it yesterday."

"We made it out all right."

"But we would have been safer if we had a plan." Peter dug a finger into the carpet. "We didn't know what the sea serpent was capable of; we didn't know about the crab attack—"

"How could we have known about that?"

"We might have known *something* if we'd done research." Peter looked up at Kai. "We don't know what we don't know."

"Exactly. We have to act on what we *do* know." Wasn't that obvious?

Peter sighed and stood. He sat in the chair Dad had been in the night before. "What if we make a mistake?" he muttered, then stood and pulled a pile of papers out from under him.

"What's that?"

"The papers Dad was looking at last night."

Kai scooted closer and looked at the top page. His eyes widened. "It's about the seals!"

"Huh." Peter sounded curious. "I guess Dad did research yesterday while we were gone."

The pages on top were a small-print, boring historical research article from some college journal. Kai almost skipped over it, but fortunately Dad had written notes along the side, and that was enough to help Kai understand the paper. It was written by a historian who believed that they'd found evidence of settlers living in Massachusetts before any known Indigenous people. The ancient structure under the Seaspire lighthouse was cited among this evidence. The paper suggested that they might have come here fleeing some cataclysm but ultimately died out or blended into later groups so their culture was now unknown.

"Looks like the Atlanteans came here," Kai said, waving the thick article.

"That would make sense. Someone had to leave the seals." Peter scanned the paper, and then turned to the next one. It was another printed page, a map of Massachusetts. Dad had circled multiple places with blue pen. The next page was a printout of a website titled Massachusetts's Most Supernatural Locations.

"Why did Dad want this?" Peter asked, holding it out to Kai.

"Not sure." Then Kai pointed. "Gloucester Harbor's on this! And Dogtown!"

Peter took the paper back. "Looks like New England, and Massachusetts in particular, has tons of legends and ghost stories for being such a small area."

"Sea monsters? Magic seals? Dad probably thought that these seals are in places that people think are cursed."

"I'd say a vicious forest and ghost ship are plenty cursed," Peter said.

Grandma stuck her head into the living room. "Still no word from your dad. I'm going to walk down to the Seaspire library and see if he's there."

"Okay," Peter said, and after the front door closed, added, "That's going to take a while."

"Be nice. She saved our lives last night."

"I know. I just—" Peter flipped absently to the next paper. "Do you think Dad's okay? He didn't go down to the ocean, did he?"

"No way," Kai said. He picked up their plates and walked them back to the kitchen. "Dad's more scared of the water than we are, now. He's the one who keeps telling us to take a step back. I think he'd go after the seals himself if he had the power to—"

Kai passed the front door. The mace Grandma used as a shoe scraper was gone.

Oh no. He *didn't*.

Kai set the plates down on the nearest surface and hurried back to Peter. "Where are the riddles?"

"What the—?"

"Just give them to me."

Peter took back half of the stack, and they both riffled through the pages until they found the poems. Kai read the third one out loud.

> *"In darkness deep beneath the stone*
> *The dead still plead for breath.*
> *In metal ground is flood of flame,*
> *And in dust destruction's crop is sown.*
> *Pits run deep with blood of death*
> *And walls are traced with like and same,*
> *So sense by scents and rock is blown."*

"Dad, where did you go?" Kai muttered.

"You don't really think he went after the seal himself?" Peter took the poem. His mouth shaped the words "dead" and "blood."

"The mace is gone. You don't need weapons at the library." Dad kept trying to keep the boys from the seals. After Grandma swept the boys away early in the morning to find the second seal, Dad must have had the idea to identify the third seal and do the same thing.

"But he *can't*," Peter said. "He can't activate the seals. No. He must be at the library. We'll just wait for Grandma to find him."

"Who says he's trying to activate it? That mace is made for smashing." Kai's hands shook. "He's going to destroy the seal so it can't hurt us. But remember Dogtown? You can't destroy them."

Peter paled. "The seals are protected. What if it attacks Dad, trying to protect itself?"

"You need to activate it before that happens."

Peter grabbed the list of Massachusetts's most haunted places. "What are we looking for?"

Kai scanned the poem. "This has a lot of mentions of blood and death. So, somewhere people have died?"

"Gonna have to be more specific than that."

Okay. What did this poem mention that others didn't? Well, the others talked about the ocean more, and this one was more interested in . . . "Fire. Fire and stone."

Peter ran a finger over the page. It stopped halfway down. "Like this?"

Kai leaned over. "The Hoosac Tunnel? What's that?"

"A bad place," Peter said, reading the short description. "It's a railroad tunnel in western Massachusetts. Built from 1851 to 1875, and during that time, 196 workers died during construction, mostly due to explosions. Because of this, the workers called it the 'Bloody Pit.' Some died by suffocation."

"*Blood*," Kai murmured. "*The dead still plead for breath.*" That sounded like suffocation to him.

"And look at this. Hoosac Tunnel used black powder in building the tunnel. *In dust destruction's crop is sown.*"

The paper fluttered in Peter's hands. "Kai," he said, "this one's going to be dangerous. Worse than the others."

Kai remembered what Mom said, about Peter handling this adventure differently than he did. "I know," Kai said. "But no one can reseal the sea creature except you. And Dad needs us."

He put a hand on Peter's shoulder. Peter tensed, and then said, "How do we get there? Dad has Grandma's car and it's the only transportation we have."

Kai thought. "No," he said. "We can take the bus."

"I don't think the bus goes to spooky train tunnels."

"Then we borrow a car."

"Even if we found a car, we can't drive it."

"*We* can't."

"You want to wait for Grandma?"

No. Grandma was great, but she was slow. She probably hadn't reached the library yet. If they wanted to help Dad, they had to leave now.

Kai imagined Dad in the dark tunnel, haunted by ghosts. Time to rescue their dad, like the heroes they were. "No," he answered. "Peter, go next door and tell Mrs. Perkins that Grandma needs to borrow her car for the day. She'll lend it to you." Mrs. Perkins, a homebody, never used that car.

Peter shrugged and left, and Kai went upstairs to do the heavy lifting. "Sophie," he called. "Wake up!"

Arriving in her room, he saw his sister stirring. "What is it?"

"We have to leave. Now."

"Why? Is the town flooding?" Sophie pushed her hair back. "Is the creature here?"

"Dad's missing. We know where he went." Kai tossed a blue shirt and jeans at Sophie. "We're going after him. Peter's getting a car. Get dressed. You're our driver."

Sophie blinked, still drowsy. "What about work?"

"Sophie!"

"Sorry. Dad. Missing." Sophie flopped back into her pillow. After a moment, she sat up. "Okay. Okay. Are we using Grandma's car?"

Kai pressed his fists against his head. "Not exactly. But Peter's handling it. Now get up."

"I'm getting up." Sophie swung a leg over the bed, then asked, "Are you sure you need me? What about Grandma?"

This was not going well, and Dad had an hour-long lead on them. Kai grabbed Sophie's arm. "She just went to the library. It could take a while for her to get back. We need to go *now*. Why are you wasting our time?"

"I'm not wasting time." Sophie closed her eyes. "Just let me get dressed. And call my boss. I'll be down in a minute."

"Great!" Kai left Sophie to get ready. Downstairs, Peter was waiting with Mrs. Perkins's keys.

"Sophie's driving us," Kai said, grabbing the platter of pancakes. "And let me tell you, it wasn't easy getting her moving."

"What, did she make you promise her your firstborn?" Peter asked.

"My soul," Kai said. He dumped the pancakes into a plastic bag. For the road. "I would have thought she'd jump to help us save Dad. But she dragged her feet getting up."

"Weird. I thought she was the go-getter." Peter found some scrap paper. "I'll leave a note for Grandma so she doesn't think the Sea abducted us or something."

A few minutes later, Sophie came down, ready to go. She took the keys from Peter and said, "Okay, let's go."

And with that, they left. They were going to save Dad, activate the third seal, and be home for a hero's dinner.

That was all there was to it.

CHAPTER 14

FIRE IN THE HOLE

PETER

Peter felt sick the whole way to Hoosac Tunnel. Dad was probably in danger. Dad was *likely* in danger. But here they were, on their way with their only backup their older sister, who was pale and silent the whole drive. Why couldn't they have waited for Grandma to come back if they needed a driver?

And did Kai even think about picking Grandma up at the library before rushing out here?

This so-called adventure was getting worse. Last night, Peter had another nightmare where he'd been forced to watch Seaspire submit to the ocean, flooding with powerful waves that knocked over the tourist center, the whale watching depot, and Grandma's house. He watched people swirl through the water, gasping for breath that would never come.

The Sea showed him *Kai*, chipped tooth and all, sliding down into the water as Peter failed to save him.

Of course *Peter* was the only one who could activate the seals. It was like the universe was telling Peter that he was needed. Peter wondered if Kai recognized that. So far, Kai had done whatever he wanted, and not listened to any of Peter's ideas, and the worst part was that it was working for him. Kai had gone after the seals and figured out the clues. Peter was left to trail behind, ignored until it was time to activate the seal. Kai got to be the hero, every time, and Peter was the sidekick with one useful skill.

For the first time, Peter wondered if maybe he shouldn't be so hesitant. Everything worked out when Kai charged forward. If Peter acted quicker, maybe he'd have a chance to be a hero, too.

Eventually, Kai pointed. "There's Grandma's car!" Dad had pulled off the road near Hoosac and parked in a ditch beside a thick forest. Peter watched the trees, thinking of Dogtown and suppressing a shiver.

Sophie pulled over and hopped out of the car. She hiked through long grass and weeds to Grandma's car and peered inside. "He's not here."

"Maybe he went for help," Kai said. He climbed out of the car.

Peter pulled on his backpack, filled with snacks and lots of water bottles. Since the tunnel mentioned explosives and fire, he wanted to be prepared. His stomach flipped. Another seal, another dangerous death trap. He could smell it coming, like smoke in the air.

But if Dad was caught in that trap . . . Kai was right, wasn't he? They had to do something.

"Where would he go?" Sophie asked.

Kai searched, then pointed at a set of train tracks barely visible through the trees. "Maybe he followed those."

"All right." Sophie didn't sound convinced, but she trailed after Kai, who had already started walking through the forest, toward the tracks.

Reminding himself of his nightmare, and that he had no choice, Peter resigned himself to his fate and followed his siblings toward Hoosac Tunnel.

The railroad led them to a gray stone tunnel entrance with 1877 written at the top. It wasn't big, but it was dark, and to Peter, it looked like a huge fish's mouth, ready to swallow a minnow like him.

"I think he's in there," Kai said.

Sophie frowned. "Why would Dad go inside a tunnel? What if a train came?"

Kai waved her away. "Thanks for the ride. We can take it from here."

Their sister's face turned as ashen as her work shirt. "You can't! Not by yourself."

"Then come with us," Peter said.

Sophie stepped back, but said nothing.

What was going on with Sophie?

Kai spoke up. "Dad's trying to destroy the next seal. We need to stop him and activate it."

A faint tremor, so small Peter wondered if he'd imagined it, shook the ground beneath his feet. A train coming?

But then Kai sniffed the air inside the tunnel. "Is that smoke?"

Peter smelled it, too. Another metaphor made real. "Dad."

Without a word, Kai took off running down the tunnel. "Wait!" Peter called. "What if there's a train?"

"Don't worry! We're fine!" Kai's voice echoed back. "Hurry!"

Peter shifted, desperately wanting to stay put. They didn't know what was down there. What if they made a mistake?

He turned to Sophie. "Come help us."

But Sophie was already backing away.

"Sophie?"

She shook her head. "I want to help," she said, her eyes wide. "I do . . . but you won't need me. Of course you won't. So I'll guard the car! That's it. I can be your getaway driver. Do some homework while I wait."

Sophie turned and ran away down the railroad track toward the cars.

Peter was alone. Gritting his teeth, he turned and raced into the darkness after Kai. Why wouldn't Sophie help them? Did she really think homework was more important than saving Dad?

The tunnel was dark, but electric lights kept it from becoming totally black. And there was plenty of room beside the train track to run.

Where was Kai? And where was Dad? As he ran, Peter peered into the shadowy darkness. He was usually good at spotting things, even in dim light, but there wasn't anything to see. Just a dark tunnel, a railroad track, and pipes, passing through.

For a moment, he wondered if the seal had been destroyed as the tunnel was modernized, but decided against it. If the Sea's attack on Dogtown only made the seal bigger and easier to find, he doubted normal human workers could make a dent.

Another tremor, this time stronger. Peter stopped for a moment and pressed against the wall. No train came.

Around him, he thought he could hear the sounds of people whispering, though maybe that was just the wind. The tunnel smelled like wet stone, though every other breath brought a wafting of something sharp and bitter, like chemicals or rotten eggs. The sound of his footsteps mingled with the sounds of stone and metal ringing together. Someone coughed.

No. Nope, no, nope. Peter was *not* going to get involved with ghosts. Not again.

He started running and found Kai beside a crack in the stone. It looked like it had been there before, but widened with a mace. Thick, acrid smoke streamed from it.

"Think Dad's down there?"

"Where else would he be?" Kai's shoulders straightened, and he edged into the gap. "Come on."

Down that way would be fire and danger. Stopping to think of a plan could only protect them. But Kai was already gone, so Peter sighed and climbed through, as well.

Beyond the gap was a dark corridor that smelled rank and sour. Ahead, yellow light flickered. Smoke fogged their vision.

Their footsteps echoed in the narrow corridor. Still, Peter could swear he could hear the sounds of people coughing and choking, suffocating in the narrow halls of the tunnel. And that sulfur smell seared his throat until he thought he, too, would choke, drowning on dry land.

The sooner they finished with this seal, the better.

They turned a corner, and stepped into an inferno.

A long, rectangular room, like an Egyptian burial chamber, met Peter's eyes. Carvings covered the walls. *Covered* them. Symbols, lines, and squiggles were etched from floor to ceiling, all the way down both sides. Only the floor and ceiling were bare. A series of bronze braziers shaped like long-stemmed flowers were the only furnishings.

The lit braziers spiked high with flames, but they weren't the only fires in the room. The walls were also burning.

Near the braziers, some carvings were gone, leaving only craters in the wall. But many of the other carvings were on fire.

And there was Dad, trying without success to beat the flames out with a jacket. The mace lay abandoned on the ground.

"Dad!" Kai rushed in, Peter close behind.

Dad looked at them, his face stained with sweat and soot. "No! Stay back!"

As soon as they stepped inside, a panel of stone slid into place behind them.

Peter's stomach lurched. *We've already made a mistake.*

"Don't worry," Kai said. "We're here to save you."

Dad looked sad. "You're supposed to be at home, safe. How did you even get here?"

"Sophie brought us. You shouldn't have left us behind." Kai turned to look at the walls. "The symbols aren't Atlantean," he said. "I can't read any of these."

"I'll take care of this," Dad said. "I'm your dad. It's my job to protect you."

His eyes widened, and he dived at the boys as one of the symbols on the wall glowed with fire and exploded, knocking them all back. Bits of rock and shrapnel flew everywhere.

Peter pushed himself up, spitting rock dust.

"Is everyone all right?" Dad's shirt was speckled with small holes and gravel, all along his back.

"We're fine," Kai said.

Maybe he was a little dazed, but Peter found himself wondering how the Atlanteans knew Hoosac would have a history of fire. Did they know the future of this place, or was there another force that shaped each seal to match the dark history of the location it rested in?

Dad groaned. "You shouldn't have come," he said. "This room is full of black powder."

"Isn't that the same stuff that killed all those workers?" Kai asked.

Dad nodded. "Smell that sulfur? That's it. Once I lit the braziers, the walls started to catch and explode. The whole room's a death trap." He put his head in his hands. "There has to be a way to get out."

"There is," Kai said. "We find the seal, activate it, and this all stops. Then we go home."

If we don't die first, Peter thought. More symbols were on fire. One was glowing bright, fully burning.

"Hey!" he yelled, and pointed.

"Oh no!" Dad grabbed Peter and Kai, and they ducked again as the next symbol exploded.

Shards of stone stung Peter's face and the arms he raised to protect himself. When he lowered them, his bones seemed to melt. "We're in trouble," he whispered.

The last explosion had really spread the fire. Now most of the wall was ablaze. The next time it exploded, it would be bigger.

Peter shook his backpack. "I have water," he said.

"I'll look for the seal," Kai said.

Peter and Dad rushed to the spreading flames. "Here." Peter handed Dad his backpack, and Dad grabbed a water bottle as the fire spread to another symbol.

"Down!" Dad said, and they both fell to the ground. Rock shattered all around them.

But Dad was up in the next moment, uncapping the water and pouring it all over the fire. The fire didn't slow.

"It must be the carvings," Peter said. "They're protecting the fire!"

"Down!" Dad grabbed Peter, and they dived for the ground again as another symbol erupted. The smell of burning sulfur stung the air.

This time, Dad stood up groaning. His shirt had been sliced with rock shards and singed with fire.

"Dad, it's going to blow again!" Peter moved forward, to pull his father from the exploding wall, but Dad motioned him away.

"New plan. You stay back. Stay safe." Dad opened another water bottle and attacked the wall again, with the same useless results.

This was pointless. They had no plan, no way to solve this. They were going to fail.

And burn.

"Peter!" Kai called. "Get over here. I'll need to you to activate the seal as soon as I find it."

Peter hesitated. He didn't want to go anywhere near walls that could explode.

"Peter!"

Fine. He ran over to Kai. "Well?"

Fire reflected in Kai's eyes, which flicked back and forth over the wall. "These aren't words in *any* language. I can't read any of it," he said. "And I don't know how it's spreading. But, oh, man, it's spreading fast."

The wall exploded three times, raining shards of rock on their crouching dad's head.

"You brought me over here, and you don't have a plan?"

Kai stared at Peter. "You're right. But I . . . I'm sure I'll find a pattern. There has to be one."

Kai pushed Peter to the center of the room and returned to examining the wall, hands fluttering over every rejected symbol.

This was not good. Both seals so far, Kai figured out a way through the trap, and Peter activated the seal. That was their job. But now, Kai was at a loss.

The fire grew, spreading light all over the wall. Dad retreated under another explosion. Kai yelled.

"I'm fine," Dad grunted. "Don't get any closer!"

"We have to find it," Kai said. "He needs our help!"

Peter pointed. "Uh-oh."

In the last explosion, some fire had crossed the room. Flames covered the first symbol on Kai's side.

The explosions had followed them.

"Kai!" Peter yanked Kai away as the first symbol on their side exploded. Both boys fell face-first to the ground.

Dust filled Peter's nose, musty and dry, but a welcome scent compared to the sulfur smell of black powder that filled the room.

The powder that must fill the explosive symbols.

Could it be that easy?

Trembling, Peter closed his eyes and stepped closer to the wall. Avoiding the spreading fire, he pressed his nose against the carvings. Yes, the sulfur smell was coming from the symbols.

But the seal wouldn't have that smell, would it? Why would it? If not even the Sea could destroy the seal at Dogtown, then the seals must have been created to last. Peter couldn't see why the trap would be set to destroy the seal, as well.

So, putting up with the bitter odor, he moved along the wall, smelling his way through. The seal had to be reachable. Humans had made this place. People, leaving a seal at a normal human height. It couldn't be impossible.

"Peter, what are you doing?" Kai screamed as another explosion rocked the air.

The heat grew in the room. There must be much more fire now. Peter opened his eyes to a disaster. Fire almost covered the wall on the other side. Dad had backed away, giving up on trying to fight it.

On their side, fire had spread over half the wall. If all these blew at the same time, Peter didn't think they'd survive the flying rock and fire.

He didn't have time to stop and think this through. He'd act like Kai, and trust that he knew what to do.

After giving the other wall a quick look for any bare spots, places where the fire wasn't burning, and finding none, Peter closed his eyes.

Don't trust your eyes. Trust your nose. You have more than one sense.

Time seemed both too slow and too fast. Kai's shouting seemed quick, frantic, but Peter felt like he was moving through a timeless zone, one where the fires and explosions were happening in slow motion.

The smell of sulfur faded.

Just slightly, but enough. Peter opened his eyes. It was mashed into the back corner of the room, and overwritten with other carvings, but he thought he recognized the binding symbol. "Kai!" he called. "Is this it?"

Kai ran over. "Yes! Get it!"

Peter slammed his hand onto the seal. That rushing feeling of release swept through his mind, stronger than at Dogtown or the ghost ship.

Images were pulled from his mind, like iron filings with a magnet. The Sea, rising from the ocean. Its attack on them at Gloucester Harbor. He felt as if the pictures channeled down his arm into the wall.

Then it ended. The seal activated, the fires in the room died, plunging the chamber into darkness.

"We did it," Kai breathed.

It worked. Peter didn't have a plan, but by acting quickly, he figured it out and saved the day. He felt like a hero.

Then, the seal sparked to life with the red-gold glow of flame. As Peter yelped and leaped back, it melted and bubbled with intense heat, like lava.

Peter just watched as the melting seal splashed with liquid heat, igniting every symbol along the back wall, and others besides.

"Peter! Kai! Get back!"

The air shattered with an enormous bang, and something huge and heavy crushed down on Peter.

Rocks rained into the chamber. They crashed and shattered with the sound of an ocean during a storm. The smell of sulfur rose with the dust around them.

And then, all was silent.

The ceiling had been shattered by the explosion. The clear light of the sun into the room replaced the red glow of fire with pure sunlight.

Peter groaned and pushed at the thing pinning him down. It groaned in response.

"Dad!" Peter struggled out from under his dad's weight and knelt beside his father.

Dad's eyes were closed. Dust covered him. Blood stained patches of his clothes red.

But he was breathing, and after a second, his eyes opened.

Peter looked around the room. "Kai?"

Coughing, from behind a boulder. Then Kai emerged. He had been farther away from the blast, and protected by the distance, but only a little.

And Dad had shielded Peter.

This is all my fault. I should have known the seal would blow.

"Dad's hurt," Peter called. As Kai scrambled over the rubble, Peter turned to Dad. "Dad," he said, unsure what to say next. *Are you okay?* seemed laughable.

Dad coughed and looked up. "Are you all right?" he asked.

"A little battered, but we're both okay," Peter said. "What about you?"

Dad laughed. "A lot battered, I think." Grunting, he scooted into a sitting position. Or at least, he tried. When he moved his right arm, he yelped.

He looked at his arm. "I think it's broken."

It certainly looked broken, bent in the wrong direction. Peter's stomach turned.

"But everything else feels intact," Dad said, patting his ribs and stomach with his good arm. He smiled. "And you're both okay."

Peter nodded, still feeling sick. Dad shouldn't have been at Hoosac, and he shouldn't have gotten hurt.

What had he been thinking? If he'd just waited a moment, he would have remembered that the seals self-destructed.

He'd failed his dad.

"I'm sorry," Peter said.

Dad wiped dust off his face and then used that dusty hand to pat Peter's shoulder. "Don't be. I came to protect you, and I did. And we're all alive. Now, come on, Rocky, let's go home."

Surrounded by blasted rubble as they were, the nickname, meant as a comfort, was anything but.

Peter helped Dad stand as Kai grabbed what was left of their bags. He handed one to Peter.

"The strap may make an okay sling," Kai said.

"Great," Dad said. "I'm not sure how we'll drive away from here."

"Sophie's waiting outside," Peter said. If she had just come in with them . . .

Then maybe she'd be hurt, too.

"Right," Dad said. "Now," he added, looking at the sunlight

pouring through where the wall used to be. "Let's find out where *here* is."

With that, Dad led the kids out. They had to leave Grandma's mace behind; they couldn't find it under all the fallen rock.

It wasn't a long hike to the borrowed car, where Sophie was waiting.

"Dad!" she yelled when she saw them.

"Just a broken arm," Dad said. "You're driving. Let me call a tow for Grandma's car."

As Dad made the arrangements, and Sophie sat in the driver's seat, staring into the trees, Kai and Peter leaned against the car.

"We did it," Kai said. He smiled, but his smile wasn't as wide as usual.

Peter just nodded.

Once the tow arrived, they left for the hospital. With Sophie driving far faster than she normally did, it didn't take long to get to the nearest emergency room.

But to Peter, it may as well have been an eternity.

CHAPTER 15

ANOTHER VIEWPOINT

PETER

Dad acted weirdly cheerful while his arm was set and wrapped in a cast. He had to have pointed at his arm and said, "I find this humerus," at least twelve times, despite the fact that the doctor, a pained expression on her face, told him, every time, that he'd broken his ulna.

Peter didn't understand it.

They returned to Seaspire and a downpour that was so violent it had turned the painted fish-man on the Fudge Kitchen to a streaky mess. Blue crabs walked the sidewalks like they owned them. Peter figured they kind of did now.

When they got home and Grandma wanted to know what happened to her mace and why a tow truck brought her car home, Dad just gave a half smile and said, "Ask the boys. I need a nap," and went upstairs.

Kai pulled Grandma into the kitchen to explain the whole adventure, and why they left without her, and how Dad broke his arm. Peter was left in the living room with Sophie.

Sophie had also been very quiet on the drive and at the hospital. Feeling awkward, Peter said, "Thanks for taking us. Without you—"

"Maybe you would have been better off without me," Sophie said. "If you had Grandma with you, she would have gone into the tunnel with you and maybe Dad wouldn't have been hurt." She rubbed her arms. "Or maybe Grandma would have been hurt. What are any of us supposed to do when faced with magical burning walls?" With that, she spun and went upstairs.

Peter felt like he was back in the cave, the oppressive darkness and the huge rocks pressing down on him.

Today, he was the one who did everything. He figured out the puzzle, and he found and activated the seal. But beyond noticing that the seal wasn't laced with explosives, he hadn't thought. He just acted, like Kai did. And, as a result, his dad got hurt.

Who would be the next one to get hurt? Sophie? Grandma? Kai?

Himself?

All Peter could think was, *If I'd remembered that the seals are destroyed when activated, I could have told Dad and Kai to leave before the room exploded.*

And if I hadn't activated the seal, no one *would have been in danger.*

Why did the room even explode in the first place? Dad had said the seals were there to prevent a great evil from attacking again, the evil that sank Atlantis. That was the Sea. The seals were there to send it back to wherever it came from. So, shouldn't they be easier to find and activate?

Peter understood the idea of protecting the seals. The Atlantean survivors wouldn't have wanted the Sea to find and destroy the seals, like it tried to do at Dogtown. They would've placed traps to stop the Sea from preventing those seals from activating.

But moving trees didn't stop the Sea from trying to destroy the seal; they just made it very hard for *Peter* and his family to find it and activate it. The sea serpent also seemed to be there to prevent *humans* from finding the seal. Although it later helped them, because they were kids, according to Grandma.

And those explosions . . . well, Peter didn't think fire could stop a being that could control oceans and storms.

What if the seals weren't there to stop the Sea? What if they had another purpose?

And what if it wasn't good? Why else would the Atlanteans build in so many traps geared to stop *people*, not ancient sea demons?

What if Peter had caused his dad harm for no good reason?

Feeling and smelling like the cold remains of a campfire, Peter wandered into the kitchen. Kai sat at the table, stacks of papers around him. Grandma leaned against the counter, polishing the shield-platter. "I heard you had an exciting day," she said.

"That's one word for it." Peter sat at the table. "Sorry about your mace."

"I have others." Grandma was quiet for a moment. "It's not your fault," she said. "Your father is an adult. He knows better than to rush into danger without thinking. He shouldn't have gone without you."

Peter just nodded and looked at the papers in front of Kai. They were Dad's printouts, including the copy of the MacHale poems.

"Three down, four to go," Kai said. "Time to figure out where we're going next."

Peter sagged. "Can't we just take a break for one night?"

"With only days left?" Kai tapped the papers. "Here's the next clue:

> *Devils play in stonework grim,*
> *As righteous folk to monsters turn.*
> *Mirror and egg, a simple trick*
> *Returned stony press and the water's test.*
> *Then voices taunt and needles prick,*
> *And visions, both wicked and stern,*
> *With twisted words the mind bedim."*

Kai slid the printout of the spooky Massachusetts locations toward Peter. "Here. You cross-reference. Do we see anything in there about devils?"

But Peter didn't move. "Are we sure we're doing the right thing?"

Kai looked up, frowning. "What else should we be doing? We have to stop the Sea."

"Why?"

Kai stared blankly and gestured to the rain slapping against the window.

Peter raised his hands. "Okay, I know why. But, then, from doing what? We don't even know why the Sea wants to attack us so badly. And that's not all. These seals . . . all these defenses are against *us*, not the Sea. So maybe there's no way to stop this. Maybe we should just warn as many people as we can and prepare for the flood."

"The flood? Like the one that *sank an entire island*?" Kai glanced back at Grandma, and then dropped his voice. "The Sea is dangerous, Peter! It will destroy Seaspire. Grandma's *home*. And it might not stop there. I don't know why the seals are guarded like they are. Maybe it's to prevent humans from trying to raise the Sea."

"But that doesn't make any sense! We raised the Sea by *accident*. Now that we're trying to bind him again, why are we facing all this trouble?"

"I don't know!" Kai scratched his neck, his gaze distant. "Maybe it's a 'pure of heart' thing. This could be a test, to make sure we're worthy of our quest."

Heat bloomed in Peter's chest. "This isn't a quest, and you're not a knight."

Kai scowled. "I could be, and so could you, if you weren't so ready to give up all the time. Like when we went rafting."

"Oh, you mean when 'giving up' and calling for help would have kept us from going over a waterfall?"

"We were fine, and now we have a story to tell."

"You can't tell stories if you're dead!" Peter clenched his fists. "These seals are dangerous," he said. "What if they're more dangerous than the Sea?"

"Then that's a risk we have to take. It all comes down to this: Do you want the Sea to flood the land?"

No, Peter didn't want that. So he sighed, and picked up the printout. "Massachusetts has a lot of devils," he said a few minutes later.

Kai glanced over. "No kidding. A devil's footprint? Do you think that's the one?"

Peter scanned that entry. "It doesn't say anything about mirrors or eggs. I don't think it's our solution."

"Grandma?" Kai said. "You okay?"

Peter looked up to see Grandma staring out the window, the platter hanging loosely from her hand. She turned around, brow furrowed. "Did you say 'mirrors and eggs'?"

"Yeah, he did." Kai held out the paper. "It's in the riddle. Why?"

Grandma set down the platter and limped to the table. She sat down and took the riddle from Kai. "*Righteous folk to monsters turn*," she read. "And mirror and egg." With a laugh, she added, "I should have guessed you'd go there eventually."

As the twins waited, Grandma looked up. "In 1692, two girls, Betty Parris and Abigail Williams, tried to see the future with a mirror and egg. Soon after, they began having fits and complained of being poked and pricked with pins. They blamed these seemingly supernatural attacks on witches, particularly three women in the town." She eyed the boys. "Do you know where this happened?"

Peter searched the paper. "Salem," he said. "It started the witch trials."

Kai slammed a hand on the table. "So the next seal is in Salem!"

"Looks like it." Grandma rose from the table and grabbed her sword cane. "I'll take you there tomorrow. I'd been planning a day trip to Salem since you arrived. Just don't leave without me."

Kai and Peter nodded, and Grandma went to the hall. "I'd better see if the others are willing to come down for dinner. If not, we'll just order pizza. I'll call early; I don't want the poor driver to feel they have to rush in this storm."

She disappeared, and Kai grinned at Peter. "Salem. That was easy."

"Good thing Grandma knows so much about history."

"So that's settled." Kai pushed the riddles aside and picked up a picture.

Peter glanced over. "What's that?"

"A scan Mom sent me. She found more Atlantean writing on her dig, so she sent me pictures so I can translate them. They look like they came from some kind of monument." Kai started making notes in the margins with a blue pen.

Peter picked at some dried egg on the tablecloth, but soon got bored. "Okay," he said. "Tell me what it says."

Kai shrugged. "Just a lot of stuff about glorifying the island of Atlantis, 'which shall be written in sunlight.' Huh," he said, bringing the paper almost to his nose. "That's strange."

"What?"

"The symbol for island," Kai said. "It has a secondary meaning. It also means 'twins.'"

"Also?"

"Yeah. Several other words in Atlantean also translate to 'twins.' Like 'sea,'" Kai explained. "I wonder why so many words have that meaning."

Twins. Two people. Like how the ritual required twins to toss the bloodied hot dog into the water.

Kai tapped the pen against the picture. "Maybe they're talking about us," he said, beaming. "We're twins. Maybe it's our destiny to stop the Sea and save the world."

Of course Kai would think that. But Peter had come to another conclusion. "Twins means two," he said. "More than one. Kai, what if it wasn't the Sea that destroyed Atlantis?"

Kai frowned. "What are you talking about?"

"*Twins*. Two! Something else could have been involved."

Kai's eyes widened, but then he smiled gently. "No way. The Sea told us that it destroyed Atlantis, right?"

Peter sank back in his seat. "Yeah, that's right." The Sea had promised to not fail *this time*. It had done something before. It *must* have been the one to drown Atlantis.

Still, the feeling that something was wrong here lingered.

How could Peter hunt down another seal when he was sure he didn't know the whole story?

Not knowing got people hurt.

Kai was still admiring the scan. "It's amazing," he said. "This copper plate has to be hundreds of years old, if not thousands, and it's really well preserved, for how old it is. No corrosion at all." He laughed. "Maybe the Atlanteans used mayonnaise to keep it clean, like Grandma with her platter."

"Maybe it's magic," Peter said sarcastically. He got up, leaving Kai to his translations. Not long later, Grandma's pizza came by way of a sopping-wet teenager and everyone trickled through the kitchen, one by one, to pick up a slice and go back to their separate corners as another storm pounded the house.

Peter sat in his room, eating a slice of pepperoni piece by torn piece, and thinking about Kai's words. *Twins*. Two. Could there be another threat out there? One that was worse than the Sea?

Then he heard a scream from the bathroom. Dropping what was left of his pizza, he rushed into the hall.

Sophie was backing out of the bathroom. When Peter looked inside, he saw why.

The shower sprayed ice-cold water. It smelled like salt. Seawater.

The toilet gurgled with more seawater. As Peter watched, seaweed slopped out of the bowl with a wet smack.

In the sink, more water bubbled out. Peter tried to plug it with a towel, water hammering against his hands and spilling out over his elbows. It held for a second before the water shot the towel at the ceiling. Peter cowered as the sink became a geyser.

"Grandma!" Peter yelled, coughing on water. Sophie had already run downstairs.

"It's happening down here, too!" Grandma called.

Seaweed floated in the growing tide in the bathroom. Peter spotted several silver fish and even a sea star.

He shut the door, but even as he did, the hall had already started to flood.

Peter splashed downstairs, where Sophie kicked water uselessly out of the front door, and more seawater gushed out of the kitchen sink. Grandma shoved handfuls of rags into the disposal. "It started without warning," she said. "This has never happened before."

There was a yell and splash upstairs as Dad discovered the bathroom.

"Sophie, honey, can you go give your dad a hand?" Grandma said. Sophie, face pale, nodded and went upstairs, struggling against the river pouring down the stairs.

Kai ran into the kitchen. "Got it!" he said, holding up a can of quick-setting foam.

"Great. Give it here." Grandma sprayed the foam into the sink. For a moment, the water slowed, and then it stopped.

The boys and Grandma watched the makeshift plug. But then, like the towel, it shot out of the sink like a blown soda cap and water geysered into the kitchen.

"Plan B," Grandma said. "Grab the essentials and get out of here."

Kai ran to his papers and shoved them into his backpack. Peter ran upstairs to grab clothes. Sophie and Dad were trying to hold the bathroom door against a tide of water that sprayed out through the crack.

"We're evacuating," Peter told them. "Grandma says get your stuff."

Sophie, wet hair sticking to her face, abandoned the door and rushed to retrieve her laptop and textbooks. Dad braced against the door, wincing as it shuddered against his hurt arm. "The Sea," he said. "It really hates you."

Peter had to agree. He scooped his clothes and personal belongings into his bag. By now, his toothbrush would be submerged in salt water.

With a loud shatter, the storm broke the windows. Water ran down the walls. In the hall, the door burst open and tides of water rushed out to fill the bedrooms.

Grandma's house was flooding.

Peter fought the waist-high current as he went downstairs. Dad was by the door, a backpack over one shoulder. "Here!" he called, waving Peter to the door.

Once Peter was out of the house, Dad escaped behind him and

tried to push the door shut, but gave up because the water was too strong.

Kai, Grandma, and Sophie were waiting outside. Seawater spilled over the lawn as they crowded into Grandma's car.

Together, they fled the rising sea.

"There's a place here in Seaspire we should be safe," Grandma said. "The Widow's Walk. It's not far."

"It better be far enough," Dad said, eyeing the ocean.

As they drove through the storm to safety, Kai threw Peter a grin.

Why? What possible reason did Kai have to smile? First Dad, now Grandma's house. Did Kai *enjoy* seeing his family get hurt because of their actions?

"The Sea is angry. We must be getting closer," Kai whispered.

So that was it. The stupid quest again.

Kai never thought about the consequences. He never thought ahead. And Peter was left to see the bad choices made and pick up the pieces. He simmered as rain pounded on the top of the car.

CHAPTER 16

WELCOME TO SALEM

KAI

"The Widow's Walk" turned out to be a touristy bed-and-breakfast on the inland side of Seaspire. According to Grandma, it had a history that went back beyond the Revolutionary War. It certainly smelled like it.

Kai felt ready to go when he climbed out of bed the next morning. They knew the next seal was in Salem, Massachusetts, so no matter what the Sea threw at them, they had the power to take action. And in such a well-known town, whatever guarded the seal couldn't be as deadly as the Hoosac trap.

Still, Kai felt a twinge of unease. What Peter had said, about the seals being protected by traps that seemed designed to stop humans, not the Sea itself, made a little too much sense. Why set them if you *wanted* people to send the Sea away?

Stories change over time. Things are lost, misunderstood.

No. There *had* to be a reason. The Sea was dangerous, and it apparently didn't like the seals. That was good enough for Kai to keep searching for them and have Peter activate them.

Dad was the only one waiting in the dining hall when Kai and Peter came down for breakfast. "Where's Grandma?" Kai asked.

"At her house, seeing how damaged it is." Dad sighed. "I hope we can save the foundation."

Kai hoped they could save her weapons.

"And Sophie?" Peter asked.

He was answered by Sophie pushing past them, in her work shirt. "I've gotta go," she said.

"Are you okay?" Kai called.

"Fine, just fine!" Sophie ran out the door.

"I guess she's not coming," Kai said. "We can meet Grandma at her place. She said she'd take us to Salem."

The corners of Dad's mouth drooped. "I think . . . I think it's best if we let Grandma deal with her house today. She has her hands full. I'll take you to Salem."

"Really?" Peter asked. "Are you sure you're up for this?"

Dad's eyes flicked to his cast. "I am. I know this is something you need to do. But listen to me right now. No lingering, no playing the hero. We find the seal, Peter activates it, and we leave. Got it?"

"Got it." This was another win for the good guys!

"Okay. Now, let's order and eat. We have a long day ahead."

After the boys placed their breakfast orders, Peter said, "Maybe we should go help Grandma."

"We *are* helping her," Kai said. "By finding the fourth seal and activating it."

"Yeah, but her house flooded. The Sea attacked her, trying to get to us. You care about that, right?"

Kai thought about how Peter acted after Hoosac. Sure, he felt bad about Dad, too, but Dad would be okay. If they hadn't gone, hadn't activated the seal, much worse would have happened to Dad, and Grandma and Sophie and everyone else. It was for the greater good.

"Of course I care. But if this means the Sea is scared," Kai said, "then I say it's a good sign."

Peter dropped the subject with a huff, and they ate breakfast with minimal conversation.

After Dad paid the bill, they left the bed-and-breakfast. They still had to go back to Grandma's house to borrow her car.

Clumps of seaweed surrounded the door at Grandma's house. Her furniture, patterned with sand, had been brought outside to dry. Grandma herself was hanging a rug on a line to dry next to a crate of old knives.

When she saw them, she smiled. "With your dad today, then?"

Kai nodded. "Sorry."

"Me too. But it's for the best. I've been meaning to clean house for a while. None of my weapons were harmed. Would you like to borrow one?"

Dad blanched. "No, Mom!" As Kai reached for the knife she offered, Dad pushed him back. "But we do need your car." After a second, he asked, looking at the house, "How bad is it?"

"We'll see. I called someone to come by and look at the damage. I should know tonight." Grandma smiled again, but sadly. She held out her keys. "Go make the Sea pay."

Dad accepted them. "Come on, boys."

Peter turned to leave, but Kai hesitated and peered inside the house. Wet sand and seaweed speckled the floor. Water damage marred the walls and floors. Everything smelled like salt and rotting fish. Could anyone fix all that up?

"Go, Kai," Grandma said, and Kai climbed into the car, vowing revenge on the Sea.

Peter was silent on the drive to Salem. This didn't bother Dad, who spent the drive explaining the history of Salem.

Kai had heard of Salem, Massachusetts, before. Who hadn't? It was a famous place, the location of the infamous Salem Witch Trials. And Grandma had explained about the mirror-and-egg trick. But as they rode to Salem, Kai looked it up on Dad's phone.

"It says here the accused witches who didn't confess were executed," Kai said. "But the ones who did, and named other witches, were set free. That doesn't make any sense!" Kai added, looking at his dad. "If they were innocent, why would they confess to something that wasn't true?"

Dad shrugged. "It was the culture of the place, and the time. The people of Salem believed in repentance over truth, in this case. But it meant that the women accused could easily save themselves by accusing someone else, and then that woman, or man, would have to either confess or be executed themselves." Dad sighed.

"'More than two hundred people were accused. Twenty were executed,'" Kai read. "Why did it happen?"

"Religious and social culture." Dad smiled sadly. "We covered this in my class, when we read *The Crucible* by Arthur Miller, which is about the witch trials. First, you have to understand that the people of Salem really believed in witchcraft. It was as real to them as, well, Grandma's Damascus knife is to us. And Salem was a very divided place. There were plenty of disputes over land, and there were feuds, and other issues that gave the people reasons to want others tormented or dead. With that, it was easy to believe your enemies were using witchcraft against you. And it was easy to get rid of those enemies by accusing them of witchcraft." Dad cocked his head. "Rebecca Nurse, one of the figures in *The Crucible*, was accused and executed as a witch, likely because of a feud her family had with her accuser's family."

Kai sank back in silence. It didn't seem real that a whole town would suddenly turn on one another, accusing friends and neighbors of dark magic. For a moment, Kai wondered if the location of the seal could have influenced them in a similar, if darker, way, like the way the gate at the lighthouse influenced him and his brother. He wondered if the "dark magic" in Salem was the very thing they were trying to find, and if the accused people were innocent of any real crime.

But then Kai looked at Peter, who hadn't spoken a word to him since they left the Widow's Walk. Peter had seemed angry with Kai even without the influence of dark magic, before this whole mess started.

They soon reached Salem. The weather was gray and bleak, and the trees bowed under heavy wind. There were people walking around, but not as many as expected of a tourist town in summer.

Kai watched the old-fashioned brick buildings pass as they pulled into the tourist center of town. Signs advertised historical locations, and shop signs boasted witchy souvenirs. Plenty of places were emblazoned with a traditional, pointy-hatted witch on a broomstick.

Dad pointed at one. "Not accurate. Your average Salem witch was a normal Puritan woman. They would look more like the Thanksgiving pilgrims than that."

"Well, the subject of witches is pretty pil-*grim*," Kai said, and Dad grinned.

Peter groaned. "No, Kai."

Kai leaned forward. "Oh, I'm just having pun."

Peter's mouth quirked, just for a moment. Then he went sober again. "Look."

Kai looked. Through the colonial-style buildings, he could see dark water. Kai shivered. He hadn't realized Salem was so close to the ocean. Suddenly, the stormy weather seemed a lot more threatening.

Dad's mouth tightened. "We won't go anywhere near it," he said. He turned the car into a parking lot by a visitor's center.

"Let's find out where we can begin," Dad said as they left the car. "We'll need a map. Let's see what we can find."

Kai and Peter followed him into the visitor's center. Peter immediately wandered off to read the displays on the history of Salem, but Kai stuck close to Dad as he was approached by an employee.

"Welcome to Salem," the woman said. "Are you from out of town?"

"Kind of," Dad said. "We're from Ohio, but are staying with my mother in Seaspire."

"Hmm," the woman said. "I would have thought you'd want to escape the bad weather, then. Today's not a great day for roaming around Salem." She gestured to the window, where a tree branch bucked with the wind.

"Well, we're only in town for so long," Dad said. He pulled Kai closer, the perfect image of a good dad taking his boys on vacation. "We couldn't leave without seeing Salem."

"No, you couldn't." The woman beckoned Dad to a counter, and Dad and Kai followed. "Well, our museum is open and safe from the elements today," she said. "And we have an informational film about the history of Salem. It isn't *all* witches, you know."

"Sounds interesting," Dad said, though to Kai it was anything but. History was great, but they were here to find and activate a seal. Which, he'd bet, wasn't in the visitor's center. Kai amused himself for a moment by reading the writing on the travel brochures, including the ones in languages other than English.

The tour woman continued. "There are also other museums in the area, if you're interested. They're indoors, as well. We also have the Maritime National Historical Site, Old Town Hall, and Nathaniel Hawthorne's House of the Seven Gables, if you have a literary bent."

Dad's eyes lit up. "Just like the book?"

The woman nodded. "The very same one that inspired Hawthorne's novel *The House of the Seven Gables*."

Kai, sensing danger, said quickly, "Where should we *not* go?"

The woman looked at him, and Kai added, "Are there areas of Salem that are really stormy today? Places that you don't think would be . . . fun?" He'd almost said *safe*.

The woman shrugged. "Anywhere outdoors, to be honest. I wouldn't go down to the bay, of course, not in this weather. Today wouldn't be a good day to visit the *Friendship*, for sure. A sailing ship," she added, at Kai's confusion.

Kai's stomach lurched. Another ship? That seemed like a good place to check.

The woman wasn't finished. "Derby Square and the Salem Heritage Trail are both outside, so I can't recommend those today. And, of course, there are the cemeteries."

"Cemeteries?" Kai thought back over the poem. *Devils play in stonework grim . . .*

What stonework was grimmer than a tombstone?

The woman nodded. "Charter Street Cemetery is near the Witch Trial Memorial, not far from here. The Howard Street Cemetery is a bit farther away. But both are outdoors, so you'd be in the storm."

We're already in the storm, ma'am, Kai thought.

"Could we have some maps?" Dad asked. "Kai, go get your brother."

Kai found Peter examining a display. "Hey," he said, running over. "Dad's getting information, but I think I know where we're going."

"Let me guess," Peter said. "It's a scary place full of death."

"Well, yeah. Maybe. Depends on your definition of scary. I think the next seal is in a cemetery. They're not that scary. Just a bunch of carved rocks."

Peter snorted. "If the seal is there, it will be scary."

"Don't worry." Kai smiled. "You handled the last seal, so this one's mine. Any scary things happen, I'll protect you from them."

"Oh, will you?"

Kai almost stepped back from Peter's glare. He thought, trying to figure out what Peter meant, but gave up. "Um, sure."

Peter didn't say anything. He just sighed. "Okay," he said. "Fine. Let's get Dad and go check out these cemeteries."

Dad found them a second later, hands full of pamphlets. They left the visitor's center, and once back in the car, Dad exhaled. "Are we all thinking the seal is probably in the cemetery, with the 'stonework grim'?"

When Kai and Peter both nodded, he grimaced. "Why couldn't it be in the House of the Seven Gables?" Dad muttered, and put the car in gear.

CHAPTER 17

REST IN PEACE

KAI

The first cemetery they visited was the Charter Street Cemetery. It was a fairly large cemetery, or maybe it just looked big because it was packed full of old gravestones.

Kai passed a sign calling the cemetery THE BURYING POINT as they wandered in. "So, any idea where to start?"

Peter shrugged. "Maybe just look around? Tell us if you see anything written in Atlantean."

So for an hour or so, that's what they did. Dad and Peter searched stones for names or messages that might connect back to the Sea or Atlantis or even MacHale's poem, but turned up nothing. Kai only used his language ability to sort through Latin inscriptions. He thought he may have found an Atlantean word, once, but it was just an old carving of an angel.

Eventually, the three admitted defeat and returned to the cemetery entrance. "So I guess this isn't it," Dad said.

Kai looked back over the cemetery. Another group of tourists were fighting the growing wind to look at the graves, but they also looked ready to give up.

"Maybe," Kai said. "But at Gloucester Harbor, we didn't see the serpent at all until after dark. Maybe it's the same here."

Dad's face fell. He was probably about to argue that this wasn't Gloucester when Peter said, "Or maybe it's not about the time. It's about something else."

Kai and Dad looked at him. Peter pointed at the sign on the gate. It said that the people buried there were people "whose virtues, honors, courage, and sagacity have nobly illustrated the history of Salem."

"These were the good guys," Peter said. "We're looking for where *devils play in stonework grim*. I don't think we're supposed to be looking for where Salem buried its heroes."

"Good catch," Dad said, but he didn't look pleased. "Then, let's check out Howard Street. According to the pamphlets I got at the visitor's center, that's where one of the Salem witches was executed."

A chill raced up Kai's spine. A cemetery with an execution. That sounded dark enough to hold a seal.

They climbed back into the car and drove toward the bay. Kai watched the choppy waves flash in and out of sight. "We're going to the water?"

Dad sighed. "This cemetery is closer to the ocean. I was hoping we wouldn't need to check it out."

Kai felt the same. Still, being closer to the ocean seemed to be another point in this cemetery's favor. The seals were there to stop the Sea, after all.

Peter squeezed his hand into a fist, over and over. He looked pale, and he didn't open his eyes once until they arrived at the Howard Street Cemetery.

This cemetery was more spread out than the first one. A few

trees dotted the area, as well as some taller monuments, but most of the space was filled by empty grass and old, gray tombstones.

Interesting, how old tombstones had that Halloween look. New ones were more like nameplates, shiny and fashionable. These looked morosely self-important. Kai touched one, and his skin crawled. He told himself it was just because the seal was probably here.

They were the only people in the cemetery. The land was ringed by buildings, houses and other edifices, but they were quiet, unwatching.

"Okay," Dad said as they stood at the entrance, tombstones on all three sides. "Same thing as last time. Let's look for any clues."

Kai and Peter nodded, and they followed Dad. No one felt good about splitting up.

Kai could almost feel the closeness of the ocean. The air felt heavy with water, and the wind smelled like seaweed, even this far inland.

When he looked at Peter, he could tell Peter could sense it, too.

Dad examined the twins and gave a small smile. "Oh, come on. Why the grave faces? Don't you know we're in the dead center of town?"

Peter grinned a little. "Dead center? It's off to the side."

Dad scoffed. "Like I haven't taught you about wordplay."

"Everyone's dying to come here," Kai said with a grin of his own.

"That's the spirit!" Dad said, and the boys groaned as Dad high-fived himself.

"I'm surprised you can crack jokes after yesterday," Peter said, and wandered away to study a section of tombstones.

The broken arm, and the flood. Yeah, those hadn't been good. But Kai knew they could make sure it didn't happen again.

Besides, as Dad said to Kai, "Laughing beats the alternative. And wordplay is a good way to keep the mind sharp." He gestured around. "See anything?"

Kai shook his head, and then looked up to check on Peter. "Yeah. But it's not Atlantean."

A thin, ghostly fog had rolled into the cemetery. It softened the gray light and thickened around the edges of the cemetery, like an imprisoning wall.

Peter, having noticed the fog, had backed away from it. "I don't like this," he said to Kai and Dad. "Look."

Kai followed Peter's finger to one of the few trees in the cemetery, which rocked and twisted in a high wind. "Have you ever seen fog this thick at the same time as wind that strong?"

Dad's cast scraped against Kai's shoulder. "What do you need me to do?"

The fog hid everything outside the cemetery. The wet chill seeped into Kai's bones. When he breathed out, he could see his breath. "Start searching," he said. "The sooner we find the seal, the sooner we can leave."

They walked deeper into the fog.

Whispering voices followed them. Kai didn't know what they were saying, but they sounded cruel. Angry. Something sharp jabbed him in the hand.

"Yow!" Kai examined his hand. Whatever it was, it felt sharp enough to draw blood.

But there was no mark. Just pain.

Peter called out, grabbing his side. And then again, twisting to rub the back of his neck. "Something's poking me."

Dad didn't cry out, but he twitched and twisted, as well. "Is this one guarded by giant mosquitoes?"

Another attempt at humor, but this time Kai wasn't laughing. The angry whispers grew louder, and angrier, with every step he took. He could almost understand them.

Almost.

Peter shrieked and swatted at his clothes. "Something is crawling on me!"

Kai reached out, trying to help Peter, when he felt tiny legs, like spiders' or ants', all over his skin. Collapsing to his knees, he swore he saw his shirt ripple as thousands of insects crawled all over him. Their footsteps added up to a hissing rattle as they swarmed him. He yelled and slapped at his skin, but felt no bugs. Only more crawling.

"What is this?" he asked as he tried to ignore the feeling. It was just a feeling, right? Nothing was real. But that crawling was *everywhere*.

Dad, pale and shaking, helped Kai stand. "Poking and pinching. A crawling sensation. It's like what the Salem victims claimed happened to them."

"It's getting worse," Peter said, hands over his ears.

The whispering voices were louder, but Kai still couldn't understand what they were saying. "It's not real," Kai said. "But it means we're getting close. We're heading toward the center of the graveyard, right? Let's keep going."

The wind rose to a howl, and a shadow blocked out what little light they had. Kai looked up to see a huge wave towering over Salem.

And on top of that wave, the Sea.

"Today I am strong, fed by the moon," the Sea bellowed out. "Now I take my revenge on the land and all its peoples."

No. No, it's too early. We still have time! But Kai couldn't deny what he saw. They were too late.

The wave swelled and fell. Dad grabbed Peter and Kai and tried to shield them, but Kai knew it wouldn't be enough. He closed his eyes, waiting for the end to come.

It never did.

Kai looked up. The wave was gone. The fog and wind roiled around them, like nothing had changed.

Peter yelled, "What's that?"

A crowd of people, dressed in very old-fashioned clothes, were bunched around a man who was almost impossible to see under the wooden planks on top of him. As Kai watched, some other men picked up huge rocks and approached the man.

Dad sucked in his breath and pulled the boys away. "Giles Corey," he said. "Look away, boys."

"What? Why?"

"Remember I said someone was executed here as a witch? Well, that was him. He was killed by pressing, placing huge stones on a person until they can't breathe."

Unnerved, Kai tried to smile. "That's de-*pressing*," he joked, but realized immediately after, by Dad's face and his own sick stomach, this pun was the wrong kind. "Sorry."

A line from the poem floated through Kai's mind: *Returned stony press . . .*

Visions flashed around Kai. He saw people, tourists in T-shirts and shorts, wandering the gravestones. He saw more old-fashioned people sobbing over graves.

Peter walked to one of the images, hand out. Kai ran over and grabbed him. "Don't do that!"

"What if that's where the seal is?"

Good point, but Kai didn't like this. Looking at people with cell phones passing people dressed in solemn, Puritan clothes, Kai didn't even know where, or *when*, to look for the seal.

"We're seeing through time," he said. "All these people, they're here. Or were, or will be."

Peter stiffened. "Then does that mean the wave *will* happen?"

Kai sure hoped not. Steadying himself, he said, "Not unless we let it. And we won't. Wait, where's Dad?"

Spinning around, he spotted Dad. His father was crouched, hands over his ears. Fog swirled around him, and Kai could see human figures in the mist. "Dad!"

"Kai. Peter," Dad said. But he didn't look at them. He mourned something only he could see.

Kai wouldn't let Dad get hurt again. Time to act. He tapped Peter. "Come on. We have to activate the seal!"

"You know where it is?"

"No. But we have to do something."

"Like we did at Hoosac?"

Scowling, Peter broke away from Kai. Kai watched as his brother vanished into the fog. "Wait!"

Great. Just great. His twin had run off, and who knew where (or *when*) he'd end up? And without Peter, they couldn't activate the seal.

Never mind that. Kai would find the seal and then find Peter to activate it.

Past experiences told Kai that where the trouble was, the seal was, so he ran toward Dad.

"I'm here," he said. Dad fought off invisible attackers, swatted at invisible bugs. Kai felt the prods and pinches, but he tried to ignore them as he stood over his father.

"Kai, where are you?" Dad looked with unseeing eyes.

"Here. I'm fine."

It was strange to be comforting and protecting Dad, the man who did the same for him his whole life.

Dad didn't respond. He had no idea Kai was there.

Faces appeared in the mist. Grinning faces, swirling around him and Dad. The whispers grew no louder, but now Kai could understand them.

Who is this child?

Is he worthy?

He is but half a man!

Kai yelled into the whirlwind. "My name is Kai! I have come for the seal. I will face whatever challenge I have to!"

He tried to feel like a knight, facing down impossible odds with nothing but his boundless courage to save his father, brother, and the world. For a moment, he did, but then the faces changed, mouths sprouting long teeth and eyes burning flaming red, and his confidence wavered.

Will you? Then come, and we shall see if you are wise enough.

The whirlwind tightened around Kai, and the invisible attacks increased. Kai closed his eyes against the beatings, swearing that he wouldn't flinch. But when the clammy air pressed against him, frigid as ice, he couldn't suppress a yelp.

Then it all ended. The frozen air faded to a warm summer breeze. When Kai opened his eyes, he was in the cemetery, but it was different. The trees were smaller, and the day was warm and sunny.

Dad was gone, but standing in front of Kai was a young girl, maybe six or seven years old, playing with a pink pinwheel. She smiled, showing gaps where baby teeth had been.

"Hello," she said, smiling. She wore a bright pink shirt (magenta, Kai remembered) with violet ruffles around the armpits and the collar, and turquoise leggings. The look reminded Kai of the time Sophie dressed up to go to an eighties decade dance, only more subdued.

"Hello," Kai said back.

The girl's smile widened, taking on a wickedness. "What you seek should never be found. And yet you seek it. What makes you worthy?" Her voice was a child's, but her words made her sound older than Grandma.

"Um, well, I can read all languages, including Atlantean," Kai said.

"Knowledge, it is? Then perhaps you will find this easy." The girl sat on a tombstone. In a singsong voice, she said:

> *"I have no mouth, and yet I roar.*
> *I have no teeth, and yet I gnaw.*
> *Though no man's knife my life can take,*
> *With windy breath, I bend, and break.*
> *Who am I?"*

Kai blinked. "What?"

The girl, smile unwavering, repeated the poem. "Surely," she said, "the answer should be easy for someone who is worthy with *knowledge*."

Suddenly Kai's answer seemed a little presumptuous. He stepped back, both literally and metaphorically. "A riddle. I have to answer a riddle?"

The girl nodded.

"And if I do, I can find the seal?"

She nodded again. "But fail, and lose what makes you worthy."

"My knowledge? But I need to read Atlantean."

She blew on the pinwheel, making it spin. "Surely your knowledge doesn't end there."

Kai's blood ran cold. All his knowledge? He thought of losing every lesson from Grandma, every fact he'd ever learned at school. And every memory, every life skill.

The price was so high.

Kai swallowed. "Can I hear it again?"

With utmost patience, the girl recited the riddle one more time.

Kai started to pace. "No mouth, and yet I roar. A speaker system? No, that makes no sense with the next line. No teeth . . . what can gnaw without teeth?"

He skipped forward in the riddle. "*Though no man's knife my life can take, with windy breath, I bend, and break.*" He exhaled slowly.

No one could kill this thing. But that was impossible! Everything could be stopped, or killed.

"Even you," the girl said. As Kai wondered how she read his mind, she added, "The unprepared should wait for knowledge. You must now pay the price and turn back."

"*No.*" Kai just had to think harder. If he failed, the Sea would win.

The Sea. Kai turned to look past the buildings to the bay beyond them. The Sea. The *sea.*

Waves that bent and broke on the beach under wind. No one

could kill the sea, at least not with a knife. And it roared and gnawed without mouth and teeth.

Kai thought of his dad's puns. Wordplay. Riddles were no different.

"The sea," he said. "That's the answer to your riddle."

The girl hopped off the tombstone. "Very good. May your knowledge increase and show you the things you are yet ignorant of." With that, she blew at him through her pinwheel.

The pink blades spun, and fog again swirled around Kai.

This time, when it cleared, Kai saw a young woman wearing men's colonial garb, like from the Revolutionary War. She carried a musket in one hand, and a scar ran across her forehead. The cemetery had changed to night, and the buildings had thinned and changed to older brickwork. The trees had become entirely different.

"When am I?" Kai asked.

"When you need to be," the woman said. She pointed the musket at him. "You challenge for the seal, do you? What makes you worthy?"

Kai raised his hands, hating that they trembled. "Um, I can read Atlantean?"

The woman fired the musket. Kai, gasping, searched for pain, but found nothing. She had fired past him.

"You cannot make the same wager twice," she said. "What makes you worthy?"

Kai's mind raced. Nothing seemed to come to mind. Because he was good at Frisbee? That didn't seem important enough.

"Because I've found the first three seals and survived those challenges," he said. "I can do this."

The woman lowered her gun. "Strength. Perhaps you are worthy. Or perhaps not. You have been weighed, but not measured. Prepare yourself."

Kai was as prepared as he'd ever be. "Ready."

She raised an eyebrow, but said:

> *"A garden of beauties, under summer sun,*
> *They spring in loveliness, every one.*
> *Under sun and in storm, they dance, smile, frown,*
> *Until the gardener comes, and cuts them down.*
> *Who is the gardener?"*

Kai took a shaking breath and rubbed his temples. Wordplay. It was all just wordplay.

If only Dad were here. He'd know exactly how to pick apart the riddle and uncover what it meant. That was the benefit of studying English, knowing wordplay.

If only Kai had tried his hands at more puns. But the time for practice was gone.

"And if I fail, I lose my strength, right?" he asked, and the woman nodded.

"All you have to lose," she said.

All his strength. Kai felt like it was already draining from his arms and legs. A garden of beauties . . . that sounded like flowers.

Was that the answer?

No, it couldn't be that easy. No riddle was.

He should have practiced more. Or maybe prepared his mind before he asked for the riddle. But time was wasting! He must have done the right thing.

For what seemed like hours, Kai thought. Who was the gardener? If the "beauties" weren't flowers, what were they?

It seemed like the more he tried to think of something other than flowers, the more the idea of flowers popped into his head.

The soldier woman didn't press him or point out how much time passed. She stood, motionless, waiting, and that unnerved Kai more than if she'd tapped a watch or something.

He sat on one of the tombstones. Hopefully the dead person below him wasn't offended.

Something in that was intriguing. The ground here was full of dead people, sleeping silently. Flowers were on his mind, so he imagined flowers springing up from the dead, sprouting through the grass.

This whole place was a garden of death.

With a laugh, Kai understood. The answer was right in front of him, and had been the whole time. "The flowers are people," he said. "Everyone lives, and then Death comes for them. Death is the gardener."

The woman nodded once. "And Death is stronger than anyone, young warrior. If you pursue this path, you will come face-to-face with him. Will your strength be enough then?"

She shoved Kai and sent him back into the swirling mists.

Rocked by the fog and shaken by the soldier woman, Kai stepped into the next vision. Now the cemetery was younger than ever, with fewer stones, and the buildings were smaller and more old-fashioned. And this time, the person waiting for him was an old woman.

She sat on the ground, skirts spread around her. She was dressed like a pilgrim. Like a Puritan.

"It's 1692, isn't it?" Kai asked.

The woman looked up at him, but didn't answer. With a wrinkled hand, she patted a space on the ground next to her. For a moment, Kai wondered if he should hold back, assess the situation. But Dad needed him. Peter needed him.

Kai sat. The woman picked up a cloth and thread and began to sew.

"Knowledge and strength," she said, "have brought you to me. But what will bring you farther?"

"I guess this is when you ask me what makes me worthy?" Kai said. He looked at the embroidery on the cloth. Waves rippled around flowers. Sea and gardens.

The woman shook her head and added another stitch to her embroidery. "This is when I ask you what you're prepared to lose."

When Kai didn't answer, the old woman continued. "The prize you seek is powerful, and power comes at a terrible cost. I ask not what makes you worthy, but what makes *it* worthy to *you*."

Kai ran his tongue over his tooth. Pay a price? He didn't think she'd accept an answer like, "Five dollars." She meant something important, and Kai couldn't even think what to offer.

So he stalled. "What are you people?" he asked. "Are you ghosts? Witches?"

The woman smiled. "The land can have a memory as long as the sea's," she said. "It can dream. We're only images from that dream. But now, here, you are as well. So you must answer my question or stay in the mists with us. What are you prepared to pay? Would you pay with your life? Or the life of your father? Your mother? Your sister? Your brother?"

Kai's mouth went dry.

The woman was still speaking. "Would you pay with failure, to save those you love but lose the ground beneath your feet? Would you succeed in your quest but fail in one you never knew you were part of? Would you save the day, but watch the world crumble because of your actions?"

Shivers racked Kai's body. "No," he said. "I'll win. I won't have to pay anything."

"Then you are not prepared. I thought as much. When you seek a treasure, or build a house, a price must be paid. Did you truly believe this would be any different?"

Kai tried, really tried, to imagine what stopping the Sea would cost, and what he'd be willing to give. He tried to imagine sacrificing any member of his family, of sacrificing Peter, but the thought made his stomach twist.

But when he tried to think about doing the noble, heroic thing and sacrifice himself, he found he couldn't speak it. What if it came true?

Scared and ashamed, Kai said, "There has to be a way we all win. A happy ending."

"And if there isn't?"

"Then I will make one!" Kai stood, shaking his head. "I'll figure it out. I'll save everyone. I have knowledge, and strength. I can do it. I *will* do it." Breathing hard, he looked down at the old woman. "I will pay no price. I won't need to."

The old woman took out a pair of scissors and with a *snip!* cut the thread. After a moment, she said:

> *"I see you, and you see me,*
> *As music, we are harmony.*
> *Wave at you, wave at me,*

As alike as land is to sea.
See your own face, look and see.
Two alike in face, me and thee.
But in soul? A mystery.

What are we?"

Kai stared at her. "That's it?"

"You answered my question. I am not here to test your wisdom."
Standing, she tossed her sewing into the air. It disappeared.

The woman patted his cheek. "And now I will leave you alone
to ponder my riddle. Answer well. Perhaps you may find what you
seek."

She spun on her heel, and vanished in a cloud of mist.

Kai sank back to the ground, the words of the riddle ringing in
his head. He sat as the mists grew, thinking, and thinking, but the
answer never came.

See your own face? A mirror? But that wasn't a "we."

As alike as land is to sea? But they weren't alike at all!

Nothing seemed to fit. Kai pondered and pondered, and as time
passed and his stomach began to rumble, and his head became
fuzzy with hunger and dehydration, he thought one last time and
decided to risk it all on a guess.

"Reflections!" he said. "The answer is reflections!"

The mist sighed and swirled. When it cleared, Kai was still in
the 1692 graveyard. But he wasn't alone.

An old woman, a different one, stood several yards away.

And Peter was with her.

CHAPTER 18

CHOOSE RIGHT, CHOOSE WRONG, CHOOSE NOTHING

PETER

When Kai said he didn't know where the seal was, Peter had already started running. Was he running to find the seal? Or was he running away from Kai?

As invisible hands poked and pinched him, Peter ran past scenes of the twentieth century, the nineteenth, the eighteenth. He was alone here, amid the glimpses of the past. Always alone.

And then the torment stopped. It was a sunny day in Howard Street Cemetery, but it wasn't *his* day. Peter had stepped through into a vision of the past.

An old woman dressed like a Puritan stood beside a grave. She didn't weep, or mourn. She just stood, looking at the stone.

Peter turned around, expecting to see his own time through a hole in space. But there was nothing there but more graves and another, old-timey Salem. So he turned back. The birds sang, and the sun was comfortably warm. In the storm, he'd found a haven.

The woman stepped away from the grave. She looked up and

saw Peter. With a warm smile, she beckoned him toward her. "I won't harm thee, child," she said.

She reminded him of Grandma, but without the collection of daggers. Peter walked over.

The woman examined him. "Thou are not from Salem, I perceive."

"No, I'm from, um . . . far away," Peter said. "My name's Peter. I'm sorry to bother you."

"I am not bothered." The woman began to walk, slowly, and Peter followed. "I am Goody Nurse," she said. "I am pleased to meet you, though you should return to your home and your parents. This place is not safe."

Peter looked at the beautiful summer day. "It's a lot better than where I came from."

Goody Nurse looked at him sadly. "Then you must have come from the Fiend's pit itself."

"It feels that way." Peter took a deep breath. "I know I have to go back. I just don't want to. Not right now."

Goody Nurse peered at him, and Peter stayed silent until he couldn't take it anymore. "It's just—I know this place isn't my ti— my home. I have to go back. But when I do, I'm going to have to face my brother."

"Your brother?"

"It's complicated." Here, in this lovely place, Peter let some of his guard down. "We're in the middle of something dangerous, and people are getting hurt. My dad, and my grandma. But my brother doesn't seem to care."

That was the core of it, the way Kai acted like he didn't see what this quest was doing to their family. But he had to, right? It was obvious.

Peter said, "What if we're wrong, and doing this—thing actually isn't what we should be doing? But on the other hand, what if *not* acting hurts a lot more people?" He sighed. "I wish I could stay here."

"Here?" The woman touched his shoulder. "Here is no better than there. Here, many people are taking action, and many people are not. Many are speaking, and accusing their neighbors, and they are causing harm. But many also turn away from the harm. Perhaps they believe they don't know enough to take action, or perhaps they simply are afraid. But are they more guiltless in the eyes of God than the others?"

Peter felt worse. "Are you saying that I'm wrong either way?"

"As Ecclesiastes says, there is a time to reap, and a time to sow. There is a time to act, and a time to wait for greater wisdom. It is not my place to say what time it is for you. It is yours alone."

Alone. Always alone. Peter felt cold, as stony as his name. Kai would want to act. But Peter wasn't ready. He needed more time.

"I don't want to choose," he whispered.

Goody Nurse frowned. "Not choosing is a choice, too."

He shook his head. "No, it's not." Not choosing was *not* choosing. It was letting Kai's tide carry him until he had all the information he needed to make a choice of his own.

Sure, he wasn't positive he could trust Kai not to cause more harm, but what if Peter acted rashly and did something worse?

"Peter!" Kai was strolling across the grass. "Hey! I wondered where you went."

Peter raised a hand.

Kai jogged over. "Who's your friend?" he asked.

"This is Goody Nurse," Peter said.

Kai frowned. "The name's familiar," he muttered, but then beamed at the woman. "It's wonderful to meet you. I think I just met one of your friends, though I didn't get her name. But anyway, I'm Kai."

Goody Nurse looked bemusedly at Kai. "Two of you, then. Strange, that two can look so similar, and yet be as different as land and sea."

Peter smothered a laugh. Yeah, that described them.

But Kai's face turned ashen. "I got it wrong," he whispered.

"What was that?"

Kai grabbed Peter by the shirt. "I got it wrong!" he yelled. "That's why we're not home yet."

Peter looked around. Goody Nurse had vanished, leaving Peter feeling isolated. All that remained was a cemetery from a dangerous time in history.

Kai seemed to realize that, as well. Expression desperate, he raised his eyes to the sky. "The riddle. The answer wasn't 'reflections.' It was *twins*."

The sky dimmed, and a shred of mist appeared between the boys. Kai released Peter and caught a piece of embroidery as it fell from the sky. Peter examined the cloth. A border of stitched blue waves ran up the sides, transforming into golden flowers across the top and bottom. In the center of the cloth was the binding symbol.

"So that *was* the right answer." Kai looked around, as if searching for someone, then shrugged. "Better late than never, I guess." After a moment, Kai held out the cloth to Peter. "The seal," he said. "It's all yours. Go ahead and activate it."

Peter reached out a hand, but stopped. These seals were holding some kind of secret Peter didn't trust. Did he dare activate yet another one?

What if he chose wrong?

But Kai said, "Peter, come on. Dad's back there, fighting who knows what. We can't wait anymore."

And Peter took a deep breath. *I'm not going to choose, not yet*, he thought, and gave himself over to his brother's wishes. He placed his hand on the embroidery.

His head felt thrown open, like windows breaking their latches in a storm. More images of the Sea's attacks flowed through him: He watched Grandma's house flood again. Deep inside his mind, a slow, hot rage built, and ebbed.

The thread on the embroidery faded and withered, like old vines. It unraveled as the cloth yellowed and aged, growing black spots of mold. The sky darkened, and the air turned colder. When Peter looked up, they were back in their own time. The fog had gone, and their dad was standing, brushing off his knees.

"Kai! Peter!" He raced over and hugged them. "I thought I lost you."

"Just a vision," Kai said. "We're fine. In fact, we've been having fun, playing games."

Games? That's what Kai had been doing while Peter talked to Goody Nurse?

Dad stared as the cloth in Kai's hand crumbled to dust. "Was that it?"

Kai nodded, and Peter looked at the cemetery. After they activated the seal, something bad usually happened. So he watched, waiting.

Nothing came. The place was as silent as the grave.

"All things considered, I liked this one better than the tunnel," Dad said. "No explosions. Now, come on. We have the rest of the day, and we're in Salem."

So they went back to the car. Dad got his wish, and they visited the House of the Seven Gables. They also visited a couple of witch museums.

At one of them, Peter found a list of the people who were executed as witches. Giles Corey, the man pressed to death at Howard Street, was on it. He touched the name, wondering if that man wished he'd done something, or hadn't done something, before he died.

As he was about to move away, another name caught his eye. Rebecca Nurse. An elderly woman, executed for witchcraft.

Feeling sick and guilty, but not knowing why, Peter left the list. He found his dad and brother, and left Salem, thinking about seals and Seas and kind old women who gave advice that no one followed.

—— ● ◉ ● ——

They returned to the Widow's Walk later that evening. Peter slumped into an armchair, exhausted. He didn't know why, really, since Kai apparently had the real adventure. He wouldn't shut up about it all the way to the bed-and-breakfast.

"I met a girl and two women and they gave me riddles," he told their dad as Peter sat in the back seat. "If I failed the riddles, they were going to take my knowledge and my strength. But I guessed them right. I solved them, all by myself!"

"That's great!" Dad had said.

Peter had frowned, though. Kai had said earlier that he'd gotten the last riddle wrong. He'd been troubled by that. Why gloss over that now?

Probably to sound more like the hero he thought he was.

Dad turned to Peter. "Rocky, what happened with you?"

Peter shrugged. "Nothing much." Meeting Goody Nurse still unnerved him. How could not choosing be a choice? That didn't make any sense.

What if by not choosing he let Kai's recklessness get someone else hurt?

Why should it matter? He never wanted a part in this in the first place.

Even though the sun was setting behind a screen of gray clouds, neither Sophie nor Grandma had returned to the bed-and-breakfast.

"That's odd," Dad said. "Sophie's shift should have ended hours ago."

Peter had expected to find his sister working on her chemistry notes in her room. "Maybe she's helping Grandma clean up."

"Yeah. Yeah, that makes sense," Dad said. He jingled the car keys. "Let's go return Grandma's car and help them finish for the night."

They made the short drive to Grandma's house, and Peter's jaw dropped. A police car was at the house, red and blue lights flashing against the growing dark. Grandma stood on the porch, talking to an officer.

Dad leaped out of the car. "Mom! What happened?"

Grandma, eyes glinting wet, reached for Dad. Peter's heart thumped. He followed Dad, with Kai right behind him.

Dad was shaking his head. He looked like he had at the cemetery: pale and hopeless.

"Dad?" Peter asked. "What happened?"

"Sir, Sophie Syracuse is your daughter, correct?" the officer asked.

Dad nodded, and the officer added, "I'd like to ask you some questions. Get a profile. Figure out if she may be with the others."

She? As the officer escorted Dad to the side, Peter turned to Grandma. "Where's Sophie?"

Grandma put her hand on his shoulder. "She came by after work, to help me clean the house. I tried to convince her she'd be more helpful hunting down the seals, and she got upset, though she tried to hide it. She hasn't been herself, starting with the ghost voices on the wind, but it got a lot worse after you boys went to Hoosac Tunnel." Grandma shuddered. "Sophie . . . Sophie said she needed to figure some things out. She went on a walk." Grandma looked at the horizon. "She went toward the beach."

It was like lightning had struck Peter in the chest, like he was both burning and freezing from the inside out. The beach.

The *beach*.

Sophie had gone to the beach.

He didn't need to ask Grandma if that was the last time she saw Sophie. He knew it was. If it hadn't been, she wouldn't have called the cops. She wouldn't look like she'd lost a great treasure.

It was all too clear.

The Sea had taken Sophie.

CHAPTER 19

LOST

KAI

Sophie was gone.

As soon as Kai heard that she was missing, he ran down to the shore, with Peter and his dad on his heels. The sand was swept clean by the frequent rain, except for a set of footprints. Sophie's footprints, leading to the water.

They ended there.

Dad pushed Kai behind him, and paced back and forth beside the water. "She must have walked in the tide," he said. "We just have to find where she left the water."

"Dad," Kai said. "You should step back."

"No, you stay back!" Dad looked almost feral. "The Sea wants you two, not me, and not Sophie. She must be around somewhere."

If that were true, Kai thought, *Grandma wouldn't be so worried.*

Kai stepped closer to the water, close enough that if the ocean wasn't shattered by waves, he would have been able to see his reflection.

Another wave surged with a sound like a deep sigh. And another.

And then, a wave came with a roar. This one dropped something on the sand at Kai's feet.

A phone.

Sophie's phone.

Kai picked it up. As he held the phone, it sputtered to life, revealing the lock screen: a shot of Sophie and her friends last Fourth of July, waving sparklers. Then the picture flickered and died, and water gushed out of the phone. More water than Kai thought even a drowned phone could hold.

The message was clear. Kai fell back to where Peter was standing. "It's got her," he said to his twin, showing him the phone.

Peter nodded and bounced as he dug his foot into the sand. Kai's twin stood perfectly straight and stiff. "Do you think it drowned Sophie?" Peter whispered. "To make us stop?"

"If it did, it's an idiot," Kai growled. "If *anything* happened to Sophie, I won't rest until that monster is locked away for good. Or destroyed."

Peter's bouncing intensified. "Something *did* happen to her," he said in a rough voice.

"Then I guess I have a promise to keep."

Kai turned around and marched back into town, Peter following behind him.

"Kai, what are you doing? Kai, stop!"

Kai halted so fast Peter ran into him. "Kai," Peter said again. "What are you doing?"

"What does it look like I'm doing? I'm going to find Sophie."

"It's getting late. It's already dark, and Dad, Grandma, and the police are already searching—"

Kai couldn't believe it. "Are you saying we just *do nothing*?"

"No, of course not. But are you saying you're just going to . . . *challenge* the Sea?"

"You know me. I like a challenge."

Kai started to move again, but Peter grabbed his arm. "Just stop and wait a moment. Think. If you anger the Sea, it might hurt Sophie. If it hasn't already."

"It *hasn't*." Kai wouldn't even entertain that thought.

"What about the others?"

"What?"

Peter took a deep breath. "The cop back there said Sophie might be with 'the others.' If the Sea got her, maybe she's not the only one. Maybe it took a bunch of hostages."

Oh. Kai searched the beach. It was remarkably empty, which could have been due to bad weather, but what if the Sea swept more than Sophie away with it?

The beach's sand was smoothed, as if a huge wave had covered it from end to end. Peter had to be right.

Kai gritted his teeth. "All the more reason to find them now. To stop the Sea *now*."

It was so clear to Kai. It would be to Peter, too, in a moment.

Kai watched, waiting for Peter to give in.

Then Peter shook his head. "No."

"No what?"

"No, I'm not going to help you. I won't risk Sophie's, or anyone else's, life just because you want to play the hero."

Anger boiled inside Kai. "That's not what this is about. This is you not wanting to actually do anything, isn't it? Our sister was captured by a monster, and you want to do nothing?"

"If the alternative is making things worse, then yes!"

"We make things worse by doing nothing."

"Yeah?" Peter leaned forward, fists clenched. "And how would you make this better? If you go off looking for Sophie, what happens? Maybe you find her. And then the Sea will try to stop you, and you'll fight it, and lose, and it will take out its anger on Sophie and the other hostages. Have you even stopped to think about the cost?"

The word "cost" cut like shark's teeth. "There won't be a cost! We're going to save them, and that's how it's going to be."

Peter stared at Kai. "Do what you want," he said. "But I'm going back to the Widow's Walk to come up with a plan. Try not to get the whole town flooded before the thought that this might not be the best idea finally makes it into your thick skull."

Peter shoved his hands in his pockets and started the trudge across town to the Widow's Walk.

Kai seethed. How could Peter sit idly by when Sophie needed their help? Didn't he care more about her than about his fear that he'd mess up somehow? Didn't he care about Sophie at all?

But what if he's right? What if you did mess this up and Sophie got hurt? What if an innocent person who just wanted to explore the beach today got hurt? First Dad's arm, then Grandma's house. The cost is piling up, Kai. For everyone. Except you.

No. Kai just had to work harder. Try harder. Starting with getting the people of Seaspire back from the Sea.

Kai was sure Sophie was still alive. The Sea was many things, but Kai didn't think it was stupid. Alive, Sophie was a bargaining chip. And that phone, washed up at Kai's feet? That was a ransom letter. *I have your sister. If you want her back, stop activating the seals.*

Nice try, but Kai didn't negotiate with terrifying sea monsters.

Well, the good thing about a sea monster was that you always knew where to find it. As the sky darkened with night and the police and Dad drove inland to look for Sophie, Kai marched down to the shore. "Hey, ugly!" he yelled. "Give me back the people you took!"

Nothing responded but the roar of the waves.

Growling, Kai picked up a huge rock and lobbed it into the surf. It sent up plumes of white water. He picked up another stone and threw it.

"I can end you," he said as he picked up another rock. "I'll keep throwing rocks. Little pieces of the land. With every piece I throw, you get smaller, and weaker, and even more *pathetic* than you already are."

A thought quietly reminded him that water volume didn't work like that, but Kai didn't care and, anyway, he didn't have time to think about physics before the Sea rose in a crash of water in front of him.

"HOW DARE YOU!" it thundered. Whirlpools formed and water spouted. Kai dived as the rocks he'd thrown, plus several more, shot back at him.

The Sea rode the waves higher into the air. "How dare you pollute my domain with shards of land? With *filth*? Do you wish death, human boy?"

Spitting sand, Kai yelled back, "How dare *you* abduct my sister? Give her back!"

The ocean foamed and seethed. "DO YOU PRESUME TO GIVE ME ORDERS?"

"Yeah, I presume!" Kai stood up. The churning water only mirrored his own feelings: turbulent, dark, and enraged. "They're not part of this. Sophie doesn't even *care* about this."

"She cares more than you think," the Sea said.

"What have you done to her? To all of them?"

"They're safe. Now you understand how it feels to have something prized stolen from you." Kai frowned. What had they stolen from the Sea? The creature continued, "Give up your quest, and I will give them back. Perhaps I will give you a day's head start to escape my waters when they come."

"No." Digging his toes in the sand, Kai glared at the Sea. "I won't run."

"I could destroy you, child."

"So do it! What, are you scared?"

The Sea just laughed. "*You* are no threat to me."

"Oh yeah?" Kai laughed. "Then why did you abduct Sophie and the others, if you're so powerful and I'm no *threat*? You want leverage over me because I can stop you. I can send you back to your prison."

"You have no idea what you meddle with," the Sea said. Kai thought it sounded a little panicked.

"I know enough to know we can defeat you." Realization struck Kai. "You can't hurt me. Sure, you can send your water, but as long as I'm on land, I'm stronger than you."

Standing firm on shore, Kai felt like a hero. Here, facing the enemy, issuing a challenge. Here, he'd save the hostages, including Sophie, and force the monster to comply.

But then the Sea bellowed with rage. "LAND?"

A giant wave plowed into Kai, slamming him into the sand.

"DO YOU THINK YOUR LAND PROTECTS YOU?"

Another wave.

Kai choked on water and sand and tried to crawl away, but the force was too strong.

Wave after wave pounded Kai. They flattened his chest, squeezing out the last wisps of air. Water smothered him. He couldn't see, couldn't hear anything but the Sea's voice and the rush of the ocean.

He couldn't breathe.

On the next wave, Kai let go. The water carried him farther inland to the boardwalk, where he clung to a splintered board until the water receded. Then he staggered to his feet and ran.

The Sea howled wordlessly behind him. Thunder boomed, and wind shrieked like a train.

Kai looked back to see lightning flash. A bolt struck the Spire once, then twice, and the water's edge raced away from the shore like it was terrified.

Then the dark sea rose in an enormous wave, and Kai turned and kept running. Behind him, wood splintered as the ocean's wrath hammered down on the beach and wharf.

The sound of water receding into a second enormous wave met Kai's ears, but this time he didn't look back.

The Sea was attacking Seaspire early, and it was Kai's fault.

What have I done?

CHAPTER 20

SCREAMS IN THE WOOD

KAI

Kai didn't go back to the bed-and-breakfast that night. He returned to Grandma's sodden house, now abandoned as Grandma and Dad searched for Sophie. There, he went up to his sea-stained room and huddled, trying to sleep, as the Sea sent tidal waves to rip the coast and a storm with thunder that shook the walls.

But he couldn't go back.

He couldn't face them, not when he'd made it worse.

He couldn't face Peter.

What have I done? What will happen to Sophie? To Seaspire?

Somehow, Kai made it through the night.

The next morning Kai woke from fractured sleep to hear something moving downstairs. *Oh no.* Had Seaspire been invaded by sea monsters?

Kai sneaked downstairs to find Grandma in the wrecked kitchen. She jumped and said, "Oh, Kai! Where have you been? I've been searching for you all night while your father handled the police. After I saw the wharf, I was so worried. Are you okay?" She hurried over and examined him.

"How bad is it?" he asked dully. When Grandma frowned, Kai said, "The wharf. How bad is it?"

Grandma was silent for a moment. "It's gone," she said. "The docks closest to the beach have sustained some heavy damage, and every boat tied there has either been swept out to sea or is in splinters. The power lines went down last night. Seaspire is out of power, and some places have damaged windows from the storm. The cleanup crew is working to board the windows in town. But we'll recover," she said, coming over and touching Kai's face. "You can't keep my town down."

So the Sea didn't destroy Seaspire completely. It wasn't at full power yet; maybe the wharf was all it could manage. Kai had been right; the land stopped it. For now.

Still, it wouldn't have attacked at all if Kai hadn't been stupid enough to challenge it.

"What about Sophie?" Kai asked sharply. "And the others?"

Grandma shook her head.

"Still missing, last we heard."

Missing, or worse. What would the Sea have done to Sophie now that Kai made it angry?

"Come back to the Widow's Walk," Grandma said. "I'll call your father from there. We can figure this out, but we'll need to work together. All of us. You, me, your brother—"

"No." Kai couldn't even imagine how painful it would be to return to Peter without Sophie, for Peter to have been right all along.

"Kai—"

"No," he said again, stepping away. "I'll be fine. I'll see you later."

Kai left the house, with Grandma calling his name from the door. He didn't turn around.

He'd find Sophie, and he'd do it on his own.

Seaspire's streets were littered with fallen branches and garbage from cans that had been blown over. People, Grandma's neighbors, including Mrs. Perkins, had come out to assess the damage and try to clean up.

Guilt stuck in his throat like he'd swallowed a sea urchin. Kai averted his eyes and hurried past. He ended up walking back to the shore.

The beach was washed away. Lifeguard towers were gone, and what was left of the wharf hung in jagged splinters. A few boats lay on their sides, dead in the water.

It was all Kai's fault.

Kai sank to the sand. If he hadn't challenged the Sea, this wouldn't have happened. And now Sophie was gone, maybe forever. Sophie, and other innocent people who had no idea the Sea was out there.

What had he been thinking?

Kai spent hours wandering the coast, uncovering more wreckage. When he saw people near, he ducked behind debris and waited until they left. He wondered if they would have seen fault, like a stain, on him.

As he walked, his thoughts turned in a circle. Maybe Peter was right; they should have let Dad and the police deal with it. But the adults would have searched in normal places, like the forest or a friend's house, and wouldn't have thought about places the Sea would keep its hostages. Where *would* the Sea keep them? They couldn't breathe underwater, so it would have to be on land. But close to the ocean. At least, they would have been there yesterday. Now, what? The Sea had raged all night. Maybe it was tired and left its hostages where it'd put them. Or maybe it took its revenge on Kai out on them.

Maybe Peter was right.

Kai's stomach growled. He'd missed breakfast and lunch and had reached the point where seaweed smelled tasty. He should go back to the Widow's Walk and get something to eat.

But then Peter, and Dad, and even Grandma, would find out that Kai had failed.

And this quest would have a cost, after all.

What choice did he have? Kai headed down the beach.

As he neared the turnoff to Grandma's, thunder rolled.

Kai startled and looked up, but while the sky was gray, it wasn't stormy. The storm had passed.

Then where did that thunder come from?

Kai searched. There. By the Spire and the lighthouse, thick dark clouds remained, shadowing the land. The trees near the lighthouse bent under wind, and lightning spiked. It was a tiny, unnatural hurricane. Even the news crews and storm watchers gave it a berth.

Odd, to see such a small storm. Especially when it was taking place at the site of the gate, a place special to the Sea, but on land.

Hope bloomed in Kai's chest. Hunger forgotten, he raced toward the lighthouse.

As he approached the park, the wind grew louder, whistling and shrieking in his ears. Was it loud enough to smother screams? Was that why the Sea created the wind?

The storm beat at Kai as he pushed through the forest on the way to the promontory. Kai had to lean into the wind to keep from being blown away, and fingernail-sized hail pelted him. Kai wrapped his arms around his head to protect it.

Soon he reached the lighthouse. The wind was so strong that when Kai tried to call Sophie's name, the howling winds stole his voice. Lightning flashed and thunder boomed in the tiny yet potent storm.

Another gust pushed Kai back a few steps. But he fought his way to the edge of the promontory and peered down at the Spire. What did he expect to find? Sophie and the others tied to the Spire like Andromeda in the Perseus myth?

She was here. She *had* to be here.

The wind screamed. Kai circled back to the lighthouse. The building had recently been soaked by the ocean; seaweed littered the ground, and sand and seawater puddled around the base. But other than that, there was no sign the place had been tampered with.

No windows broken, no doors off their hinges. So maybe Sophie wasn't taken here, and Kai had messed up completely by rushing in, once again.

But then a flash of color met his eye. In the window, at the top. Bright, vivid pink.

A torn sleeve of a magenta shirt, waving in the wind.

Kai let out a cry that was taken by the wind. He went to the lighthouse door and started kicking at it.

The door shook but didn't break. Kai kicked again, and again. Nothing.

The wind screamed again. Or was it Sophie?

Kai clenched his fists. With a roar silenced by the wind, he threw his whole body at the door. On the third blow, the lock snapped and the door swung open.

A small group of waterlogged people, men and women, old and young, pushed past him, desperate to escape the lighthouse. Once outside, they stopped and peered at Kai. "Who are you?" a drenched woman asked.

"Just someone passing by." Kai searched the group for a vivid pink shirt. Sophie wasn't with them. "Did you see anyone else in there?"

"Why would anyone stay in that place?" The woman shivered. "Look, I just want to go home."

Kai nodded. "Then go now. Get help, report this to the authorities."

The woman blanched. "As if anyone would believe us. Believe what happened." The rest of the group looked just as scared. With a final, fearful glance at the lighthouse, they left. As they disappeared into the woods, Kai turned and went inside. He had to find Sophie.

The lighthouse smelled like rotting wood and fish. Kai touched a wall, and his hand came away wet. How had water gotten inside, when the outside was still sealed?

There was an iron staircase leading up. Kai ran to it and put one foot on the first step. "Sophie?"

Here, inside the lighthouse, the wind had quieted.

No response. Kai took another step and then heard a trembling voice beneath the staircase say, "I'm here."

Sophie.

Kai jumped off the stairs and ran to where his sister sat huddled against the wall. "Hey. Your group already left," he joked, pointing toward the open door.

But Sophie didn't laugh. Her torn shirt was iced with dried sea salt, and her eyes were red. She shuddered with every breath. "Where's Peter?"

The spiky guilt turned to anger inside Kai. If Peter had his way, Kai would have stayed home and Sophie would still be missing. "Not here," he said. "Come on. Let's go home."

"Home? Last I checked, home got flooded. Let's go to our hotel." Sophie tried to laugh and failed, then rubbed her face. But she stood up.

Kai put his arm around her, more for comfort than support. He led her out of the lighthouse and into the screaming wind. Together, they entered the forest and left the Sea's unnatural storm behind.

Once they were far enough away from the ocean to hear each other again, Sophie started speaking. "It should have been dusty in the lighthouse," she said. "I mean, no one's been there for years, right? It should be dusty. Not washed out by the ocean." She took another shuddering breath. "It ripped us from the beach, and then we were here. I don't know how we got inside. I don't. Only water can fit through the cracks. Did we become water? Don't tell me. Don't want to know."

Sophie patted Kai's hand and looked at him with tired eyes.

"I tried," she said. "When all this started. When you woke up . . . *that thing*. I tried to be brave."

"You've always been brave," Kai said. "Like, at rafting, and then at the cemetery."

"*Been*. But not now. Rafting, getting you boys out of trouble, those are easy. Normal problems, the kind everyone faces. The right answer is out there if you know where to look. But there's no right answer here. Those ghostly voices told me. They told me stories of ships wrecked on coasts, of tsunamis and monsters and storms that no living mortal knew about, because no one survived. They told me about young boys swallowed up by the water, never seen again. They told me about the power of the Sea and mocked me. 'Can you plan for this when we could not? Can you, who are *so* clever?' they asked. 'If you are not smart enough to protect your brothers, what hope do they have when the wrath of the Sea comes for them?'"

Sophie took another shuddering breath. "I tried not to listen." Sophie looked at Kai with wide eyes. "It's an ocean god, Kai. With magic and power unlike anything I can understand. This isn't a locked cemetery or a bully at school. I . . . tried. But I can't do it. I'm sorry. I'm so sorry."

Kai was shocked. He'd thought Sophie was a skeptic, that she didn't care about the quest. He never imagined that his brave, capable older sister had found the one thing that frightened her in the supernatural.

He hugged Sophie. "It's okay. Thanks for trying."

She hugged him back, and Kai warmed. Things were looking up. Yes, the Sea attacked Seaspire, but it didn't level the whole town, and like Grandma said, they'd recover. They'd survive.

And he'd found Sophie. He'd beaten the Sea, and he'd done it on his own. He might have done it faster if Peter had helped him, instead of running back to bed, scared.

But the point was that everyone was fine. The family was safe, and Sophie and the other hostages might not have been if Kai had waited any longer to find them. Taking quick action was the best thing he could have done.

Sophie's head dipped, and she said, "Thank you. I tried to face my fears. That's why I went to the beach. I wish . . ."

She didn't finish the thought. Kai hugged her again, and, silently, they walked back to the Widow's Walk.

CHAPTER 21

WATER UNDER THE BRIDGE

PETER

Peter spent the night agonizing. Kai hadn't come back, and a new storm rattled the Widow's Walk. All night he listened to the Sea's storm tear at Seaspire. Whenever he looked out the window, he saw the eerie glow of Saint Elmo's fire on the rooftops and the streets flowing with water. Occasionally, he swore he could see crabs and other sea life in the gutters.

He made plan after plan, each one sounding more desperate than the last. Then he pulled out Sophie's laptop and researched all he could about Seaspire and storms and ancient ocean deities, but nothing seemed to help. At one point, he summoned up the courage to leave, go look for Kai, but his dad told him to stay put.

"Grandma and I will go search," he said. "We need someone here to call us if they come back."

So Peter kept researching until he fell into an uneasy sleep.

The next morning, Peter woke up with his face on the laptop. When he looked outside, Seaspire's wharf was gone, ripped away by the storm. Such violence . . . what had happened?

Kai. Kai had done something, and the Sea retaliated. And where was Kai? Where was Sophie?

Maybe Peter should have gone looking for them. But what if disobeying his father was the wrong choice? What if it only ended in the whole family washed out to sea?

Should he go out now?

Before he could decide, the door crashed open and Kai and Sophie, both crusted with sand and smelling like the ocean, burst in.

"Kai! Sophie!" Peter set the laptop aside and went to them. "Where have you been?"

"Around." Kai pushed past Peter. "I need a shower."

Peter grabbed Kai's arm. When Kai glared at him, Peter said, "Let Sophie go first."

Kai bit his lip, nodded, and let their sister shuffle to the bathroom. After the door closed, Peter eyed Kai. "So, where was she?"

"The old lighthouse. The Sea had her trapped. Her, and a bunch of other people. They should be home by now." Kai kicked off his shoes. "What about you?" he asked Peter. "Have you been here this whole time?"

The question had an edge to it. Peter narrowed his eyes. "Dad told me to stay. Someone had to be here in case you came back."

"So you stayed. Never mind that Sophie was out there. Never mind that *I* was out there."

Peter shuffled his feet. "I researched. I planned. What else was I supposed to do?"

"More than you did."

"Like what, exactly? Annoy the Sea so much that it raised another storm? What exactly did that accomplish?"

Kai reddened. "Nothing."

"Really? Because I can see the damage from here. The wharf is *gone*, Kai. That's on you, isn't it?" When Kai looked away, Peter added,

"And you could have gone with it. Sophie, too. Then what was I supposed to do?" Tears stung Peter's eyes. "Did you even think of that?"

Kai gaped. "At least I tried something. At least I didn't sit around waiting for things to magically get better. You should have been with me."

"And what if the Sea got us, too? All I asked was that you stop and think before you made a move you might regret. Did you ever, at all, consider the cost before you charged out there?"

Kai went very still. Then he said, "I'm going to call Dad and Grandma to tell them we're all here now." And left.

Peter sat back on the bed and rubbed his face. A sick, guilty feeling flooded him. Kai had gone and saved Sophie all by himself. Sophie probably thought only one of her brothers cared. Which wasn't true; Peter just didn't want to push the Sea into doing something awful to her. Maybe Peter should have gone; he and Kai might have found Sophie sooner, working together.

But Kai had also antagonized the Sea. It had attacked Seaspire. The only reason nobody was hurt was sheer luck. And Peter knew he had a point; if anything happened to them, they lost their ability to find and close those seals, and the Sea would win anyway. As much as Peter wanted to help, he didn't want to be responsible for a worse thing happening.

Peter pulled out the poems. He may as well get started on looking for the next seal. It might take his mind off Kai's stupidity.

5.

Fear the holy land of death,
Where spirits roam and devils dwell.
Within this land inscription strange,

Words of power, lost to time:
Island mineral may river's path stay.
Marvel at what time doth not change
And dread the light beautiful and fell.

Then, thinking that if solving one riddle was good, two was better, Peter read the next poem:

6.

What unhallowed beasts dwell in mire!
What deception lurks 'neath noxious ground!
Brambles trap or earth's mouth gapes,
And serpent and hound stalk every step.
Their master walks with mammoth tread.
Mind, though solid become sand without whole spring,
The dark is only dispelled by fire.

Well, this was encouraging.

Holy land of death? Another graveyard? But which one? Massachusetts had many. Words of power? Was that a reference to a spell? Were they going back to Salem?

That would mean there were two seals in one place. Was that possible?

What would a place with two seals look like? Probably super creepy. Salem might qualify. It seemed like the best option.

Should he tell Dad to take them back to Salem?

A knock, from behind him. Peter turned to see Sophie, freshly washed but looking like she'd been awake for a million years. "You trying to solve the riddles?"

Peter nodded, and Sophie closed her eyes. "Let me help."

"Why?"

Sophie's eyes popped open. "Because I need to *hurt* that thing."

Peter stared at his sister, then handed over the poems.

Sophie read the poems and then handed them back, saying, "You're looking for a river and a swamp."

"What? How do you know?"

"The fifth one actually says 'river.' As for the sixth, 'mire' and 'noxious ground'? That's a swamp. That should narrow your search."

"Thanks," Peter said.

"Don't mention it. Ever."

Sophie fell on her bed and rolled over to face the wall. Was it possible that his sister had been . . . scared? Well, that fear seemed to be giving way to something else now.

Peter bit back a thousand questions. Better to focus on the riddles.

A river and a swamp. Peter could work with that. He searched the printout and a moment later had his target.

Target. Singular. Peter spent several minutes cross-referencing the riddles and the lists Dad had printed out, and still came back to the same conclusion. The best fit for both riddles was one place, one location holding not one but two seals.

The location was massive. Huge enough to hold two seals, and, believe it or not, the place fit both the fifth and sixth riddles.

Bridgewater Triangle.

Peter had never even heard of it before, but when he read the description, he wondered why.

The Bridgewater Triangle was listed as "the most dangerous supernatural place in Massachusetts." It earned the name "Triangle" for the same reason as the Bermuda Triangle: a history of disappearances and other spooky phenomena. People had reported UFOs, strange lights, monsters, ghosts, and even demons. There was a section inside it that settlers in the area called "the Devil's Swamp."

If they were looking for places of spooky power, Bridgewater sure was one of them.

And there was a swamp inside, the most famous swamp in Massachusetts. That *had* to be the sixth riddle solved.

But also, one of Bridgewater's attractions was called Dighton Rock, a stone found in a river that was covered with old writing no one could read.

Peter felt a chill. *Words of power, lost to time.*

That was the fifth riddle down, too.

With both seals in the same place, no wonder Bridgewater was so dangerous!

Peter set down the papers. Bridgewater was the next location. But it was more dangerous than Dogtown, than Salem, than even Hoosac Tunnel. People, adults and experts, went into the Triangle and never came out. With the seals' traps attacking them, Kai and Peter would have even more odds to face.

Peter looked out the window. The sky was dark. Kai probably had contacted Dad and Grandma by now, but it was still too late to go to Bridgewater. They'd have to wait until morning.

Two seals, one place. What kind of protections would the seals have?

A horrifying thought struck Peter. What if there were *three* seals there? Three seals in the Triangle made a nasty kind of sense.

Peter looked at the final, seventh riddle.

Six must fall before the last appear.
The prize is at hand, the curse at heart.
A dream turns nightmare with revealed price,
For who can pay that which asks for all?
Will you reach for peace or truth?
I set down my pen, the choice is yours:
Once land may grow, but, too, more sea.

It didn't make much sense, but at least it didn't seem to point to Bridgewater. Peter read it again.

"Prize at hand, the curse at heart," he muttered. That seemed to suggest a possible cost. Same with the line, *For who can pay that which asks for all?*

It was like he'd feared: This quest was going to cost them something serious. And it felt like Peter was the only one worried about what that cost would be.

At that moment, Kai returned with Dad and Grandma. Dad hurried to Sophie's side and started grilling her about where she'd been and, more importantly, if she was okay.

As Sophie reassured Dad she was all right, Grandma and Kai came over to Peter. "Find anything?" Grandma asked, gesturing at the papers.

Peter showed her the riddles and pointed to the entry on Bridgewater, and she sucked in her breath. "I knew I should have brought my vampire hunter's kit."

"You have one of those? Never mind. What's Bridgewater?" Kai asked.

"I've been trying to figure out number seven," Peter said, "but I've got nothing."

Grandma squinted at the paper. "*Six must fall before the last appear.* The way I read it, we won't know where the last seal is before we take out numbers five and six. Then we'll be able to find it."

"Yeah, but where?" Peter asked.

Kai shook his head. "Doesn't matter. We go to Bridgewater and activate the next two seals. That's our next move."

"Are you sure?" Grandma put a hand on his shoulder. "Bridgewater isn't something to take lightly."

Kai nodded. "We have to do this."

Peter looked outside. Rain had started falling again. Another attack by the Sea, though hopefully not as bad as the night before.

"You won't be alone," Grandma said. "If no one else, I'll be there."

"I know." Kai looked at Peter. "And Peter will be there, too."

Peter felt uncomfortable but nodded. "I'm going to get some sleep," he said, "if we have such a big day of *heroics* tomorrow."

"Heroics get the job done," Kai said at Peter's back.

And maybe they did. They'd strike out tomorrow, activate two more seals, and then find the seventh and last seal, just like Kai wanted.

But Peter felt sick. He was sure there was more to this story, and Dad, Grandma, and Sophie had all been attacked. Was it worth acting when one foolish mistake could doom their family, or Peter or Kai themselves?

Was one of the twins the next price to be paid?

CHAPTER 22

SPLITTING UP

PETER

Peter tossed and turned with nightmares, same as he had for days. However, instead of seeing his family hurt or taken by the Sea, like he thought he would, Peter saw something else.

It didn't make much sense, at first. It was dark as night in his dream, but then the sky cracked and Peter realized he was underground. Clods of dirt and stones rained around him.

As the sunlight poured into the pit, vines snaked out of the ground. They twisted and grew, rising toward the light. At first, Peter felt comforted by the little green tendrils. But then, as they thickened into twisted ropes, sprouting thorns and bristles, his ease vanished. He tried to run, but the vines grabbed him, hoisting him out of the pit and into the air.

Bound, he struggled. In front of him was the ocean, dark, veined with green energy and churning. The Sea was out there, ready to attack.

But below . . . Peter strained to look down. Below, something was moving.

A dark shape, writhing with vines. It strained against several cords. No, *seven* of them.

Four cords snapped: *pop pop pop pop*. Three were left.

A hand reached out of the pit. It was knotted and woodlike, with sharp slate claws. It reached for Peter. A claw pricked his skin right over his heart.

He woke up, sweating. The sunlight was pink and blue, just the crack of dawn.

Kai was twisting in bed, torn with his own nightmare. Peter walked over, ready to wake him. Did they have the same dream?

Kai moaned and rolled over, and Peter grabbed his shoulder. "Wake up," he whispered. The others were still asleep.

With a gasp and a grunt, Kai did. His eyes focused on Peter. "Oh, it's just you. I thought it might have been the Sea for a moment there."

"Another nightmare."

"Yeah. I don't know about you, but I'm getting pretty sick of seeing Seaspire drown." Kai sighed and swung his feet off the bed.

For the first time since they woke the Sea, Kai had a different dream. Peter would have been pleased by this, only he didn't understand why it changed. It couldn't bode well.

"Mine was different," Peter said, and explained what he saw.

Kai played with the edge of his blanket. "Huh," he said. "I guess the Sea isn't messing with you anymore."

"You don't think it's some other warning?"

"It's not about the ocean, is it? Or Atlantis? So it's not our guy." Kai stood up and went to the bathroom.

Peter wasn't so sure. Kai hadn't seen the dream. He didn't know what it was like. He didn't see the earth creature reaching for him. Even awake, Peter couldn't shake the feeling that the thing was coming for him, that it knew him and wanted him for something.

There was more going on here than they knew. They needed to take some time and plan before closing the next two seals.

Peter went down for an early breakfast. He'd need the energy to figure out how to get out of going to Bridgewater. Maybe he could stay back with Sophie.

But then, when Dad and Grandma woke up and packed lunches of leftover breakfast foods and a selection of weapons Grandma had rescued from her house, Sophie arrived, wearing hiking boots and carrying a backpack. She looked pale, but determined.

"You don't have to come," Peter told her.

"Yes, I do." Sophie rubbed her shoulder. "I don't want to, but I can't let this stop me. Not anymore, not when you might be safer if I'm there." She glanced back upstairs. "I should pack the drone. We might need an early warning signal."

Then Peter pulled Dad aside and tried to explain that he didn't think they should go. He described his nightmare, but Dad also thought the dream was a sign the Sea had stopped harassing Peter at last, told him it was just nerves, and handed him a backpack.

Fine. Whatever. If no one wanted to listen to what Peter had to say, then fine. Let them deal with the consequences.

Kai didn't say a word to Peter during the drive to Dighton Rock.

Or where Dighton Rock used to be. Grandma explained that the rock had been moved to a museum in 1963.

"But it used to be in the Taunton River bed, near Berkley," she said. "Since that's where it was when MacHale wrote his riddles, then we should start there."

"Are you sure?" Peter asked. "Hoosac Tunnel wasn't built when the riddles were written. What if the next seal is at the museum?"

Sophie joined in. "Then we would have heard about hauntings at the museum, not at the Bridgewater Triangle."

"Ignore him," Kai told them both. "Peter's just scared."

As Peter stiffened, his dad said, "Cool it, Kai. We're all scared."

"Not me," Kai muttered, then turned to face the window. He didn't move until they arrived.

Dad pulled the car into Dighton Rock State Park and found parking, and then the family climbed out. As Sophie assembled her gear, drone and all, and Grandma readjusted her cane sword, dagger, and a small shield, Peter grabbed Kai. "*Scared?*"

"Well, you are, aren't you? Don't think I didn't notice you dragging your feet as we left this morning."

Kai jerked away from Peter and strode into the woods. Peter threw one glance over his shoulder at the rest of the family (who were apparently too distracted to notice Kai leaving) and followed him.

"Stop it! We need to wait for the others."

"Why? They can't read Atlantean or activate the seals. We can do this alone."

Peter hurried to block Kai's way. "I don't think we should do this at all."

Kai scowled. "I knew it. You're scared."

"Okay, yeah, I'm scared. Why aren't you? You're the one who went face-to-face with the Sea and lost."

"Whoa." Kai raised a hand. "I got Sophie back. I'd call that a win."

"But it could have been a loss! If even one person was hurt in *our* war . . ." When Kai didn't answer, Peter went on. "Something's not right with these seals. Why all the defenses? And why do I feel like every time I touch a seal, I'm *releasing* something, not locking it away?"

"You never told me that."

"Well, I'm telling you now." Peter couldn't stop thinking of that earthy hand, reaching out. "We should just go home. The risk is too much."

"*I'm* willing to take that risk," Kai said, glaring at Peter.

"Why don't you understand that it's not just yourself you're risking?"

"Want to talk about risk?" Kai pressed a hand against Peter's chest. "The Sea's hostages had been stuck in that cold, wet, smelly lighthouse for about twenty-four hours. Who knows if the Sea was going to move them or let them go? *Sophie* could have been left there, unheard, for days. That was the *risk* you took when you decided your own safety was worth more than hers."

Peter arched back, like he'd been hit. "That's not how it was."

"Then explain it to me."

"I . . . I." Peter struggled to find the words that would make him not sound like a selfish jerk. "I wanted to help Sophie. But not by charging in without a plan. You don't seem to notice how people get hurt when you're reckless."

"I'm not reckless!" Kai's cheeks burned red, and he dropped his hand. "But we don't have time to sit down and write out a twenty-stage plan. The Sea will attack tomorrow. If we stand by and do nothing, we let it win."

"Maybe it should win, if our beating it means we're responsible for something worse happening." Peter thought of his nightmare.

"Worse than raising the Sea? Because we're responsible for *that*. It's our job to fix our mistake."

Anger, hot and thick like lava, pushed through Peter's limbs. "Who says? Who says this is our job? And even if it is, we acted too fast. We should have held back and waited and learned more before we ran off to Dogtown."

"Yeah, well, I think we did the right thing." Kai stuck his chest out and stood on his toes, making himself a little taller than Peter.

Peter didn't let that intimidate him. He looked Kai in the eye and said, "*Your* definition of the right thing isn't the same as mine. Despite what you might believe, Kai, I'm not you. Being your twin doesn't mean I agree with you on everything."

Kai chewed his lip but didn't respond.

Peter went on. "We're not the same. We're not even a *team*. Not with how you just assume you know best and I should follow your every whim. I'm done trying to make you see that *I'm not your other half*."

Kai didn't say anything for a moment. Then he shrugged. "If that's how you feel, then why are you tagging along after me? Don't you have somewhere better to be?"

"Like what? Finding a seal?"

"There *are* two of them."

Peter clenched his fist. "Fine. We'll do it your way. Looks like I have a seal to activate."

With that, Peter tucked his thumbs under the straps on his backpack and marched deeper into the trees. If Kai wanted a seal activated, then Peter would do it. Alone. Let Kai take responsibility for the consequences.

Footsteps pounded behind him, crunching dead leaves. Peter stopped, surprised that Kai would have come after him.

But it was just Sophie, drone in hand.

"I saw you two leave," she said. "Dad and Grandma are still bickering about which one of them should stay with the car."

"You don't need to be here."

"I know. But special ability or not, I might be helpful."

Peter considered her. As much as he'd like the company, he didn't want to put anyone else in danger. "What about Kai?"

"He sent me along to you. He said you needed to 'make it up to me.'"

Peter grunted and headed deeper into the woods. Sophie followed.

After a moment, Peter said, "I wanted to help you. I just didn't know what to do."

"I know," Sophie said with a smile. "That's typical Peter."

That only made Peter feel worse.

"Come on," Sophie said. "We have a lot of ground to cover." She lifted the drone. "This can help us find the seal, right?"

"You doing okay?"

Her face was grim. "Yeah. Let's finish that fishface."

She activated the drone, and they walked on in silence. Sophie was watching the display on her phone, scanning for trouble with her eyes in the sky. Peter, on the other hand, just seethed.

How *dare* Kai just think Peter would go along with this? Well, he was, but only because he wouldn't be responsible for whatever happened. If activating the seals was the right choice, then Kai could be the big shining hero, just like he wanted. Peter wouldn't argue.

But if Kai was wrong and this whole thing blew up, then whose fault would it be? It would be Kai's, because he insisted they rush in.

When there was no good option, no way to know whether to act or not to act, then the smart thing to do was to do nothing until you did know. Why didn't Kai see that?

Because Kai would rather act first and think later. And he expected Peter to think exactly the same way just because they shared a face.

Sophie grabbed Peter's shoulder. "Stop," she said.

He shook her off, but stopped. The drone wasn't too far ahead of them, but he watched as it dipped and fell out of the sky, crashing into the growth. Same as at Dogtown.

Through the trees, sunlight gleamed on the river. Dighton Rock must not have been too far away from here. But in the trees, the Triangle had darkened almost to twilight. Peter looked to see if the trees had moved, closed in on them, but they hadn't. It was like the sun refused to shine on this cursed ground.

He and Sophie stood, waiting. "So, what was the story about Dighton Rock?"

"Grandma didn't say much," Sophie breathed. "It's a rock with petroglyphs on it. You know, ancient writing? Except no one knows who wrote on it."

"Maybe it was the Atlanteans." Had Kai seen a picture of the rock? Could he have read the writing?

Maybe leaving Kai behind had been a bad idea.

Sophie's hand tightened on Peter's shoulder. "Look!"

A light had appeared in the shadows. It looked like a firefly, only so white it was almost blue, and larger. It hummed and whistled.

"A UFO?" Sophie whispered. Peter was tempted to agree.

Then another light appeared, and another. And another. Soon there was a small swarm of them, bobbing and whistling.

The lights flashed and weaved, dancing like fairies. Sophie's eyes gleamed. She seemed enchanted. "This isn't so bad," she said.

And then one of the lights dived at the fallen drone. When it touched the drone, the machine spouted sparks and caught on fire.

"No!" Sophie's yell caught the lights' attention. In a mass, they rose back and swarmed toward her and Peter.

Peter wasn't about to wait to see what the lights would do if they touched *him*. Pulling on Sophie's shirt, he yelled, "Run!"

They charged deeper into the Triangle, unearthly lights whistling like sirens behind them.

CHAPTER 23

SWAMP CREATURES

KAI

After sending Sophie after Peter, Kai stormed in the opposite direction, fuming. Did Peter really think that they *shouldn't* activate the last seals and stop the Sea? Did he *want* the land to flood?

Was Peter right that this quest was already costing them too much, and would only take more?

No. Peter just didn't want to get involved, again. This was typical; he preferred to sit back and think instead of getting the job done. And Kai was over trying to convince Peter to take part in the adventure. Maybe they could never go back to the way they used to be. Maybe that divide couldn't be breached.

It didn't matter. Kai'd find the seal and—

And do what? He needed Peter to activate the seal, and Peter had selfishly run off into the woods.

So what did that leave Kai to do? Run after Peter and apologize.

Which he wouldn't do. Apologize for what? Trying to save the world? Trying to save his family? He'd sit on the seal and play paper football with Grandma before doing that.

So he hiked his backpack higher on his shoulders and walked faster.

They'd parked close to Dighton Rock's location, so Kai had a longer walk to the swampy areas of the Triangle. Kai watched the trees and path for signs of danger, since he didn't have Sophie's early warning drone. He tried to be vigilant, but his mind kept turning to the quest, the riddles, and the possible cost.

As much as Kai tried to remind himself that what they were doing was right, that the Sea was *absolutely* going to drown the land, and therefore *had* to be stopped (and deserved it, for what it did to his family), there *were* some details that nagged at him.

Like, how the Atlantean word for "sea" also seemed to mean "twin." That didn't make sense. When he'd looked at the scans Mom sent over of the relics she'd found in the North Sea, he'd noticed more that stood out. Lots of references to "sacred sunlight" and "heart of the earth" that didn't seem to have anything to do with the odes to the ocean they belonged to. It almost seemed like they were talking about something else that Kai couldn't identify.

Add that to how the rhyme scheme for the MacHale poems changed riddle by riddle, and there was too much that didn't make sense. Maybe the rhyme scheme was a clue of some kind, pointing the way to some deeper pattern Kai couldn't see?

And if it was, what if that meant Peter was right?

Then that meant there'd be a cost beyond the attacks their family had suffered so far. What if it was a cost Kai couldn't pay? One *no one* could pay?

Kai really hated thinking about that. Instead, he turned his attention to resenting that he and Peter couldn't both read Atlantean *and* activate the seals. It would have made the quest much easier, and, after all, they were twins. They should have the same abilities.

Kai stumbled on uneven ground. Just a paw print. Though, it seemed ... bigger than the paw of any dog he knew about.

Beside the paw prints was an S-shaped squiggle through the dirt. It looked like a snake trail.

Kai knelt beside it. He put his hands on either side of the squiggle, measuring its width. When he pulled his hands back, they were shoulder-width apart. "That's one huge snake," he muttered.

Nothing native to Massachusetts grew that big. The thought occurred to him that maybe he should have listened when Peter wanted to stop searching for the seals.

But he had to be strong, and brave, and save the day. So he took it as a sign he was on the right track and trekked deeper into the brush, looking for more signs of strange animal life.

He didn't have far to go. Another snake trail, also massive, crossing the first. More paw prints so big that Kai could fit his whole foot inside one. And a dark shadow like a bird passed overhead, but it was so big it could have carried off their car.

"I think I hate this," Kai said to himself.

He searched for the seal, but with all the undergrowth and animal tracks, it seemed impossible to find a pattern like the binding word in all the chaos.

And even if he found it, he couldn't do anything about it until Peter showed up. That left him alone in the forest, waiting, while the creatures that lurked in the shadows got closer and closer—

Kai's shoes squelched in swampy mud. Mosquitoes buzzed around him. He was deep into the swamp now, and the daylight had faded into a yellow haze. The air was rank with the smells of decay and thick animal musk. Kai pulled his shirt over his nose and tried to breathe shallowly.

The seal was probably here. This place was creepy enough for it.

Kai heard a loud crack and grumble from his right. He spun, knife out. "What was that?"

No response. Kai crept toward the sound. He wouldn't back down now.

Kai pushed aside a bush and saw it. A tall, hairy figure, like a large ape, crouched by some manna grass. It looked like it was searching for a lost phone, and it would have been funny if Kai didn't notice the thing's feet.

Human or ape feet, but huge. *BIG* feet.

Bigfoot.

"Bigfoot?" Kai said. Out loud. Too loud.

Bigfoot paused and looked around. Seeing Kai, it stood, rising up and up and up.

It had to be at least ten feet tall!

There!

On Bigfoot's chest, there was the seal, marked in dark brown like a tattoo.

So now what?

Kai had no idea. He couldn't activate that seal, not without Peter. And how could anyone even get close enough to touch it, when it was about seven feet in the air, on a legendary ape-man?

There had to be a way. A secret, a clue, a pattern. Kai had solved multiple puzzles protecting the seals. How different could this one be?

Kai scanned the ground, the trees, and Bigfoot himself.

Nothing.

Kai didn't have time to wait! He strode out toward the creature. "Hey!" he called. "You! I need that seal!"

This felt uncomfortably like how he'd challenged the Sea. But maybe this time it would work out better.

Bigfoot roared.

The swamp water bubbled. The reeds and buttonbushes quivered.

And Kai realized he'd made another huge mistake.

From the ground, spiders the size of Kai's hands, put together, crawled from under the leaves. The water spit out giant rats, and then the surface rippled with scales.

Snarling, huge red-eyed dogs emerged from the trees.

Kai backed away from the growing horde. A pattern? Something? A trick to stay alive and safe until Peter arrived?

If there was, Kai couldn't see it. He just saw the creatures scuttle, slither, and prowl toward him.

He was surrounded. Any moment, those racing spiders would crawl up his legs, and the dogs would leap, and it would be over.

There was nothing else to do but run.

Kai tore back through the forest. Behind him, an army of enormous, monstrous creatures followed, guided by Bigfoot himself.

CHAPTER 24

WISPS AND LIGHTS

PETER

Peter threw himself to the ground and spat out a leaf. Above him, the lights dived and wailed. He rolled over as another one attacked, and it grazed his skin.

The pain was like a thousand bee stings, all over his body. His muscles spasmed as electric energy filled them.

"I've got you." Sophie pulled Peter back as he gasped and tried to remember what his face felt like.

Her shirt had burnt patches where she'd taken her own electrocutions. They'd both tried to dodge the lights, but there were too many of them. As soon as Peter avoided one, another slammed into his back.

There was no time to make a plan.

Peter looked, searching for something familiar, or anything he could use. After the lights attacked again, he closed his eyes, trying to use his other senses, like he had at Hoosac. But all he could smell were normal forest and swamp scents, and the whistling and humming of the lights drowned out any other sounds.

He got another shock, this time on his leg. Crawling, dragging the leg, he made it to a rock and leaned against it. Sophie was on the other side of the cloud of lights, playing her own unearthly game of dodgeball.

The daylight had faded to nothing. This was a haunted swamp, after all. If it wanted to be midnight at two in the afternoon, it could be.

Maybe it was absolute darkness around him, but the glow of the lights was also absolute. Peter couldn't see anything other than the lights and the area right around them. And he couldn't hear anything else.

If there was something out in the woods that would help him fight them off, he would never find it.

Sophie tried to run into the woods, but a handful of lights drove her back. Peter yelled as she got shocked again, and then he screamed when at least three lights attacked him, stinging his back and legs.

One was bad enough, but three? Peter put his hand to his heart, which beat quickly and, he feared, out of rhythm. How much more could he take?

Sophie appeared and pulled him behind the rock.

"We—we're not safe here," Peter wheezed.

"We're not safe anywhere." Sophie picked up a stick, but then tossed it away. It wouldn't be that easy. "Do you see the seal?"

Peter shook his head. "I've looked. I swear. I'm sorry for dragging you into this."

"You couldn't drag me anywhere. I came willingly." Sophie yelped and pulled Peter down as another crowd of lights attacked. These missed them both, but Peter smelled ozone and felt a light buzz as they passed over.

"We have to do something!" Sophie said as they sat back up.

"I don't know what to do!"

Peter wanted to run. He was willing to give up the seal, but the lights wouldn't let them leave this area. He was stuck, getting shocked again and again until he couldn't survive another, all because he got mad at Kai and went after a seal alone.

If Kai were here, would *he* see a way out?

Sophie pulled Peter out of the way of another light. She eyed the swirling mass. "It's strange," she said, her voice barely louder than the din.

"What?"

"That—watch out!"

This time the warning was just a bit late. Two lights rammed into him and Sophie, and they twitched until the electricity went to ground. Every muscle aching, Peter lay on the dirt. But Sophie sat up. She stared at the lights.

Then she grabbed Peter and pulled him standing. They ducked under another wave of the lights. "Listen to me. You have to go into the middle."

"That will kill me!"

"It won't."

"Can we think about this?"

"Now!"

Sophie pushed Peter into the middle of the lights. The pain made his vision flash red as multiple dancing lights brushed his arms and legs, though none seemed to hit him directly. He fell over, gasping, trying to calm his heart.

"Do it!"

"What?"

"Do what you do! Activate the thing!"

Why? Peter saw no binding word.

"Peter, please, trust me!"

Well, it was worth a shot.

Peter dug his hands into the soil and opened himself to the rush that came with activating another seal. To his surprise, it came, filling his mind with images of the Sea and his nostrils with the smell of warm dirt.

The lights around him blazed blue and halted midair. They rearranged themselves and sank into the ground around Peter, forming the binding symbol he was becoming so familiar with. The seal shone and vanished, and the false nighttime brightened back to a sunny day in the forest.

Head reeling from both the pain and the sheer rushing power of the activation, Peter looked back at Sophie.

"How'd you know?" he croaked.

"I didn't. I mean, I had a good guess, but I didn't see the seal or anything. I'm not Kai." Sophie sank onto the rock. "But the lights were flashing in a pattern. As they got closer to the center of the swirl, they blinked faster and faster, like they were more . . . agitated, I guess. I figured that was working like an arrow to the seal, so I pushed you in. I should have been more careful."

"No." Peter sat back on his heels. "No, you did the right thing."

Sophie could have gotten him killed, pushing him into all those balls of lightning. But if she hadn't, the lightning would have gotten them anyway, sooner or later. Not acting was killing them both.

If Sophie had waited to make a plan, how much worse would the attacks have become?

No matter what, he was glad she'd chosen to come with him.

Peter moved to stand, but as he planted his foot, the ground beneath it shifted. Bits of dirt sank below him, like he was standing on a sandcastle.

Right. The seals were destroyed after each one was activated. And Peter was sitting on a giant seal.

He tried to run, but the earth split below him, sending him tumbling down into darkness as Sophie yelled above him.

Fortunately, Peter didn't fall far. He slammed into a pile of loose dirt, which hurt, but not as badly as it would if he hit the rock floor to his left and right. As dust billowed around him, clinging to the inside of his nose and bringing tears to his eyes, he coughed and tried to look around.

"Peter? Peter!" Sophie's face peered over the side.

"I—I'm fine." He sat up to prove it and waved at his sister. "I just don't know how I'll get back up." The pit wasn't too deep, but at ten or fifteen feet of smooth stone and loose dirt, Peter knew he couldn't climb it.

"Grandma packed a rope. We'll get it and pull you out."

"Okay. Where is Grandma?"

"I don't know. Maybe at the car?"

"At least those lights are gone."

"There is that."

Peter looked around. Now that that fake night was gone, the sunlight illuminated the pit pretty well. A large tunnel headed down to one side, and while it wasn't bright that way, it wasn't dark, either. "I'm going to explore down here," he said. "I won't go far. Call me back when you have a rope."

"Be careful, Peter."

"I will."

The tunnel remained well lit, even though Peter had left the huge hole behind. Small cracks overhead let enough light in.

And then there were the crystals.

Crystals in all colors were scattered along the sides and floor of the tunnel. No, it wasn't a tunnel. It was a chamber. A huge room that only looked like a tunnel if you fell into one end of it.

Red, green, yellow, blue, violet, clear white, deep brown, and black. Crystals of all colors, some the size of Peter's hand, some only the size of his pinkie nail. He picked up a clear one and tried to figure out if it was a diamond.

What was this place doing here?

Light sent a prism of rainbow from the crystal to the wall. Peter followed it, and dropped the crystal. On the wall was a mosaic of crystals.

A mural of the Sea.

Its snaky body rose from rich, blue waves, curving over an island set in amber, red, gold, and green. The waves started small but sharp beside the Sea, but they grew into mighty tidal waves over the second half of the island.

It was the sinking of Atlantis.

Seeing this after the Sea's recent attack on Seaspire made the danger feel more real to Peter. The Sea had destroyed a whole island. Now it wanted to do the same to Seaspire and all the land it could drown.

Peter noticed a little figure, arms raised, about to be swallowed by the wave. That would be him, and his family, if the Sea had its way.

It *had* to be stopped.

Peter stepped closer to the mural and noticed an odd structure in front of it. A strange, treelike web of reddish metal. Many of the holes were empty, but a few of them had crystals set inside them.

"What are you for?" Peter murmured.

Beneath the structure, crystals lay scattered and loose. They must have once been set in the metal, but they'd fallen out over time.

Peter walked up to the structure and picked up a fallen green stone. He examined it for a moment and then placed it in the hole where it fit.

Nothing happened. The walls didn't shake, and no traps sprang. A crystal now shone in its setting. That was all.

Peter's skin tingled with a different kind of electricity. If the mosaic was the story he knew, maybe this structure, once completed, could illuminate the secrets he sensed were lurking in the shadows.

He picked up another crystal.

CHAPTER 25

PIECES COME TOGETHER

KAI

Kai ran. The spiders skittered behind, rustling over leaves without any sign of slowing down. The snakes crossed back and forth over the path, forcing Kai to stumble over them, and the dogs sped up, clearly enjoying the thrill of the hunt.

How long could he hold out? Kai had visions of tripping and being torn apart by massive animals, failing the quest and never seeing his family again.

As he passed a large stone, a strong hand grabbed his arm and pulled him to one side. Kai struggled but stopped when he saw it was Grandma.

"Keep your back to the rock," she said, unsheathing her sword cane. "So we can't be surrounded."

"What are you doing here?" Kai asked.

There were shapes in the sky Kai didn't like. Although that strange darkness had settled on them even more, he could see, flying above, huge birds against the twilight.

"I've said it before and I'll say it again. We're not going to succeed unless we work together. You boys shouldn't have run off on your own. Where's Peter?"

"He went for the other seal."

"*You split up?*"

The forest around the woods spilled out its monsters. Grandma pushed Kai back and raised her blade. "That's not good," she said. Kai thought she meant the animals until she added, "We need Peter to break the seal."

"I know."

"Did you find it, at least?"

"Yes. It's on—"

Bigfoot emerged from the trees, seal obvious on its chest.

Grandma's jaw dropped. "My word," she muttered.

Bigfoot roared and the animals attacked.

"Let me handle this, Kai!" Grandma took a swipe at a striking snake, which hissed but backed off. "You come up with a plan."

A plan? Get the seal on Bigfoot. That was the plan.

But how could he do it?

Kai kept thinking there had to be some pattern to the movement of the creatures. If he could see a pattern, he could use it to bypass them and get to Bigfoot.

But as he watched the snakes slither and dogs run and those huge spiders crawl, he couldn't see anything. No pattern, no design. It was chaos and randomness, with nothing he could use.

A spider put its front leg against Kai's foot. Shuddering, he drove his heel into it, smashing it with a smear of green goo.

"Very good!" Grandma said as she waved her sword at a dog. "You're on plan-and-spider duty."

So, shaking, Kai stepped on another spider and another. But they were coming so fast! He was quick footed playing Frisbee, but could he be quick enough to squash spiders?

And could Grandma keep fighting off the larger animals? She loved using her ancient weapons, but she was still old. And human. They'd both tire soon.

And Kai had no plan.

A blaze of blue light, like a lighthouse beacon, shot out of the trees to the west. It flared brightly, causing Kai to stop and stare. Then it faded.

"What was that?" he asked.

"Who cares?" Grandma said. "It made the creatures back away. See?"

Kai looked, and sure enough, the creatures had shied away from the light. But they were regrouping.

One spider clung to his leg, so Kai slammed it against the stone. The crunching sound it made nauseated him.

"Hold them off with this." Grandma opened her backpack. She took out a bronze dagger, passed it to Kai, and continued to rummage through the bag.

Kai cradled the blade. "Why?"

"I have a plan."

A red-eyed dog leaped at Kai. Yelling, he slashed at it with the knife. He managed to keep it from biting his neck, but its weight carried them both to the ground.

The knife slipped from his hand. The dog snapped at Kai's throat.

A bright light shone right in both of their faces. The dog whined and jumped away. Kai stood up next to Grandma, who held a halogen flashlight.

"Stay back!" she said, waving it around. "This is as good as Greek fire to you, isn't it? So stay back!"

The creatures leaped back from the light. Even the spiders cowered, scuttling under the safety of fallen leaves and undergrowth.

Bigfoot roared. Emboldened, the creatures moved forward after the light passed them. A spider climbed on Grandma's backpack, which she'd left on the ground. Kai kicked the spider off and grabbed the backpack.

"Everything has its weakness," Grandma said, spinning around to blast a new group of creatures with the flashlight. "If you look carefully, you see what it is."

Peter was the careful one. If he'd been here, would Kai and Grandma have gotten into this mess? Was there something Peter would have seen that would have let them reach that seal on Bigfoot's chest?

"We have to get the seal," Kai said.

Grandma smiled at him. "Leave that to me. Just hold the light right there."

Kai took the flashlight, balancing it and Grandma's pack in his hands. Grandma pulled a road flare out of the bag, and, grinning, lit it.

Then Kai watched as his grandmother, wearing a sweatshirt that said FUN IN THE SUN with a picture of a smiling beach umbrella, and carrying her cane sword and road flare, yelled, "For the Library of Alexandria!" and leaped at Bigfoot, bad leg and all.

Kai didn't expect it. And clearly Bigfoot hadn't, either. Bigfoot collapsed as Grandma struck him right below the seal. When Kai shone the flashlight on them both, he saw Grandma's sword stuck in Bigfoot's shoulder. It was in deep, pinning the beast to the ground.

"I've got him!" Grandma said. "Go, Kai! Take the light. Find your brother. Let's end this." She swept the flare along the ground beside her, lighting a fire and keeping the creatures at bay.

Coolest. Grandma. Ever.

Kai tore away, the flashlight in one hand and Grandma's bag in the other. Kai had been useless during that fight, unable to act. Without Grandma's help, he would have been toast.

And now Grandma was still there, fighting off those creatures alone. What if Kai couldn't find Peter in time? What if getting the seal cost them *Grandma*?

Kai ran harder, chasing the place where he'd seen the blue light. If it was weird and magical, it was probably Peter.

He skidded to a stop when he saw Sophie sitting by a large hole in the ground, trying to twist vines into a rope. "Sophie! Where's Peter?"

Sophie pointed into the hole. Sick, afraid of what he'd see, Kai looked down.

"He's fine," Sophie said. Her shirt was covered with burn marks, and she looked exhausted. "We both are. We found the seal and activated it. But then the ground fell. He's down there. I didn't want to leave for help, in case I couldn't find this place again, but we need a rope."

"I have Grandma's." Kai handed her Grandma's backpack, and Sophie pulled out a length of rope. "I'll go get him," Kai said. "You tie this up so we can get out."

And then Kai climbed over the side and slid down the wall into the pit below, flashlight tucked under his arm.

He had to find Peter. Grandma needed his brother now, and after Kai had failed her so badly, he could actually *do* something.

Kai turned a corner and found Peter, sticking colorful crystals into a metal matrix. "Peter!"

His twin turned around. "Oh, hey, Kai. Look at this."

"We don't have time. Grandma's in trouble. We found the seal, but—" Kai noticed the mural on the wall. "Is that what I think it is?"

"Yeah, it's the sinking of Atlantis. I think this metal thing is part of it, though."

Kai examined the mural. The sea creature was depicted on the left side, rising from the water over the island. Atlantis itself was crumbling, a deep crack cutting through its center as it split apart. But what Kai found interesting was that at the bottom of the crack was a structure that looked like an ancient Greek temple, with an empty pedestal inside it. It too had split in half. Tiny human figures stood on each side, but whether they were trying to put the temple back together or tear it apart, Kai didn't know. Without a written language, he couldn't interpret the story the mural was telling.

"What was that about Grandma?" Peter asked.

"Grandma needs our help, like, immediately. Once Sophie finishes tying off the rope, we need to leave and help Grandma. I don't know how long her fire will protect her."

"Right." Peter bent and picked up another crystal.

Kai wanted to strangle him. "What are you doing?"

"This is the last one. It will only take a minute. And I need to see."

Peter put the last crystal in its slot. Nothing happened.

"Okay, you fixed it," Kai said. "Let's go."

The metal web, now full of crystals, looked like stained glass. Was that the answer? Kai raised the flashlight and shone it through the matrix.

There was the mural showing the Sea, raging over the island

of Atlantis, sinking it. But, a second image, created from light, had appeared on the right side of the island.

It was a tall, humanoid being that looked more like a tree than a person. Leafy vines covered its body like clothing, and it stretched long, knotted arms over Atlantis. While the Sea flooded Atlantis with waves, this creature seemed to be tearing it apart with stony claws.

Kai sucked in his breath. "What is that?"

Peter walked toward the mural. "I don't know. But I think that's what we've been releasing with all these seals."

"No, no. We've been sealing *away* the Sea. Why else would the Sea try to destroy the seal at Dogtown?"

But the answer came to him as soon as he asked the question: *It hates that thing.* It wanted it locked away for good. He could see it in the way the waves rose against the other creature, in the way the tree creature swiped a clawed hand at the Sea. They were fighting each other. Atlantis just got caught in the middle.

All the strange pieces that didn't fit came together for Kai at that moment. The way the sign for "sea" also meant "twin." All the doubles and pairs in the messages and poems. The riddle the last woman at Salem gave him: *as alike as land is to sea.*

The way the Sea only seemed to lose its temper when Kai referenced what it called the "filthy" land.

These two beings were Sea . . . and Land.

"They *both* sank Atlantis," Kai said.

But why? How did the island fall victim to a fight between gods—the literal embodiments of Land and Sea? Kai looked at that image of the underground temple again. He rummaged in Grandma's bag until he found her camera. He snapped some pictures of the mural. Maybe later, he could compare them to the scans Mom sent and figure out what he was missing.

By the mural, Peter touched the creature made of light. "Every time I activate a seal, I feel a release. Not a binding. We're letting something go. We have the whole time."

Kai nodded. Peter was right. All this time, he'd been right.

Peter ran his hand along the picture, stopping at the small figure of a human at the heart of the light image, its hands raised in a strange echo of the land creature's grasping reach. "We have to stop activating the seals," Peter said.

Kai was about to nod again, and agree, but then he remembered. "No! We have to activate one more. Grandma's in danger. If we activate the sixth seal, she'll be safe."

"And after that?"

"We stop." Kai looked at the mural, of Sea and Land fighting, tearing an island apart. "We can't let this happen."

But what about the Sea? How do we stop it?

Kai would have to figure that out later. For now, Grandma needed Peter, and they needed to prevent this Land creature from escaping its prison. They'd already raised one monster. Kai wouldn't do it again.

"It can't escape with only six seals broken," Kai said. "Right?"

"I guess," Peter said. "Okay. Let's help Grandma."

Peter ran back toward Sophie, but Kai lingered a moment longer. They'd almost set this other monster free, all because Kai wouldn't listen to Peter. He could have unleashed another creature that would have cost them everything, all because he didn't stop to think.

But now he knew better and everyone would be safe. They had a whole extra day to find another way to put the Sea back.

Yeah. They could do this.

Kai switched off the flashlight, banishing the Land creature, and left the chamber.

CHAPTER 26

THE SEVENTH SEAL

PETER

Sophie was waiting with the rope by the time Peter got back to her. Without a word, he jumped up onto the rope and started climbing, bracing his feet against the wall of the pit. Sophie helped, pulling him up.

"Where's Kai?" she asked.

"Coming," Peter said. "I have to find Grandma, now. Kai said she lit a fire?"

They both looked around until Peter noticed a column of smoke through the trees. "There. I have to go. You stay and help Kai up."

"Are you sure? Do you want me to come with you?"

Peter shook his head. "I've got this. See you soon."

With that, he ran into the trees toward the smoke and, hopefully, Grandma. He made sure not to pass the parking lot where Dad waited.

Peter didn't want Dad involved. Not with his bad arm. And he wasn't going to let Grandma get hurt, too, because he was late arriving with his ability to activate seals.

This would be six seals down, one to go. Six seals holding

back another monster, broken, and only one keeping the line. But it would be okay. Peter wouldn't activate the seventh, and Kai was on his side now. They'd stop, and no one would be hurt again.

As long as they stopped the Sea, too. Peter pushed his frustration into his feet, running harder. He had no idea how to stop the Sea. But there had to be a way, right?

Wow, he was thinking like Kai, expecting a solution to just exist. Odds were good they'd just have to sound an alarm and get everyone to move far enough inland to stay safe while the Sea threw its tantrum and hope it ended soon.

At least they wouldn't have to contend with *two* monsters.

Peter turned a corner and saw Grandma kneeling on top of what seemed to be a huge, mossy log. Fire encircled her, as did a crowd of enormous spiders, snakes, and dogs.

Peter stumbled back. So this was what Kai had been facing?

Every time the creatures attacked her, Grandma hacked at them with her sword. Her face was stone, set in an expression of determination, but her arms shook and sweat gleamed on her face. She was tiring.

"Grandma!"

She turned to face him. "About time, Peter. Get over here!"

Grandma tossed him a bronze dagger, which fell at his feet. Peter picked it up. The weight felt almost too heavy, and its edge was stained with blood. He wasn't sure he wanted to use it.

But what choice did he have? Swinging the blade in front of him, Peter raced toward Grandma. Spiders crunched under his feet, and a dog yelped when Peter grazed it with the knife.

The fire blazed in front of him. Peter hesitated for just a moment, and then gathered his will and jumped even before Grandma told him to.

Then he was on the log with her. Nope, not a log. The moss was thick hair, and the thing below it had arms and legs and a torso that bucked and squirmed. Peter was amazed Grandma managed to stay on for so long.

Peter looked at the thing's apelike face. "Is this Bigfoot?"

"It's on his chest," Grandma said. "The seal. Get it!"

There it was. Dark brown, like a brand, against the fur. Peter narrowly avoided being thrown off Bigfoot and brought his hand down on the seal.

That smell of warm earth, stronger now. This time, as the images of the Sea poured through him, Peter sensed another mind, one burning with anger, watching the memories. And watching Peter.

It knows I'm here.

Then the connection ended, and the chaos of the horde of animals stopped like an instantly muted TV. Peter looked around and saw nothing but dust and ash floating in the air where the monsters once were.

Bigfoot stopped moving, too. When Peter looked back, the brown fur turned gray and Bigfoot, too, collapsed into dust. The seal was broken, and he and Grandma were safe.

"Very good, Peter," Grandma said. The fire around them was dying, and Grandma stepped over the last embers to wipe her sword on the closest patch of nondusty grass. She examined the blade. "First time this thing has seen battle, other than some gentleman's duel. Now *this* is how you respect a weapon." She raised it high, arm still shaking, and then sheathed the sword.

Then she sank to the ground. Peter rushed to her, but Grandma waved him off. "Don't worry about me," she said. "I just overexerted this leg of mine. A small price to pay for getting another seal. One more to go, right?"

No. That was the last one. Peter brushed dust off his hands. "Let's just go," he said. "Is Dad at the car?"

"He lost the coin toss. Probably still pouting about it." Grandma smiled, and she stood shakily. She wrapped Peter in a hug, and then they wandered back to the parking lot.

When Dad saw them, he got out of the car. "Where's Kai?"

"I had him, but we had to make a switch," Grandma said. "On account of Peter being the only one who can activate the seals."

"Hey!" Kai was emerging from the trees with Sophie, carrying her fallen drone, at his side. "We got both seals. Time to leave."

Dad smiled. "One to go, right? When it shows up, we'll end this once and for all."

Peter and Kai shot each other glances. "Um, about that," Kai said.

"We're not breaking any more seals," Peter said.

The others stared at him. "What?" Sophie asked.

"Because you don't know where the last seal is?" Dad asked. "The riddle said it would appear once the first six were activated. That should be anytime now. We just have to watch."

Peter shook his head. "The seals aren't what we thought they were. They're not sealing back the Sea. They're stopping something else."

Kai stepped in. "There's another monster. We're not activating seals. We're *breaking* them. If we keep going, we'll release another monster. One I don't think the Sea likes very much."

"What are you saying?" Grandma said, arms folded. Her gentle, grandmotherly demeanor had been replaced with the warrior Peter saw fighting off the giant creatures. "You're just going to stop? You're going to let the sea monster flood the land?"

Grandma's house was just a taste of what would happen to her whole town if they didn't stop the Sea. Peter's stomach twisted and goose bumps broke out over his skin. He sat on the hood of the car.

"No, of course not! I'm just saying that Peter and I found this cave that told us there's another creature and Atlantis got caught in a grudge match and *that's* why it sank! See, look!" He pulled out the camera and passed it to the adults. "I got pictures. We don't want the same thing to happen to Seaspire."

Grandma took the camera and opened the image. Her brow crinkled, and she showed the pictures to Dad.

"It's ... concerning," Dad said. "But I feel like I'm missing something. Why would the monsters fight over Atlantis?"

"We don't know, but they did. *Two* huge monsters. Now we know activating the seals isn't the right way to save the world. We have to find another way."

"The full moon is tomorrow!" Sophie said.

"Are you sure you're right?" Dad said to Kai. "Are you absolutely sure that your interpretation was correct?"

"You can see it. Make your own interpretation." Kai rubbed his face. "From the start, something hasn't been adding up. There was always more to the story. Now we know what it is."

Peter's head spun. He felt like he'd been swimming for too long, dazed without air. He pressed a hand against his heaving stomach and took deep, careful breaths. His skin prickled, and he wondered if he was about to throw up.

Dad touched Kai's shoulder. "Did you see an inscription telling you all about this other creature?"

"No. But the mural is pretty clear."

"It does look bad. But we don't know why Atlantis got torn apart. Maybe they did something wrong, and we can avoid their mistakes." Dad stepped back and rubbed his cast. "Look," he said. "Let's look into the history, and when the seventh seal appears we'll make note of it. We'll make our decision then."

"It doesn't matter where the seventh seal appears," Kai said. "Peter and I aren't going to activate it."

"Not even to save the world?"

"It won't save anything! It will only make it worse. Right, Peter?"

Peter fell off the car, clutching at his shirt.

He wasn't nauseous. This was something else. His chest *burned*.

"Peter!" Kai was next to him in an instant. "What's going on?"

"I'm . . . burning." Peter felt like someone was carving his skin with a hot knife.

"Stand back, Kai." Dad was there, helping Peter sit up.

The burning, itching feeling was unbearable. Peter, gasping, pulled up his shirt, expecting almost to see fire ants crawling all over him. Weirder things had happened in the past week.

Instead, the whole family fell silent, staring. Peter looked down at his own chest, at the bright red binding symbol vivid on his rib cage.

It was him. Peter was the seventh seal.

CHAPTER 27

PEACE OR TRUTH

PETER

The drive home from the Bridgewater Triangle was awkward, with Dad refusing to look anywhere but the road, Kai staring at the binding word but trying to pretend he wasn't, Grandma talking a mile a minute about ancient rituals and how they worked or didn't work, and Sophie holding Peter's hands so he wouldn't accidentally touch the seal and break it.

Not that he would. As tempting as it was to touch the seal, see if it felt like the rest of his skin, Peter knew very well that every other seal he'd touched had been destroyed.

And the rest of his family knew it, too. That's why everyone was yelling now. They'd gone back to the bed-and-breakfast and locked the door while they debated what to do next.

Peter sat against the wall, hands behind his head, eyes closed, seal no longer painful but still there under his shirt, branded on his chest.

"If he touches that thing, he could die!" Kai said. "We can't allow that."

"Bigfoot had a seal on its chest, too," Grandma said. "When

Peter touched it, Bigfoot turned to dust. That could happen to Peter."

"It might not," Sophie said, but she didn't sound convinced. "Kai, what *exactly* did you see in that cave?"

Peter listened as Kai told them all about the mural and the metal matrix with the crystals, and what it revealed when they shone the flashlight through it.

Which was interesting to Peter. The Atlanteans who made that chamber had put the Sea in the wall as part of the mural. Wouldn't it be just as easy to put the Land in there, too, the same way? Why bother creating a light show?

Kai was still talking. "It all makes sense. Some of the Atlantean words have multiple meanings. One that means 'twin' comes up a lot. The Atlantean texts don't really make it clear if they worshipped one creature or two. They refer to 'sacred metal' and 'day flowers' and other things that *don't belong to the ocean.* They belong to the land. The signs were always there."

"We just saw them too late," Dad said. Springs creaked as he sank into their chair. "We should have stopped before Bridgewater. But now . . . do we think the seal will just go away?"

No one spoke. Peter, for one, didn't think it would. He'd always carry, always *be* the seventh seal, until it was broken. And then what?

"Maybe we risk it," Grandma said. "It seems cruel that the gate binding the Sea would gift you with the ability to read languages, and Peter with the power to open the seals, and then require one of you to be destroyed. Why do that? Maybe activating it is the only way to get that seal off Peter."

That was a good point, Peter thought. The Atlanteans might have built into the ritual a sacrifice to prevent people from opening doors they shouldn't. But that didn't explain why opening the gate granted Kai and him powers that helped them raise the Land, too.

And why did the ritual to raise the Sea involve bringing a twin? There was more here. He could feel it.

"We can't risk it." Kai sounded angry. "The ritual to raise the Sea required a sacrifice. Maybe this is the same. I'm not going to sacrifice my brother."

"We might either way." Sophie's voice cracked. "If we don't do something, we all die when the Sea comes for us. Including Peter."

"Are you saying we sacrifice Peter for the greater good?" Kai shouted.

Sophie raised her hands. "No, of course not! We . . . we can get it off Peter. And then open the seal. That way we can save everyone."

Peter wondered if her words sounded as hollow to everyone as they did to him. If there was going to be an easy way out, they would have found it already.

"*A dream turns nightmare with revealed price, for who can pay that which asks for all?*" Kai said, quoting MacHale's last poem. "It's obvious. The price here is Peter's life. I can't . . . I can't make that choice. I can't do it."

With a pang, Peter realized that no, Kai couldn't. Neither could Sophie or Dad or Grandma. Only Peter could make the choice to activate the last seal.

Himself for the rest of the world.

In terms of math, it made sense. But there were so many

variables. What if bringing back the Land didn't stop the Sea? What if it made everything worse?

But what if it *did* save everything? What if there was a reason MacHale, sensitive and sleeping, was able to put to pen the seals' locations and protections? What if, somehow, in trying to protect the town through the lighthouse he stumbled upon how to protect the town from the monster beyond the gate he lived next to?

Could Peter choose not to act this time, knowing what came next was his fault?

A choice. Act, and possibly save or doom everyone. Don't act, with the same possible results. How could he choose?

He thought about that mural, with the solid Sea and the lightshow Land, that small figure under the Land, hands raised.

Maybe there was still more to the story.

Peter's eyes snapped open. He stood up, and the arguing stopped. He faced his family. "I'm going outside," he said.

Dad nodded. "Okay. Do you want anyone to go with you?"

Peter shook his head. "I'd like to look at the papers, though."

"Sure." Kai scrambled to his bag and handed Peter the folder with all the Atlantean scans and the poems.

Peter took them and headed outside. It was a cool night, not yet stormy. It was like the Sea was getting a good night's sleep to be ready for the morning's attack.

Peter sat on the curb and opened the folder. MacHale's poems. Dad's research. His mother's discoveries, scanned and sent to Kai, marked up with Kai's translations. How convenient.

There was that symbol Kai mentioned, the one that meant "sea" but also "twin." And now they knew why. Peter picked up another scan and read the inscription by the almost-full moon.

"On the eve of summer gold, we met the being of stone and tree. Our liege is now encircled with light, and, in return, we receive bounty of sun."

"Sun" was circled, with multiple meanings written next to it, from "strength" to "beauty," but Peter was more interested in the phrase "encircled with light." It reminded him of the mural in the cave, the little human figure under the creature.

Could that little human figure from the mural be that leader, that "liege"? It was covered with the light image of the Land. What did it mean?

Why was the Land rendered in light? Why wasn't it physical like the depiction of the Sea? And what did this inscription mean when it said the writer's leader was "encircled with light"?

Peter didn't think it was anything good. After all, the Land had been bound with seven Atlantean seals, and you didn't do that to friends. Yet the inscription didn't say it was bad, either.

He picked up another page. This one was only partially translated. In Kai's handwriting, Peter read, "In memory of the Shattered Isle, of the Schism, of the Flooding." And that was it.

A eulogy or memorial? For Atlantis after it fell? The Schism could be the Land tearing the island apart, and the Flooding would have been the Sea's attack.

The bed-and-breakfast door opened, and Kai stepped outside. "Hey," he said.

Peter just waved the paper in greeting.

Kai sat next to Peter. "How are you doing?"

"Fine, I guess. It doesn't hurt or anything."

"Yeah, but don't touch it." Kai grabbed his knees. "You know, I was warned that this quest would have a cost."

"I always knew it would. Maybe that's why I was chosen."

"Really? Because *I* was warned. Not you. It's not fair."

Peter shrugged and waved MacHale's poems. "It's like the riddle says. *Will you reach for peace or truth? I set down my pen, the choice is yours.*"

"Peace or truth," Kai muttered derisively, but Peter was intrigued. He hadn't thought about it like that.

Odd, that there was only the choice to reach. MacHale didn't allow for sitting back, waiting. Maybe, in its own way, waiting *was* reaching. Making a choice by refusing to choose.

So what did he want? Did he want peace? Or truth? Which one would breaking the seal release?

And what would happen to him if he did it?

Peace or truth. Odd that they didn't come together as a package deal. Maybe you couldn't have truth and have it easy, too.

"I'm sorry," Kai said. "This is all my fault. If I hadn't gotten my blood on that hot dog, this wouldn't have happened."

Peter snorted. "If I hadn't wiped my sweat on it, it wouldn't have happened."

"If I hadn't gotten a hot dog in the first place."

"If I hadn't said, 'Get up, Kai.'"

"If I hadn't bloodied my nose."

"If *I* hadn't bloodied *your* nose."

The boys grinned. "I guess we're both guilty," Kai said.

Peter laughed. "Well, we are twins. We share everything."

Kai looked away. "Not everything." Peter knew he was thinking of the seal.

It was weird, having to be the optimistic twin. Peter handed Kai one of the scans. "We still have time. Maybe there's more to the story. What does this say?"

Kai took the paper. "It's a tragedy," he said, and tried to hand it back.

Peter didn't take it. "But what does it *say*?"

Kai sighed. "'In memory of the Shattered Isle, of the Schism, of the Flooding. May our families forgive us our greed, and may the gods forgive us our pride. The unworthy shall break upon the rocks as once the stones broke upon them.' Real happy stuff."

Peter thought. "The Sea mentioned greed, didn't it? When we raised it."

"Yeah, it said, 'I had dreamed of humans who would not take back what they once gave so freely. Who would honor me, and what I could bring them, instead of giving in to their greed.' Why?"

"Because it might be important. What happened to Atlantis? Why do the Atlanteans blame their greed and pride if the Sea and Land got into a poorly placed grudge match, like we think?"

Kai scratched his arm. "No idea. It doesn't really fit."

No, it didn't. Once again, too many things didn't add up for Peter. The creature depicted in light. This reference to greed, and another to pride. Atlantis fell so long ago that it was impossible to actually know what happened. The Sea might, but it was not going to answer any of their questions.

Peace or truth? The choice was Peter's.

And amid the maelstrom of questions and confusion, Peter found the eye of the storm. In a moment, he knew what he had to do.

"Kai," he said. "Do you trust me?"

Kai didn't answer for a while. By the time Peter was about to ask again, Kai said, "Don't."

"Don't what?"

"Break the last seal. I know you're going to do it. We don't know what will happen to you!"

"I know. But," Peter said, "we're not *going* to know. And I have to choose anyway." His hand hovered over his chest. "If I don't choose, I choose not to act. Not choosing *is* a choice." He looked at his brother. "I choose this. Do you trust me?"

Kai's mouth gaped, opening and closing. Then he looked at Peter's shirt, hiding the seventh seal, and then at Peter's face. Peter tried to look defiant.

It must have worked. "Yes," Kai said. "I trust you. But I'm not letting you go alone. And promise me you'll sleep on this. Don't run off tonight without letting yourself think this over. And sleep with gloves on."

Peter laughed. Odd that Kai was the one telling him to be cautious.

"Whatever you say. Well, good night, then."

"I'll bring these back in." Kai gathered the folder of papers and stood up. "Good night."

"See you in the morning." Peter waited until Kai left, watching the moon and listening to the distant sound of waves. Then he went back inside.

When he told the family that he wanted to sleep, they moved their argument outside. Except for Kai. He was nowhere to be found.

Twins, one with the ability to read all languages, including Atlantean, and the other to open seals. They both had choices to make. Peter saw that now.

Peter didn't have gloves, so after he set his alarm for early morning and climbed in bed, he put socks over his hands. He was more grateful than he thought he'd be for one more night of rest; he could put off thinking about the seal for a few more hours. But he'd made his decision. He didn't know every angle, or if what he was about to do was right. He just knew that if he did anything else, he'd regret it for the rest of his life.

However long that may be.

CHAPTER 28

A PATTERN OF WATER

KAI

Kai was not giving up so easily. After he left Peter, he carried his papers back inside, heading to the empty bed-and-breakfast dining room.

The others spotted him as they came down the stairs. "Well?" Grandma said. "How is he?"

"He's fine. For now." Kai looked at Grandma.

Dad frowned at Kai. "You didn't tell him to break the last seal, did you?"

"No! I told him to get some sleep. But I'm going to be up late. I have work to do so don't bother me."

Dad's shoulders fell. "Are you sure? Maybe we can help."

They couldn't. "Can any of you read Atlantean? I have to do this alone."

When they didn't answer, like Kai knew they wouldn't, he hiked the papers higher under his arm and went into the dining room.

Answers. He needed answers. They thought they needed to seal the Sea back with seven seals, but they were wrong. Now, they thought they were doomed either by Land or Sea, when Peter broke that last seal.

Why did Peter have to pay the price? It was Kai's quest, and Kai was the one who wanted it. If anyone paid for this adventure, it should have been him. Now he was the only one escaping unscathed. All he could do was sit helplessly by as his twin broke the last, deadly seal.

No. He wouldn't be helpless. He could still read and make a plan. So he did.

Kai read the scans his mother sent him until his eyes ached. He heard Dad, Sophie, and Grandma finish their futile argument and go to bed, creaking up the stairs but mercifully not bothering him. He circled hieroglyphs that had multiple meanings and tried to figure out the message behind them.

A pattern. There was always a pattern. Here were the symbols that meant "sea" and "twin," and another that meant "land" and also "twin." They'd always been here; he just never saw it.

Why twins so much?

One message, down. But Kai also noticed a pattern of references to sunlight, usually discussed as something sacred or valuable. Did the Atlanteans love the sun that much? Was that a clue; could the sun save Peter? Or did it refer to something else? The only other word used next to "sacred" was "metal." What if it wasn't actual sunlight at all?

Kai's head hurt from chasing the same dead-end ideas again and again, so he scowled, tossed the scans to the side, and pulled out MacHale's poems. He tried to examine the last one, the one about the seventh seal, but it made his stomach knot, so he went back to the first one about Dogtown.

If land in common meets the sea,
And find ye path of trunk and tree,

What man has built, Mother sets free.
Inspired past and future see:
Mongrel town, lost history.
'Neath pine and boulder find the key
Then fire burn, and seeker flee.

Interesting, that rhyme scheme. At the end of every line, the exact same rhyme. And then there was the second poem:

Where sailors return with fishy tale
To sun's shore from sacred wave,
Where crest glitters with golden scale,
And Charles Curtis failed to save,
Upon spectral boards and under sail
A song reverbs from watery grave
Let ocean roar, and woodwork fail.

And suddenly there was a second rhyme. In the first poem, every line rhymed with "sea." But in this one, half the lines rhymed with "tale" and half with "wave." Two rhyming sounds, instead of one. Why?

It was a pattern. He could feel it. There had to be a reason.

Every poem added another rhyming sound. One, then two, then three. To mark which poem it was? Seemed silly, when except for the seventh, all the other seals probably could have been found in any order.

No. There was another reason. With any pattern, you looked for what changed, and what repeated. The pattern of increasing rhymes repeated. But in each individual poem, the rhyme changed.

Looking at the second poem, Kai focused on the second line, where the rhyme switched from "tale" to "wave." He read it again and again. Nothing seemed to be strange about it, except it was interesting how it mentioned the sea. "Sacred wave" and all that.

Hold on. Kai went back to the first poem. The first line of the first poem also mentioned the sea! First line, then second, and what about the third?

> *In metal ground is flood of flame,*

Flood. Not the ocean, but still water. So, yes!
What about the fourth?

> *Returned stony press and the water's test.*

Water!
Kai continued with the fifth, sixth, and seventh:

> *Island mineral may river's path stay.*

> *Mind, though solid become sand without whole spring,*

> *Once land may grow, but, too, more sea.*

River, spring, and sea.
But why? Why include all these references to the sea, especially if the poems were about the seals binding the Land?
Because it stands out.
Kai felt like he was staring down off the Point into the water by

the Spire, just inches away from an exhilarating plummet. In poems about land, the sea stands out. It's *meant* to be noticed! Running his tongue over his chipped tooth, Kai quickly wrote down the words about the sea and water, from their corresponding lines.

"Sea, wave, flood, water, river, spring, sea."

No pattern in that. At least, not that Kai could see. They were just words about water. "Sea" was repeated at the start and finish, but Kai wasn't sure if that was meaningful. He decided to come back to that later.

What if these words weren't important? What if they were markers for *other* words that were?

Kai went back to the first poem. "Meets the sea." "Sea" ended that line. So the only other word that it could be pointing to was "the."

"The" was a good start. So Kai tried the next word. "Sacred waves."

"Sacred." Kai's eyes roamed to the scans. That word again. Another pattern!

The word before the water word. That was the key!

Kai wrote them down. "The sacred is the may whole more."

That didn't make much sense.

Perhaps it was another riddle. Kai sat, thinking, researching any possible multiple meanings for "sacred" and "whole," looking for cross-references in the scans and *their* possible multiple meanings in Atlantean, just searching for some possible answer to this riddle, some conclusion that would stop the Sea, prevent the Land from rising, and save Peter.

He didn't even notice falling into a dreamless sleep until he woke up at sunrise to find Peter standing beside him.

CHAPTER 29

THE BROKEN SEAL

PETER

Peter woke before his alarm. He'd had no dreams, but that was okay. It meant that for the first time in days, he was fully rested.

He would have liked to know more about the Sea's plans, but they wouldn't really change his mind. He knew what he had to do.

So he pulled the socks off and sneaked downstairs, passing his sleeping dad, sister, and grandmother. Kai wasn't in bed when Peter woke up, so he expected to find his twin downstairs.

This wasn't Dad's, Grandma's, or Sophie's fight. But Peter and Kai had to see this through together.

So Peter found Kai in the dining room, sleeping on a pile of papers.

Peter touched Kai's shoulder. "It's time."

Kai snorted and sat up, pen marks on his face. "Oh, good. So excited."

Peter smiled as Kai shook himself awake.

"All right." Kai scooped up his stacks of paper. "We started this thing together. Let's end it the same way."

Peter waited for Kai to grab a backpack for the papers, and then both boys crept out of the Widow's Walk, making sure the door didn't make a sound. They ran down to the beach.

The storm chasers and news crews hadn't begun their day yet. Why would they? There was nothing obviously strange or exciting. Yet.

The morning was so similar to that first day when they raised the Sea. Except, of course, that instead of a bright, sunny afternoon, it was a cold, windy morning. The sky was mostly overcast, clouds lit with a bloodred sun.

"*Red sun at morning, sailor take warning,*" Peter murmured. He didn't know where he'd heard that, but it seemed all too appropriate.

The waves clawed at the sand before roaring and trying again. Farther out, the sea leaped like wildfire, blazing copper with the red sun.

The water surged past the wrecked wharf, the ocean level unnaturally high. Peter recognized the early signs.

The Sea was beginning its attack.

"To the Spire," Peter said. Kai's face fell, but Peter shrugged. "That's where it has to end."

Peter aimed toward the forest, and the lighthouse, and ran.

Kai ran beside him.

They didn't say a word until they'd reached the barren rock in front of the lighthouse.

"Ready?" Peter asked.

Kai hunched his shoulders. "If you are."

Together, they faced the water.

The ocean frothed. It had become high enough to overwhelm the Spire with every tide. Huge waves washed over the Spire.

The wind bellowed in Peter's ears. He searched the red-lit water and soon saw it: the Sea.

It rose out of the ocean just beyond the Spire. The waves circled it like a whirlpool, but the Sea was unmoved. It raised its hands toward the shore.

"The moon is with me," it said, its voice carrying with the stormy gale. "And today, the Land falls to me. Finally, I can be at peace."

Peter swallowed. He hoped he was making the right choice.

Leaving Kai behind, Peter stepped to the edge of the Point. "You!" he called. "Sea demon!"

The Sea turned to face Peter.

"Peter, what are you doing?" Kai hissed.

Peter turned around. "Get back. Get where it can't see you."

Kai's jaw dropped. "What? No! We're facing it together, remember?"

"We are." Even in the storm, Peter felt calm. He'd made his choice. Even though he didn't know what would happen next, he'd take the action he'd chosen.

He thought of that mural, the Sea and Land fighting, the little figure caught in the middle. Then he looked at his twin. "But if I'm right, I'll need you later. Don't risk yourself now when there's no reason to. Please, Kai. Wait."

Without looking to see if Kai did as he said, Peter turned to the Point to see the Sea right there, standing on a column of water right in front of him.

Oh, man! Peter resisted the urge to scream and fall backward. His hands shook, so he clenched them. "You will stop," he told the Sea. "Now."

The Sea laughed. It grew in size until each of its fingers was as tall as Peter. "You come here, little human," it boomed, "and presume to give me orders?"

Peter licked his dry lips. They tasted like salt. "You will stop," he said again. "And you will leave us all alone."

With a sudden movement that didn't seem possible for something so big, the Sea snatched Peter up in its huge fist. Peter held perfectly still as the giant fingers closed around him and lifted him into the air.

The Sea raised Peter to its face.

"Arrogant human," it said, its voice almost deafening. "Even blessed with gifts from Atlantis, you have failed. You have done nothing to stop me, all this time. You come to me with no weapons, no bargains, as the Atlanteans did. You simply come with demands, showing your greed."

The fingers tightened, and Peter choked. He tugged a hand free and pointed at the Sea. Trying to keep his breathing steady, pretending to be Kai, he said, "It's not greed. If you're smart, you'll forget your stupid grudge and go away."

The Sea laughed. "Is that a threat, tiny human?"

"No," Peter said. "But this is."

And with that, Peter reached under his collar and broke the final seal.

—— • ◉ • ——

Energy rocked Peter from the inside, bursts of light encircling him from head to toe. The seal hardened and spread, protecting him from the explosions erupting inside him like volcanoes generating continents from nothing. He was vaguely aware of the Sea's grip releasing him, and of the Point's edge giving way beneath his weight as he grew, and grew, and grew.

A small human figure, overlaid by the Land, hands raised as if in fear. Or in combat.

A host.

Peter's arms lengthened, turning to knotted brown wood shot through with gray stone. His feet plunged into the ocean, which now only came up to his knees. Steam burst from the water. Peter was burning with lava, with the red-gold light of the fires of creation. His fingers changed as well, with stone claws emerging from each one. The better to attack the Sea with.

And oh, he wanted to attack the Sea. Memories of its cruelty flooded his mind: how it destroyed the edges of continents, eroding away the land until there was none left. How it struck without consideration, tearing land apart. How it was cold, and dark, and wet, and everything Peter hated.

No. *Peter* didn't hate the Sea. But there was another mind in here, one ancient and brutal and blazing.

Peter pressed deeper into the being's memories. The Land remembered. It remembered being part of a great island, once inhabited by people. These people discovered gold and silver and other metals and used them to build a grand city.

At first, the place was blessed. Both land and sea provided bountiful wealth, which was shared among the people. In honor of the island, the earth and the water, the people built a shrine in a sea cave. The Land remembered feeling their warmth, love, and unity until they became its own. They were its people, and it was their land.

But time passed. Something changed. The people became divided, the wealth no longer shared. Pride led to conflict and bloodshed, and the Atlanteans just wanted more, more, more.

And then they came to the shrine.

They took something vital, something precious. Sacred, even. His soul—

No, not his soul. But something just as important. And then, and then—

A rush of ocean and a glint of scales in the sunlight. An earthy presence possessing of the nearest Atlantean, the leader of the thieves. The hatred and division in the Atlanteans mirrored in the Land's mind as it turned on the Sea. As it viewed the Sea, once other half, now hated enemy. What could it do, then, but follow the Atlanteans' lead and attack?

Peter watched the memory of the Land tearing apart an island just to get at the Sea. He saw the Sea bow and vanish under the power of the Atlantean magicians, bound with a ritual intended to be lost to the ages. But things have a way of making themselves known.

He felt the Land likewise stripped from its host and locked away with seven seals, so it could never possess a human again, never attack those who once loved it. Land and Sea, an island divided, imprisoned separately when they were once totally united.

An ancient voice washed over Peter's consciousness. *We are not one*, it said, images of the Sea filling his mind. *It is unstable and cold and cruel, not steady and warm and life giving as I am. I am not that creature, and it will never be me!*

The force of the creature's mind was overwhelming. Peter rode a tide of its rage, trying to keep his mind free, to remain himself. A small human bathed in the light of the Land.

But he was unable to stop himself from giving over to the Land as it swung those slate claws at the Sea, striking it in the face. After all, he was here to stop the Sea. If nothing else, this would keep it from attacking Seaspire.

It may have been the Land's choice, but it was Peter's, too.

CHAPTER 30

THE PATTERN OF LAND

KAI

Holy mother of salt water and salt water taffy, my brother just turned into Groot!

Kai, hidden behind the lighthouse, pressed against the wall for strength. Had he just seen—

Was Peter—

Had Peter just—

What was Kai supposed to do now?

As the Land creature that was once his brother roared and clawed at the Sea, Kai forced himself to look away. Gaping at the monster fight happening in front of him wouldn't save Peter.

But what could he do? It was excruciating, being unable to act, to protect his brother. He wished he could have been the one with the seal. It would have been easier than this.

There had to be something he could do to save Peter.

And if he had any chance of finding it, it would have to be in the notes and codes. Kai gathered rocks and used them to hold down the pages, so he could look over them all.

The ocean crashed as Land and Sea clashed. It should be him

out there, not Peter. Peter never wanted to be part of this quest, and Kai had enjoyed it from the beginning. Now he was stuck on the sidelines.

That old woman in Salem had asked Kai what he was willing to pay. He wished he'd told her "himself," because that's all he wanted to do now. Pay for his own mistakes and leave Peter out of this. But it was too late for that.

Focus. Kai searched the papers, looking for some pattern, some clue he might have missed.

Sea.

Twin.

Land.

Sacred.

Sunlight.

Kai looked up, wind whipping his hair against his face. Red sunlight set the paper on fire.

As much as he tried to focus on the poems, Kai's eyes were drawn back to the *huge monster battle* in front of him. The Sea and Land, clashing and fighting. And his brother caught in the middle of it all.

Sea and Land. Kai watched for a moment, feeling a little perplexed. But why? Why was it strange that two beings that were so different would fight? The Land was warm and dry, and the Sea cold and wet. One was sunlight, and the other darkness.

A paper fluttered, and Kai grabbed it. The Atlantean word for "sea" stuck out. It had so many meanings. Including "twin."

Twin. Peter and Kai, alike but different. Land and Sea, so different, and yet . . .

Kai looked at the Point. The gate here, on stony land, right on the edge of the Sea. The shore. And there, out in the water, even below the waves there was more land. And on the land, rivers and lakes and rain kept the ground alive. Sea and shore, land and water, they were two halves of a whole.

Two halves of a whole. Kai frantically searched for MacHale's poems.

There! He read the first line of the first poem: "*If land in common meets the sea.*"

Land.

Both land and sea had been referenced in this first line. And when Kai looked at the second poem, he saw the same in the second line: "*To sun's shore from sacred wave.*"

Shore! Wave! Land and sea! Two things, together, as a whole.

Was that also true for the riddle? So far, each line with one clue held another. Kai searched for the words that came before the land-related clues in each line that held the water-related clues he had already found.

"If, sun's, metal, returned, island, become, once."

Then, as the world roared around him, Kai put them together with the sea's clues:

"If the sun's sacred metal is returned, the island may become whole once more."

There.

That was it.

Kai sat back. The island? Atlantis? Was this a way to bring Atlantis back?

That wasn't what he wanted!

Or was it? Why would the gate gift the boys with powers meant to *help* them raise the Land if the Atlanteans wanted it locked away? Why would MacHale dream-write the instructions to reunite Land and Sea? What if this was always the goal?

Then why did the Atlanteans lock the creatures away and leave the job undone until Kai and Peter arrived?

The Sea channeled water at the Land, throwing it backward. Kai yelled and was relieved when the stone-tree creature withstood the blow.

Land and Sea. Two halves of a whole. The island could come back together, Land and Sea reuniting. Then they would be at peace, right?

This was the only clue he had, the only lead. He had to take it. So, what was it telling him to do? Find the sun's sacred metal, return it, and maybe restore a lost continent?

Would that save Peter?

He didn't know. And he didn't know what the "sun's sacred metal" was. But, fortunately, he knew who might.

Kai gathered his papers and ran past the growing crowd of storm chasers back toward the Widow's Walk.

He'd only reached the park by the church when he saw his family hurrying toward him. Grandma's car was parked on the curb.

"I told you they'd be here," Sophie said. On her phone, in her hand, was Mom's face, frowning with worry. They must be burning data to stream a call to Mom.

"Where's Peter?" Dad asked. He'd wrapped the cast on his arm in plastic, preparing for a water showdown.

"Fighting the Sea," Kai said. "I'm glad you're here."

He walked to a picnic table, the same one his family had eaten lunch at a week ago, and put his papers on the table.

"Peter?" Sophie asked. "*Our* Peter?"

"And you left him there?" Mom asked.

"Yes! Please, don't ask. There's no time." Kai found MacHale's poems and read out the secret message. "*If the sun's sacred metal is returned, the island may become whole once more.*"

He looked at Dad, Mom, Grandma, and Sophie. "I found this hidden in the riddles. It references the 'sacred metal' the Atlantean relics talk about. We need to find this metal and return it to . . . I don't know. But we need to do it!"

Dad reached for him. "Slow down, Kai."

"No!" Kai knew he should have slowed down, before, and thought about the clues more. He might have seen the truth. But now, Peter was in danger, the world was in danger, and this was as slow as he could stand. Sometimes, waiting *was* better. But he knew this wasn't one of those times.

"Peter needs us *now*," he said. "I'm not going to sit here wasting time arguing when I could be out there helping him, so does anyone here know what are they talking about when they refer to the 'sun's sacred metal'?"

His family looked at him, and then looked at one another. Kai was ready to explode with impatience when his mom and dad, at the same time, said, "Orichalcum."

Sophie and Kai frowned. "What?"

Mom sighed, her voice cracking through the phone's speaker. "Orichalcum. According to legend, the Atlanteans had some kind of precious metal, like gold, that they used and traded with. They called it 'orichalcum.'"

"Some stories about it call it a precious metal," Dad said, playing with the plastic wrap on his bad arm, "but others describe it as magical, or powerful, somehow. Either way, though, what it really was is unknown."

Kai's heart sank. Unknown? Peter was out there, trapped in the middle of a giant monster fight, and he didn't have time to go hunting for some unknown metal.

Besides, what if Land or Sea actually *won* the fight? Right now they were stuck fighting in the ocean, away from any people. But once the battle was over, what would the victor destroy next?

"Well," Mom said, "actually, that's not entirely true."

Kai looked at the screen. Mom's eyes were red with exhaustion, but she smiled. "We have a pretty good idea of what kind of metal orichalcum is. It's an alloy of copper and gold."

"Copper and gold?" An alloy? Two different metals, melded together into one? That made sense to Kai. And the writings always referred to the metal as related to sunlight. Gold and red, like fire, like sunrise. "That's it!"

"That's rose gold," Sophie said. "Or red gold, depending on the alloy composition. I just learned about it in my chemistry tutoring. It's gold, so it doesn't corrode, and apparently it gets redder with time." She looked up at her family. "They sell it in any jewelry store."

"Great!" Kai said. "So we need to get some red gold. We'll just go to the nearest jewelry store, and—"

"It's six in the morning," Sophie said. "They're all closed. Unless you're suggesting we rob the place?"

"No. Well . . ." As Kai pondered the value of committing a crime to save Peter and Seaspire, Grandma gasped.

"My shield," she said.

"Which one?" everyone else asked in unison.

"Oh, you know the one! It's the one I use as a platter. The reddish one. It's very old," she said. "I thought Greek, maybe older. But I've never had to clean corrosion off it, not once. And you've seen how bright it is."

Sophie said rose gold doesn't corrode.

At that moment, a huge wind swept through the park, coming from the sea. It was followed by the sound of an enormous splash.

The family faced the sea and saw the two creatures fighting. The stony land creature had fallen into the water, where it was being pounded by waves.

"Peter," Kai breathed.

Sophie stared at him, then pointed at the land monster. "*Peter?*"

"Um, yeah. I'll explain later," Kai said to his astounded family. "But if we want to help him, we have to get that shield. Where is it?"

"Still at my house," Grandma said. "In the kitchen."

"I'll go get it," Sophie said. "Mom can tell me if it's Atlantean or not. And, no offense, Grandma, but I run faster than you."

"None taken, sweetie. Meet us at the beach," Grandma called to Sophie's retreating back. "Besides," she said to Kai and Dad, "I have other plans."

Grandma limped to her car and opened the trunk. Inside was her top collection of ancient weapons.

"That rock thing is Peter, you said?" When Kai nodded, Grandma pulled out her harpoon. "Then we need to keep that sorry excuse for a sea god off him until Sophie gets the shield."

"Mom." Dad walked over to the car and its trove of weapons.

"Not the time for this conversation, Alex," Grandma said.

"No." Dad reached into the trunk. "Any of these good for a one-armed fighter?"

Grandma grinned. "Whatever happened to 'protect the relics'?"

"Looks like today I'm respecting *them* and protecting *Peter*." Dad pulled out a spear, tested its edge, and tossed it back. "Come on," he said, closing the trunk. "No time to lose."

Kai climbed into the car and, armed to the teeth, they drove down to the beach.

* ● *

When they reached the boardwalk, Kai was out and running before Grandma stopped the motor.

Land and Sea still fought. But now, one of the Sea's arms hung loosely at its side, and it was missing patches of scales. The Land dripped molten lava from numerous cuts, the drops plunging into the water with hisses of steam. Both looked exhausted, but the fight still raged.

"Peter!" he yelled at the giant land creature.

Was it just him, or did that thing seem to hesitate and look his way?

But doing so opened the Land to another attack from the Sea. It punched the Land square in the face.

Kai shouted. How could he just wait by while his brother needed him?

Dad and Grandma arrived, carrying armfuls of weapons. "Hey, ugly!" Dad yelled. He waved a bronze spear. "This way!"

"We are officially done with you," Grandma added. She held her harpoon in one hand and a crossbow in the other. "You know what they say about guests and fish."

"They both smell after three days," Dad said, responding to Grandma.

"You've worn out your welcome," Grandma said.

With that she fired a dart at the Sea. Kai watched it arc through the air, carried by the strong winds, until it struck the Sea in the arm.

The Sea snarled and sent a wave toward them, but the family retreated to the ruined shops along the boardwalk. Once the water receded, Dad and Grandma attacked again. This time, Dad threw a spear and while it didn't hit the Sea, it distracted it enough for the Land to get a hit in.

Peter. Kai bounced on his toes, feeling like someone had filled his veins with boiling water. He wanted to attack, too, but he couldn't, because sooner or later, that shield would arrive, and then he'd have to move fast—

"Kai!" Sophie arrived, carrying the large shield-platter under her arm. "Here." She handed him the shield.

Kai took it. It was heavier than he'd expected. He turned it over, to the rounded side that held a word he'd seen before but hadn't been able to read. Yet.

Now, he could. A single word in Atlantean: SUN.

Kai clutched the shield to his chest. "Thanks, Sophie. Sorry, Grandma," he said as Grandma and Dad retreated from another wave. "I don't think you're going to get it back."

"That's fine," Grandma said, but Kai barely heard her. He was already running back to the Point.

The weather had gotten much worse since Kai was there. The wind was so heightened Kai thought he'd fly away if he caught a gale in the chest, and several times, the shield in his hands felt more like a kite. There seemed to be no reason to the wind's direction. Kai felt it blowing against him and then with him, seemingly at the same time.

Rain fell, in both drizzles and downpours. Sometimes it was cold, sometimes hot enough to steam. But Kai didn't stop. He held the orichalcum shield over his head and kept going, until he reached the lighthouse and the battle that raged in the sea beyond it.

Down below, Sophie had joined the fight. She'd picked up an ax and was banging it against an iron shield, yelling like a Viking warrior.

They were a great distraction, but they couldn't defeat the Sea, even with all of Grandma's weapons.

That was Kai and Peter's job.

Breathing heavily, Kai looked at the shield. The precious metal, sacred to Atlantis, about to be returned. A price repaid. And then what? What would happen next, and would Peter be okay?

There was a price. There had been for Peter, and there was for Kai, too. The price he paid was risking Peter. It was being forced to leave the fight in someone else's hands, not affecting the outcome himself.

He couldn't defeat the Sea. But maybe he could still save Peter. Looking at the shield, Kai knelt and picked up a sharp rock. He cut his hand, beside his thumb, and smeared the blood across the shield.

Blood has power. To raise, and to bind. This began with my blood, and it will end with it.

Kai had to try whatever he could to bring Peter out of this alive. They were twins. They shared the same blood. Maybe that would matter.

He pushed against the wind to the broken edge of the Point. He held the bloodied shield in front of him, rounded side up, like a Frisbee. He waited, watching the fight in the water, until he felt the wind at his back.

And then, he acted.

"Peter! Heads up!"

Kai threw the shield, spinning, out over the water. Then he staggered back, toward the safety of the lighthouse, to watch. He'd done his part.

It was all up to Peter now.

CHAPTER 31

STONE AND SEA

PETER

Peter felt caught in a hot whirlwind as the Land raged against the Sea. Fighting against the emotions and memories that battered and threatened to absorb him was a chore, and, anyway, wasn't he *supposed* to fight the Sea? Wasn't that what this whole quest was about?

It was easier to let the Land be in charge. Let it fight. Let it make the choices. Once again, Peter didn't know what he was supposed to do.

If I knew what caused the split, maybe I could stop this fighting before it destroys Seaspire.

More memories of Atlantis surged through Peter's mind. The people digging, discovering a metal as golden as summer wheat and as rosy as sunrise on the waves, and falling in love with it. They admired its beauty and the way its dual nature made it strong, impervious to corruption. So they took the first of it and crafted a tribute to land and sea, two things united to create the island they lived on. The metal symbolized that unity.

The rest of the metal, they took for themselves to decorate their homes and bodies, and even to write their histories on.

But it was never enough. They wanted more, and, soon, so did their trade partners. Peter felt the hammers and pickaxes rip through him, like his body *was* the island. In a way, it was, as long as he was tied to the Land.

The Land didn't mind the mining as much as it minded that the people forgot to honor it. They forgot to take joy in the island except as a source of wealth. Then the Land and Sea's wealth began to dwindle, and the people took what they wanted from one another. Theft replaced trust. When greed and desperation grew, turning into division and warfare, they came for that first offering.

The Land didn't know which side of the conflict came and stole that first gift. It didn't care. But the metal itself had ceased to be only metal; it had become a reflection of the Atlanteans' unity, and of the unity of land and sea. Stolen away in an act of hate, the division spread until Atlantis itself broke in two.

Land and Sea, born. Diametrically opposed. Peter felt the stinging heat of the Land's rage that the Sea never had to feel the pain of the digging, that the Sea always bounced back without injury. It loathed the Sea's changeable nature when it itself was so solid. How dare that thing exist, and how dare the Atlanteans ever regard it and the Land as equals?

Peter thought of Kai, adventurous, adaptable Kai. The one he shared a face with, but who surged forward when Peter saw wisdom in holding steady.

Still, they weren't that different. They both wanted to protect their family, even if they had different ideas on how to do it. And they needed each other. Without Kai, Peter would never have gotten this far. Without Peter, Kai couldn't have found and broken as many seals as he had.

They needed each other, as did the Land and Sea.

Peter was no longer sure breaking the seals was a bad thing.

Where was Kai? Was he safe? Was he nearby? Peter thought he heard Kai call his name, but when he turned the Land's head to look, the Sea hit him.

And then the Sea faltered, its fight separated between Peter and . . . something else. Peter couldn't look. The Land had only one target, and that was the Sea.

Had Kai figured out a way to defeat the Sea? Was that what was distracting the Sea? Peter didn't know. He could only trust in Kai.

Through the rushing wind and the Land's turbulent memories, Peter heard his name again.

Kai.

Again, Peter took control, turning the Land's head toward the Point just in time to see Kai throw a shining red-gold disk. *Grandma's shield?*

The shield spun through the air, a perfect throw, carried by the wind. Time to act.

As the Sea turned to deal with the distraction on the shore, Peter flexed the Land's fingers, pouring every ounce of his will into making the huge creature how *he* wanted. Then he raised his (the Land's?) arm and caught the bloodstained shield.

It was made of the same metal that the Land remembered being mined away, so many centuries ago. Removing this from a temple of both soil and water had caused the Land and Sea to separate.

A gift, taken in division. Returned in unity.

The Sea had been freed from its prison at the Point by Peter and Kai. Twins. Two people. It took two people, united but with different gifts, to find and activate the seals. Why? So that one day, this gift could be returned to Land and Sea in the spirit of unity in which it was once given.

It had taken some time, but Peter and Kai had united. Like land and sea, working together to create and destroy, to bind and break, together. And now, Peter felt synced with Kai in a way he hadn't for a long time.

The Sea's skin was lacerated with all the attacks the Land had dealt it. Its scales were burned, and an old spear hung loosely between two of them. The distraction dealt with for a time, the Sea howled and brought its huge hand up to throw another punch at its true enemy.

Peter was ready. He raised the shield, as small as it was in his stone hand, and brought it to meet the Sea's blow. The Sea struck the shield with a sound like a bell ringing, and Peter dug his feet into the sand as the force of the attack made his (the Land's?) bones shake.

The shield glowed like sunlight. The Sea's eyes widened, and it tried to pull away but was stuck tight to the shield. "What is this?" it roared.

The shield had fastened to Peter's hand, as well. Now he could sense the Sea's violent emotions and memories as he had the Land's. He could see the Sea's rage at the Land for blocking its path, for never moving, for being so *still*.

But he also felt the freedom of movement, the lively energy

in the waves and currents, and thought, maybe, he and the Land understood the Sea a little better.

Peter looked the Sea in its slitted eyes. "The only binding that matters," he said in a voice like a rock slide.

And then the light filled him, glowing like the sun yet fizzing like sea spray, and vanished, leaving Peter fading into darkness.

KAI

Kai watched it all from the lighthouse. He saw the Land catch the shield and strike the Sea with it. He saw the flash of light erupt from the shield, and had to turn away to cover his eyes.

When he looked back, both the Sea and Land were gone.

"Peter? Peter!" Kai ran to the edge and looked down. The ocean beat against the promontory, just as it had before the boys raised the Sea in the first place.

But farther out, around the Spire, was a new island. Not big—certainly not a continent. But maybe the heart of one, dotted with trees and ringed with grayish sand. An island that owed its existence to the land that formed it and the sea that shaped it.

Land and Sea had reunited and returned to peaceful sleep.

Kai ran down to the beach. Dad, Grandma, and Sophie had gone, leaving one Viking ax half-buried in the sand that was now visible as the ocean returned to its normal level.

The island wasn't far. He could swim to it.

And Peter would be on the island. He had to be. He couldn't be gone.

Kai threw himself into the now-calm waves. The salt stung his cut hand.

It wasn't far. He'd fight the tide, just long enough to find Peter.

There was a price for victory, but last Kai checked, there were prizes, too.

It was a hard swim, but not a long one. Kai finally touched his feet on the sand beside the island and stumbled onto shore. Peter wasn't on the beach, so he had to be farther inland.

If he was here.

Of course he was! He had to be. Kai had paid with blood, and blood bound them. Surely it was enough to keep Peter in this world.

Kai raced into the trees, toward the Spire at the new island's center.

"Peter!"

No answer.

What if he was wrong? What if the price *was* Peter, all of him forever, and the only prize was saving the world?

He reached the Spire. It was strange to see the huge rock surrounded by land yet still stained with ocean spray.

"Peter!" Kai yelled again.

He heard a groan. "Shut up, Kai. I'm resting."

Kai ran around the Spire and found Peter, alive but bruised, lying in its shadow with his arm over his eyes. He was smiling. "I feel terrible," his twin said.

"You look terrible." Kai sat down next to Peter, trying not to sag from relief.

"Thanks."

"I mean, anyone would, after that—" Kai stopped. "Grandma gave up her weapons for you."

"Really?" Peter took his arm away from his face. His eye was starting to blacken.

"Yep. And Dad used them, too."

"No way. If I wasn't so sore I'd think I'm dreaming." Peter grinned. Sitting up, Peter pulled down his shirt collar. Under was an unusual red welt, starting to fade. It would heal completely in no time. Looking at it, Kai felt different. He bet he wouldn't be able to read Mom's Atlantean texts when it was over.

It was over.

Peter tried to use the Spire to help himself stand. His arms wobbled, and Kai grabbed his shoulder and pulled him up.

"How did you know you needed to catch the shield?" Kai asked.

"I didn't." Peter stretched and winced. "But I trusted that you threw it for a reason. Man, it feels good to be myself again."

"What was it like?"

"Weird. I was inside it, I saw what it saw. I had its memories and its rage." Peter rubbed his neck. "The Atlanteans plundered a temple to Land and Sea. That's why they broke apart. We had to replace the relic they stole to reunite them."

"Huh." Kai doubted Grandma's shield was the actual relic from the temple. But the metal was the same.

"I think that was the point of all of this. Not to lock monsters away, but to keep the world safe until the right team came. The Atlanteans needed people who could work together to bring the creatures back together. The ritual needed two people to raise the Sea, and the Land needed two people to activate the seals. We needed one person to channel the Land and one person to help bind it and the Sea together from the outside."

"You're going to have to fill me in on what the Land's memory showed you. And why you didn't think activating the seal would kill you instantly."

Peter closed his eyes. "The mural in the cave. The Land creature was made of light, and there was that little figure under it in the same pose as the Land. The Atlantean writing talked about someone going into the light. And I figured that while the Sea was physical, the Land had to have a host, and that's why the last seal was on a person."

"Figured?"

Peter opened his eyes. "Well, I couldn't know for sure. I just had to trust my gut and act."

Kai wanted to roll his eyes, but didn't. "You sound like me. You shouldn't have taken that chance without knowing for sure."

"And now *you* sound like me."

Kai raised his hands. "What can I say? We're twins, after all."

Peter nodded. "Twins."

"Hey! Boys! Are you out here?" It was Dad, calling from the island's beach.

Kai and Peter looked up.

"Where are you?" Dad called.

"We rented a boat as soon as we saw the island appear. The storm chasers are going wild right now." That was Grandma.

And Sophie. "How did you do this?"

The boys looked at each other. "We probably owe them an explanation," Peter said.

"Yeah. You're giving it, since you clearly understand this better than I do." Kai stuck out his uninjured hand. "Can you stand?"

"I'd better." Peter took it, and together they stood.

Peter wobbled, and Kai caught him. "You okay?" Kai asked.

"Yeah. Just tired." Peter took a step with Kai, and another. Kai felt Peter getting stronger by the second.

Kai wanted to say something, about how he was proud of Peter, or something else an adult would say. Instead, he just walked next to his twin and said, "Do you think Dad will let us stop for hot dogs on the way home?"

Peter shoved Kai into a bush. After Kai picked himself out of the branches, he saw Peter running, slowly and lopsidedly, to the beach.

Laughing, Kai ran after him. The sun shone on the sand, and on the sea, as the waves pulled at the shore and the shore gave the water a place to rest. It was a beautiful day.

ACKNOWLEDGMENTS

Writing a book is like casting a spell, or like breaking a seal: You can't do it alone. I know I can't. I'd like to thank my agent, Lauren Abramo, for giving my story its first polish, and for finding the best home for it. Thank you to my wonderful editor, Mekisha Telfer, who took what was in my head, polished it, and helped me put it to paper. Thank you Jo Rioux, for the hauntingly beautiful cover art, and Veronica Mang, for the design. Also, thank you to my copyeditors. I hope you know the miracles you work.

I would also like to thank Mike Thayer and Benjamin Hewett, for workshopping this book with me, as well as Madeleine Dresden, Sarah Allen, and the rest of Writing Group of Wonders. This story wouldn't have reached its potential without your feedback.

As this is a book about family, special thanks goes to my family. My husband, Spencer, for listening to me talk out the plot and the writing snags I encountered, and my sister Grace, for being one of my first readers, as always. Thanks to my parents and siblings, for being the template for the Syracuse family: loving, united, and willing to help each other with their problems. And thanks to my many-greats-grandmother Rebecca Nurse. I found it impossible to mention Salem without honoring her.

And finally, thank you to the state of Massachusetts. There is a magic in that land and its sea that inspired my imagination and, I believe, will never cease to do so.